READERS LC
JACKIE

CW00505157

JOB HUNT

Job Hunt is a very well-written, fast-paced, action-packed, thrilling piece of entertainment that kept me glued to the pages. – Prism Book Alliance

This book was fun to read and damn hot. Just reading it set my sheets on fire. – MM Good Book Reviews

GHOSTS

...a mellower, slightly introspective read with a beauty all of its own. – Boy Meets Boy Book Reviews

This book was a different kind of wonderful than the first, quieter, slower, more down to earth and less cyberspace-high. I read it with a wistful smile and closed it with a happy sigh. – Prism Book Alliance

HOUSE HUNT

This next part of Jack's journey to finding a man to love and a real home remains thriller-level exciting, emotionally engaging, and has more twists and turns than I thought possible. – Rainbow Book Reviews

House Hunt is another double thriller from Jackie Keswick. It's suspenseful, fast-paced and action packed, and keeps you on the edge of your seat. – The Novel Approach

DWIGHT & CONRAD CASEFILES

WHEN THE LAW
Needs Help

JACKIE KESWICK

This is a work of fiction. Names, characters, places, and incidents either are the product of author imagination or are used fictitiously, and any resemblance to actual persons, living or dead, business establishments, events, or locales is entirely coincidental.

When the Law Needs Help, Dwight & Conrad Casefiles Volume One
© 2023 Jackie Keswick.

Cover Art
© 2023 Jackie Keswick.
Cover content is for illustrative purposes only and any person depicted on the cover is a model.

Warning: This book references the sexual exploitation of children.

Mouse Hunt

For Aviva,

who made sure that Jack didn't turn into a baby koala.

ONE

A phone ringing in the middle of the night was rarely good news. Jack's phone singing out *Ghost Town* into the darkness meant trouble. Only one other ring tone woke him faster.

Jack shoved his hand under his pillow and yanked the phone out, rolling out of bed as he put it to his ear.

"Listening," he said in a low voice, mindful of Gareth buried in his customary heap of pillows, his breathing deep and slow. "What's wrong?"

Echoes hollowed Alex Marston's voice, told him her phone was on speaker. Jack caught the hum of a car engine in the background and then the meaning of her words registered.

"Say that again." He rubbed his eyes as if that could improve his hearing. "Jonathan Briggs is dead? I expected to see him at *my* funeral."

"Same here." Alex's voice was so low, Jack struggled to make out her words over the static on the line. "He was so impervious to change, so much part of the fixtures. He didn't even seem to age."

That was true. Jack had been thirteen when he'd first heard Briggs' name. The man had been a legend even then. Rio used to call him one of the Grand Old Spy Masters, the capital letters unmistakable even when Jack hadn't known whether the Jamaican was serious or sarcastic.

1

Jack had met Briggs a year later, after backing up Rio on the mission from hell, where everything had gone wrong—right from Rio walking into a target location crawling with guards. Jack had spent four uncomfortable days in Rio's blacked-out den, trying to be of use.

He feared he'd never see Rio again, never again hear the comforting lilt of Rio's accent while they worked side by side. That they'd have their last ever conversation online, in hurried snatches. That he'd be alone again, with no place to belong.

Once back home, Rio had praised Jack's cool-under-fire performance, even though Jack had felt anything but cool and collected. Rio had listened to him, had nodded through Jack's hesitant admission of his fears and had wrapped him in a hug once Jack had got everything out.

A week later, he'd taken Jack to meet Jon Briggs, making sure Jack understood this was a reward for work well done.

Jack's first impression had been one of height. Jon Briggs was well over six feet and slim as a reed. He was also clean-shaven, and his skin looked baby-smooth. His lean body, dark blue eyes, and thick thatch of straw-pale hair made him a fit for many things: a marathon runner, a maths professor, or even the local vicar. A semi-retired, high-level civil servant in his fifties wasn't the first thing that came to mind.

Jon's eyes twinkled whenever something amused or interested him. And he didn't move like a man who'd broken almost every bone in his body and had only survived because he'd been too stubborn to keel over and die.

"Never show weakness, boy," Briggs had told him that afternoon so long ago in a cosy living room filled to the brim with books and papers.

Comfy armchairs loaded with colourful cushions and

heaped with woollen blankets dotted the place. Jack had curled up in the one beside the bookcase and listened to Rio and their host dissect the ill-fated mission.

"Never show weakness. Doesn't matter who or what you're up against. Never show fear and never give them what they want."

"You're wasting your breath." Rio, coming into the room with the tea tray, had heard the end of their discussion. He'd wrapped an arm around Jack's neck in a loose hug, surprising him. "This one doesn't need telling. He's got steel for a spine and he's the stubbornest son of a bitch I've ever had the pleasure to meet."

Briggs had looked at him for a long time, a look that had seared Jack's soul. "That's good," he'd said in the end. "Never enough survivors in this here pit."

It had taken Jack years to understand what Briggs had meant, but he'd never forgotten that afternoon in the whitewashed cottage, as cluttered with books and papers as music and electronics cluttered Rio's place.

Briggs had been Rio's mentor, the same way Rio had been Jack's, and Rio had been out of sorts for weeks when Jon Briggs had left the service and retired for good. The men had kept in touch, regardless, and Jack knew that the news of Jon's death would devastate Rio.

"Jack?" Alex's voice made him realise he was drowning in memories, never mind that he had the phone to his ear.

"Wait." Jack slipped into the dressing room he'd built between their bedroom and bathroom. A corduroy-upholstered love seat at the far end turned it from a space to store clothes into a convenient hideout. He closed the door and switched on the strip light over the chest of drawers. The soft yellow glow was sufficient for him to see his way, but not bright enough for the light shining under the door to wake Gareth.

"Accident?" Jack curled up on the love seat, knowing it

wasn't likely. Alex wouldn't call at half past three in the morning if Jon had died in his sleep.

"Blunt instrument. A neighbour found him in his garden around ten last night. Fatal head trauma. We don't yet know whether he was the target, or whether he surprised an intruder. Rio is abroad. Do you think you can go through Jon's computers and papers to see if anything's missing?"

"Was Jon still working on his memoirs?"

"Yes. Which is why Rio suggested I call you. He's convinced the kids in IT won't have the faintest idea what to do with Jon's equipment."

"He's not wrong." Jack pulled clothes from hangers and piled them on the dresser on his side of the room. "How's he taking it?"

"Rio? Badly, even if he won't admit it. Will you go?"

"I'm packing. Anyone there to let me in?"

"I'm liaising with the police until Rio gets back. I'll make sure they know you're coming. The garden's a crime scene, but I'll keep them out of your hair and out of the house. Once you get there..."

"D'you want me to pack up his stuff and bring it back, or shall I check it out while I'm there?" Jack found his bike's panniers and filled them with socks, underwear, and long-sleeved tops. He was reaching for his favourite woollen jumper when Alex answered.

"It might take you a while, but... Check it out and pack up anything sensitive? I'm calling Pam and Nigel next, and they're bound to want to fly over. I'd rather they're not faced with a house that's been stripped bare."

"Fair enough. Unless Nancarrow goes up in flames, I'll stay for however long it takes."

"I'll square it with Julian. And Gareth."

"Good luck with that. See you..." Jack checked his watch and calculated distances and traffic. "Around seven."

"I'm going to be with the coroner in Northampton," Alex said. "The autopsy is this morning. Someone will be at the house. They'll have your name."

She hung up, and Jack chose enough clothes for a few days away. He moved from drawer to drawer while his mind remembered a man with a cherub face and ocean-deep eyes that had never lost their twinkle.

The snick of the latch drew Jack from his thoughts. Gareth stood in the half-open door, eyes sleep-shadowed and silver hair a dishevelled mess. He was barefoot and hadn't even belted his short terry robe.

"Are you alright?"

"I'm sorry." Jack met Gareth's concerned gaze. "I didn't mean to wake you."

"You're packing. What's up?"

Jack leaned on the nearest chest of drawers. Jonathan Briggs was dead. The thought had hung in the back of his mind while he packed. Having to explain the matter to Gareth made it real.

"Alex called," he said. "About an old friend of hers and Rio's. He—Oh fuck!" Jack took a deep breath, let it out slowly. Breathed until he had the sudden spike of rage under control. "He died last night. Rio's abroad, and Alex needs someone to check out Jon's computers and papers to make sure nothing's missing."

Gareth stiffened, and Jack bit back a tiny smile. He knew what Gareth was thinking. "Don't start. Everything's legit this time, cleared with the local law. They know I'm coming and what I'm there to do. Knowing if anything's missing might help explain why he's dead."

"He was murdered?"

"No idea. Maybe. Possibly. If he wanted to off himself, he'd have found a better way to do it than bash in his own head with the proverbial blunt instrument." Jack didn't want to imagine Jon Briggs like that. The fierce loyalty and courage extinguished like the last spark of a bright, warming fire.

Gareth saw it, of course. He stepped closer. "Did you know him?"

"Yes. Rio introduced us when I was fourteen. I met him on and off after until he recruited me to the service."

"I thought Rio recruited you."

"Yeah. Rio wanted me to join him. Jon Briggs made me see it was a job worth doing. He did that. Made me notice things, I mean."

It didn't hurt to remember the cottage with its comfy armchairs and heaps of knitted blankets, the visits when Jon had always seen more than Jack had wanted to reveal. For years it had been a game between them, cheerful arguments over topics that concealed the matter Jack wanted to discuss, close combat made from nothing more than words and allusions. Jon gave sound advice, even when Jack wasn't ready to hear it until weeks or sometimes months later.

Jack hadn't been to see Jon Briggs in two years—they'd stuck to emailing and Skype calls once Jon had retired—but that didn't make the thought of him being gone any easier to accept. For as long as Jack had known him, the man had never been further than a phone call or email away.

He folded the jumper he held, then changed his mind and shook it out again. The forecast had mentioned frost. It'd be wise to wear it under his leathers and over his thermals.

"Jack."

The snap in Gareth's voice brought his head up. Gareth watched him. Waited for a reply if Jack read his expression correctly. "Yes?"

"I asked you where you're going and how long you're going to be there."

"Oh. A little way up the M1. Jon lives in a village not far out of Towcester. As for how long I'm gonna be... end of the week, maybe? I'll be back as soon as—"

"I'm not worried about that. If you need more time, we'll come up at the weekend and bring you extra gear. You're leaving right away?"

Jack nodded. Alex's call had ruined any chance of rest. "Once I'm packed."

"You want breakfast before you go?"

"No, but..."

"I'll make coffee." Gareth's smile was soft, knowing. He tied the belt on his robe and returned to their bedroom.

He wouldn't bother to dress, Jack knew, but he'd find his slippers. The old flagstones flooring the kitchen were bone-chillingly cold, even in the summer, and installing underfloor heating was high on Jack's list of home improvements. He'd have done it already, but Gareth refused to be without a usable kitchen during the coldest part of the year. He'd rather put up with cold feet.

Once he'd packed clothes and tools, Jack showered and dressed. To no one's surprise, Nico and Daniel sat with Gareth when he came downstairs. The plumbing in the old house needed some TLC, too.

Halfway up the M1, the rain turned first to sleet, and then to snow. Huge wet flakes drifted like feathers on a breeze, snagged on currents and downdrafts, and whirled in a hypnotic dance in the beam of Jack's headlight. He passed strings of lorries at a steady pace while his thoughts swirled like the snowflakes in patterns that were just as hypnotic.

Jack found it safer to live his life in the present. Yet when he allowed himself to remember, he unearthed a store of memories that featured Jon Briggs.

Funny ones like the morning when he and Rio had woken to Jon in their kitchen brewing coffee, with Danishes and croissants on the table and their raft of alarms and protective measures undisturbed.

Serious ones, like discussions about ethics and loyalty when decisions needed to be made.

And downright scary ones, like the night Jack had been on his knees in a tiny storeroom with wire cutters in hand. Instead of the signal he'd been waiting for, he'd suddenly had Jon's voice in his headset yelling for him to get the hell out of Dodge. Jon Briggs had been nowhere near the chain of command for the op, but Jack hadn't hesitated to follow his orders.

He owed the man his life.

Jack slowed the bike and moved into the inside lane, keeping pace with the lorries for a while. He knew where his thoughts led, and he wasn't ready yet to go there. The effects of Gareth's coffee were wearing off and as his clothes grew damp, cold seeped into him to join the disturbing thoughts.

The previous night's weather forecast hadn't mentioned snow. Big flakes thawed as soon as they touched the ground, but the fall didn't show any sign of slowing down. Stopping for coffee and a chance to warm up was as much a temptation as Gareth's offer to take the Range Rover had been.

Jack had stuck with his bike, and he didn't let snow and maudlin thoughts stop him halfway. He was about forty-five minutes from his destination, traffic gods willing, with a service station at his exit from the motorway. He'd stop there before heading into the maze of tiny roads that led to Holton Wick, the village that had been home to Jon Briggs.

The coffeemaker stood empty; the hotplate turned off, and the carafe washed and dried. A beacon proclaiming Jack wasn't home. Not that Gareth needed the reminder. Even when Daniel, Nico, and their friends ran riot in the old house, the place felt cold and silent without Jack.

He'd noticed not long after they'd moved in how Jack's enthusiasm for making the house theirs echoed through the rooms. When he was out, the house existed in limbo. As soon as Jack stepped over the threshold, it came to life.

He ran a cloth over the dark granite worktop, removing the last signs of their far-too-early breakfast. Behind him, the dishwasher took care of plates, mugs, and frying pans. The rest of the kitchen was spotless, from the grey flagstones to the granite worktop to the window seats with their comfy pads and the cinnamon-coloured cushions Jack had found in a tiny nook of a shop in Chelsea. Nothing else here needed his attention, but Gareth couldn't bring himself to leave the room. He hovered, listened to the rain lash the windows, and finally switched on the kettle to brew another pot of tea.

When the water hit the tea leaves and fragrant steam rose to soothe his mind, Gareth reached for the phone and dialled.

"I expected you to call me the moment he was down your driveway."

Alex Marston's voice was half wry, half indulgent, and

Gareth scowled. He was predictable. What of it? After seeing Jack off, he'd sent Daniel and Nico upstairs to get more sleep or get ready for the gym. He'd even cleaned the kitchen and made more tea before he'd called. As far as he was concerned, he was the poster boy for patience and restraint.

Gareth poured himself a cup of tea. "And your answer is?"

"He's the only one I could call for the job, unless I want to spend hours explaining to some kid barely out of uni how a mainframe works."

"In English, Alex. It isn't even five o'clock yet."

"Jon's been keeping notes for fifty years, Gareth. On paper and on computers. Kids in IT these days can't remember a time before the internet. They won't know what to do with floppy disks or data cartridges."

"And Jack does?"

"He's ace with old tech. Got that from Rio, I suppose. Forensic IT has been gunning for the two of them for years. Rio helps them out now and then, but Jack's not interested. He's more the social justice type."

As if Gareth needed telling. "And you're really just making him go through old documents and flag anything sensitive? I find that hard to believe."

"I don't blame you," Alex said.

When she'd pulled the OSA card and sent Jack to retrieve an encryption key without the chance to let anyone know what he was doing, she'd damaged a string of bridges she'd so carefully built.

Jack had shrugged it off. Gareth wasn't that relaxed about it. He understood need-to-know and chains of command, but he'd never worked in a world where trust was doled out in careful measures. He'd forever question her motives.

"Tell me, Alex."

"Jon was old-school. Careful not to compromise security. He took pains over even simple communications. But like I said, kids these days don't understand how people worked during the Cold War. They'll regard what happened to Jon as a random burglary and investigate it as such."

"Whereas you..."

"I need to know it wasn't a revenge killing, or that he died because someone somewhere has something to hide. I want to make sure he didn't become a target because someone wanted his notes."

She took a breath, and Gareth waited.

"Jon's son and daughter-in-law are flying in from Canada. It's bad enough they've lost their father. I don't want them to be in danger. If Jon died because of something he's kept, Jack will find it."

Gareth finished his tea as he thought. "How close was Jack to the... Jon Briggs?"

"Rio introduced them when Jack was—"

"I know. He told me. It doesn't answer my question."

"Neither can I, Gareth. I don't know whether they were friends or just colleagues. Jon and Jack've known each other for almost twenty years. I know they kept in contact after Jon retired and even after Jack left the service."

"You think that's significant?"

"I do. But Gareth ... I called because Rio's out of the country. He'd have wanted to take care of this himself. Jack is the next best choice. There's nothing else to it."

"Fine. I'll go with it. We'll drive up at the weekend to see him if he's not done."

Alex signed off, leaving Gareth standing in the kitchen, holding a mug of cooling tea. Dealing with death was never easy. Especially when it came unexpectedly and claimed a friend.

TWO

"You're Dr Horwood?" The officer looked shocked when Jack pushed up his visor and introduced himself.

"Yes. You knew I was coming, right?"

"Oh yes, sir." Swathed in at least four layers, stood guard outside Jon's half-timbered, thatched cottage like a damp mountain. "We were told to expect you, but we didn't think we'd see you quite so soon. With you coming up from London and all."

"They told me it was urgent." Jack parked the bike. His ears rang and the long, boring trek up the M1 echoed through his legs and hands. He liked his roads curvaceous in three dimensions, not straight, three-laned, and packed with lorries. He set his helmet on the Gixxer's seat and removed his gloves. "Do I have clearance to go inside? I'm supposed to check Jon's files."

"Did you know the victim?"

Jack saw no reason to lie. "He was an old friend."

"I'm sorry, sir. Shocking business, this."

"Yes. Do you have any information about what happened?"

"Only that the neighbour found him in the garden last night. The forensics guys are waiting for better light to start work."

That made sense. What with the ambulance and then

the police, enough people had trekked through the scene to make finding anything worthwhile a tricky proposition. "Who found him?"

"Mrs Rowntree." He pointed to the cottage adjoining Jon's on the right. "She went to get a spare lightbulb from the shed and saw him lying there. Called it in right away, tried to help, but ... you know..."

Jack nodded. "So, can I go in?"

"Yes, sir. Nobody's been inside yet. I'm supposed to give you this." He held up a single Yale key. "You have the run of the house, and you decide who's allowed inside. I'm to remind you that the garden is a crime scene and out of bounds until forensics release it. If you need access to the garden, you should—"

"Hang on, hang on." Jack stopped the official recital. "If nobody's been in the house yet, then how come you have a key? Jon didn't need a key to step into his own garden and—at any rate—he used to have his keys on a bunch."

The man's eyes twinkled like Jon's used to. "He was on a list. The police station in Towcester was holding this key."

"Thank you." Jack took it from the man. He grabbed his bag from the bike and headed up the gravel path, key at the ready. Letting himself in as if he owned the place felt strange. He'd always knocked before.

Warmth and the spicy-sweet smell of pipe tobacco greeted him. For a crazy moment, Jack thought of calling out a greeting, convinced he'd get an answer.

Then a light came on, bright white and blinding.

Intruder deterrent.

On automatic.

He hadn't been prepared for that.

"Damn it all to hell!" Jack squinted, unable to make out anything through the glare. The light flickered and flared, more disorienting than unrelieved brightness. He groped along the wall for the switch to disable the alert before Jon's security measures escalated. He didn't want to have to call Alex and tell her the house had gone up in flames.

His head throbbed in time to the light's flicker when he finally touched the switch. He ran his fingertips over the plate and then around the outside edge until he found the tiny rocker that turned off the glare.

Then he stood, head hanging, and breathed in and out to counts of five until the rush of adrenaline died down. The fury that had spurred him up the M1 didn't fade when the shivers did.

"Damn you, Briggs! Why did you have to get yourself killed?"

The silent hallway had no answer.

Jack shed his riding gear and boots before he carried his bag into the kitchen. He'd better start with a circuit of the house. Make sure nothing had caught fire while he'd bumbled around by the front door.

From the outside, the cottage didn't appear that large. The inside was a different matter. While he owned the cottage, Jon had rearranged the layout and converted the entire space under the thatched roof until he had a house with two cosy bedrooms, a bathroom, and a study with a desk, bookshelves, and filing cabinets.

Jack, who had to duck under a roof beam or two during his exploration of the study, wondered how often Jon Briggs had banged his head on those beams. The top of the house made an unlikely workspace for such a tall man.

Jack put the study on his list of places to explore in

more detail later and clattered back downstairs. The living room ran along the front of the house, the kitchen took up the space towards the garden. Nothing was out of place in either room.

Books filled the shelves, and knitted cushions and blankets softened the sofa and armchairs. The heating was on, the rooms warm and tidy and the house lay as serene as if its occupant had just stepped out.

Jack had a lump in his throat when he returned to the kitchen.

The pipe sitting on the small table beside Jon's favourite armchair, the novel and reading glasses on the bedside table, even the jar of half-wilted flowers on the bathroom windowsill made the house feel alive and lived in. It was the mug on the kitchen worktop beside the kettle with a tea bag and sugar in it, ready for tea before bed, that finally made him accept Jon was gone.

Jack blinked against the sting of tears.

He needed coffee.

Needed to bury himself in work, forget whose house this was and focus on why he was here.

He located the coffeemaker and ground beans, ran water into the jug and started a large batch. The gurgle and hiss of brewing coffee was as comforting as the aroma of Dutch coffee, the beans roasted to near black and ground medium-fine.

Rain lashed the windows, the brief flurry of snow gone as quickly as it had arrived. As he poured coffee, Jack thought of the man standing outside in the cold guarding the gate.

"Can I interest you in a mug of coffee?" he asked from the open door.

"We're not supposed to set foot inside that house, sir."

"No worries. I'll bring it out." Jack was halfway down the hall when he turned back. "How do you take it?"

15

"White with two, please. And strong as sin."

"That won't be an issue." Jack doctored the coffee and carried it outside. "Any more of your colleagues out here? I've made a large pot."

"No. Nobody's expecting trouble. My relief comes at ten." He sipped his coffee, hands wrapped around the mug to soak up a little extra warmth. "Can I ask you something? I didn't know Mr Briggs well, but his address was flagged and rumours in the station said he was a spy."

He left his words hanging, but Jack heard the question. "You could call him that. He did dangerous work in a time of danger. And he was damned good at it."

The empty mug looked lost and lonely sitting in the sink, so Jack washed it, dried it, and put it away. He topped up his own mug, then he drew a deep breath and set to work.

An hour later, he called Alex.

"You got there quickly."

"It's hardly something I'd dawdle over."

"No, I suppose not."

"Guess what? His security system nearly got the better of me."

"Out of practice?"

"Too right." Jack no longer swam in that cesspool of lies and suspicion. He had a home now, and a family to take care of. Elaborate security measures still featured in his new life, but paranoia did not. "I didn't expect him to have it on when he'd just stepped out of the house into the garden," he said, more reconciled to this job Alex had landed him with. "I should have known better."

"Anything else?"

"Yes." Jack switched to report mode. "There's no evidence that anyone's been taking an unhealthy interest in his Wi-Fi. He'd Fort Knox'd the setup and anyone attempting to break in would have to be determined. They'd also have left footprints."

"Good to know."

"Yes. Nothing's out of place inside. No sign that he was worried, felt threatened, or expected an attack. I'll get started on his papers. Maybe they'll give us something to go on. I suggest we pack up the electronics and deal with them offsite. Unless you want me to render them unusable?"

"No. Not yet, at any rate. We may need his notes. I'll send someone over with packing crates. Pull everything that appears sensitive, even if it's a long shot."

"Understood."

"I've declared the house out-of-bounds until you're done. I leave it up to you to call it. The officer in charge is Detective Superintendent Peter Wynant. He may want to have a word."

"Give him my number. What's his clearance?"

"You can talk to him. He knows who Jon was and what you're doing. Keep anything service-confidential to yourself unless it's critical to the investigation."

"Don't worry. I'll run it past you if I find anything," Jack assured her and hung up.

"Do you think Jack's friend was really murdered?"

"I don't know." They'd started the day with a gym session and were the first customers in the small cafe across the street from the dojo. Gareth handed out mugs of hot chocolate and plates of muffins, their traditional second breakfast on gym mornings. Despite the familiar ritual, Jack's absence hurt like a sore tooth. And Nico, as was his habit, was poking at it.

"What do you mean, you don't know? You called Alex while we were getting ready."

"I had to make sure she wasn't landing Jack in the mire again." Gareth didn't have to explain that one. Nico and Daniel had been there when Jack had made contact after escaping his kidnappers, and both knew that the relationships between Alex and Gareth and especially Alex and Aidan had been difficult ever since. They also knew that Jack thought Aidan and Gareth were being silly. Or something a lot more colourful to that effect.

"What did Alex say?"

"That it's legit." Not that he believed it. But until he spoke to Jack, he'd take Alex's word for it. "It's cleared with the police and they're waiting for Jack when he gets there to give him keys and information. Jack promised to phone tonight, so then we'll know."

"He's gonna be sad."

"Or angry," Daniel said.

"He'll focus on his job first, I imagine." Gareth remembered Jack's solitary wake for Ricky, the boy who'd died the night they'd rescued Nico and Daniel. Jack hadn't allowed himself time to grieve right after Ricky's death. He'd locked his emotions away and focussed on the job that needed doing. He'd do the same thing now and grieve for Jon in his own time and space, out of sight and earshot of anyone else. "But Jack didn't have many people growing up, and he's known Jon for a long time. Losing someone like that will hurt."

"Can we do anything?"

"Talk to him when he calls. Tell him things that will cheer him up. If he's not done by Saturday, we'll drive up to see him. It's not that far. A couple of hours up the road."

Daniel nodded. "We should take cake. And maybe a blanket. To remind him he has us, you know?"

"Good idea. One thing, though... When you talk to Jack, don't ask him about the case. Don't ask him what he's doing, either. Jon Briggs worked for MI6."

"Was he a spy?"

"I don't know. He retired, but he could be dead because of his former job. Jack won't be allowed to talk about any of it."

"Is that why Alex wanted Jack to come and help? Because he worked there, too?" Nico was reducing his muffin to crumbs instead of eating it. Gareth knew what that meant.

"Jon Briggs was Rio's teacher, like Rio was Jack's. Rio is away working, though, or she'd have sent him."

"It's all so messy." Daniel put his chin on his fist. "I wish Jack would call already."

"Yeah, so do I."

It had taken Jack two hours to search Jon's living room. The harvest was pitiful. One laptop, one tablet, Jon's phone, one SD card, three memory sticks—one of which he'd extracted from the spine of a cookery book—and four bits of paper filled with numbers that Jon had used as bookmarks.

Or not.

Jon's diaries, taking up two entire rows of the bookcase, were his next target.

Removing the diaries wholesale would leave Jon's son without his father's personal notes, a solution that didn't appeal to Jack. He armed himself with a pack of Post-It notes, a marker, and his phone, curled up in the chair beside the bookcase and read.

By the fourth book, still reading about Jon's life in the early sixties, he felt like a voyeur.

If it hadn't been for the tone of the journals, the hint of irony that Jack glimpsed in the detailed accounts, he would have stacked the whole damned lot of them into a pile to be taken away and made himself forget that he'd wanted to leave the diaries for Jon's son.

This was Jon's voice, though, and the way he talked about people and events made it appear as if Jon was right there in the room with Jack.

Jon had never taken the easy way out, so Jack didn't either. He took snapshots of suspect passages and mailed them to Alex, marking the pages with post-It notes before he continued reading.

One after another, his emails received answers.

Benign. Benign. Benign.

Jack read on.

A few of his queries came back with a different label: *redact*.

For those, Jack blacked out the words until the text was unreadable, then took a snapshot to confirm his actions.

The longer he worked, the more he changed his mind about Alex Marston. The woman either had an encyclopaedic knowledge of MI6 history and operations, or a clearance much higher than he'd ever suspected.

He breathed a sigh of relief when he neared the end of the first row of journals, though the painful work was just around the corner. The remaining books covered the time Jack had known Jon Briggs, and Jon wrote about discussions Jack remembered.

They'd argued about bureaucrats taking over the service, about bigotry, racism, and the dangers poor decisions posed to field operatives. They'd discussed events that masqueraded as threats when they weren't and others, where the opposite was true. Until, during one weekend in winter, Briggs had told Jack to get out of MI6 while he was still sane and human, and Jack had felt like a deserter for entertaining the idea.

The matter had weighed on Jon's mind even after Jack had ended the call. The journal entries he'd made in the following days kept referring to that charged discussion.

Jack's thoughts had been equally weighty. Years earlier, he'd walked away from his chosen career and from the one man who mattered to him, because he'd feared he'd become a liability. It had been one of the hardest choices he'd ever made, and it had taken him months to accept his decision and start over.

Ever since, walking away bothered him.

When he'd sought Jon's advice, he'd known that one day Gatting or another career bureaucrat would push him too far. Issue orders he couldn't follow if he wanted to live with himself after. Leaving before that happened was the wisest course of action. He knew it, but he hadn't been able to make that call. Hadn't been able to walk away.

Until Tom Gatting forgot that Jack's willingness to let him choose cases for their career-enhancing potential didn't mean Jack wasn't thinking for himself.

Jack set the journal on the coffee table and closed his eyes as memories came rushing back.

"Leave the kids. They're not important. We'll come back for them later."

Jack remembered staring at Gatting in disbelief. He'd worked with the man since the day he'd joined, and Gatting dared to say *that* to him? When he'd heard the screams on the recording just as Jack had?

He'd turned and left the room, leaving the service right there and then. He'd been so *done*, that everything that came after—rescuing the children, finding a piece of hospital stationery to pen his resignation so he'd have the pleasure of throwing it in Gatting's face, even the commendation they gave him and the discussions to change his mind—was nothing more than window dressing. Jack had made his choice and anyone who spoke to him after that moment could see it.

Jon had heard of it, of course. He'd left a message on Jack's phone. Just his name and a *call me if you need to.*

Jack hadn't called. Not then. Not until the day before his interview at Nancarrow Mining.

The day before Gareth had returned to his life.

Looking back, it fit. Jack had joined the service after he'd walked away from Gareth, and once he was done with that idiocy, Gareth had come back. If he didn't know better, he might believe in fate.

But then... no twist of fate could justify Jon losing his life.

The knock on the front door was a welcome interruption from the deluge of memories.

"I'm Detective Superintendent Peter Wynant from Northampton CID." A tall, broad-shouldered man stood on the doorstep. "You're Dr Horwood?"

"Jack. Come in out of the cold." He waited until Wynant had shut the front door, then headed for the kitchen. "Can I interest you in a cup of coffee? Or tea?"

"Coffee please."

Wynant shed his coat, revealing a charcoal suit, with a dark grey shirt and a silver tie. The clothes complemented his dirty blond hair and deep blue eyes and reminded Jack of Gareth, who pulled off the same colours to perfection.

He missed the damned man. Especially after reading Jon's notes. Recalling his decision to leave MI6 had brought back echoes of the days before he walked away from Gareth, when they had argued for hours before

22

Gareth accepted Jack's choice. Gareth had fought for him back then, and Jack now had the urge to pick up the phone and call Gareth to apologise.

Which was idiotic.

A chair scraped on the tile, and Jack shoved the memories back into their box. He'd examine them when his work here was done.

"Do you have news?" he asked when he'd poured coffee and offered milk and sugar.

Wynant had a notebook open beside his mug and flicked through the pages. "Found in the garden last night around ten by the neighbour, Mrs Rowntree. Pronounced dead on scene by the physician attending. Suspected cause of death is blunt force trauma to the back of the head. The autopsy is this morning."

Jack saw the sketch in the notebook, the position of the wound on Jon Briggs's skull. "No chance it was—?"

"Self-inflicted? No."

"Could it have been an accident?"

The detective hesitated. His eyes narrowed, but what Jack saw was sympathy. "If we'd found him indoors... maybe. A vase or jar falling from a top shelf, or something similar?" He considered each word before he said it. Jack liked him for it. "We found him face down in a bare flowerbed. Nothing resembling a weapon nearby."

"Why would he have been out in the garden anyway? It gets dark around half four. He'd not been there all that time, right?"

"No. Doctor estimated the time of death between seven and nine. Closer to nine. And before you ask: the neighbour didn't move him. She merely brought a cushion and blankets to keep him warm. She was worried about spinal injury."

"She didn't see he was gone?"

"More like she didn't want to believe it. I've asked the

local GP, that's Dr Wilcroft in case you need to know, to look in on her. She's been baking all night."

"Baking?"

Wynant waved a hand. "Cakes and biscuits. She said it helps settle her mind."

"She saw nothing?"

"No. She came out to fetch a new lightbulb because one of hers blew. She kept wondering whether she could have saved him if she'd come out sooner."

"Could she?"

"The doctor says not."

"Right." Jack topped up their coffee mugs. "Jon was six three, six four? Takes a big guy to club him over the head."

"Not if he'd been gardening."

"Which he wasn't, since it was well dark even by your earliest estimated time."

The detective smiled a little. "You do this a lot?"

"Homicide isn't my bag," Jack said, not offering anything further.

"Can I ask questions?"

"Knock yourself out." Jack nodded towards the notebook. "I'll tell you when I'm withholding information. Fair enough?"

"You've only been here a few hours, and you already have data to withhold?"

"If you're going to ask me detailed questions about the content of his journals, then yes."

Wynant sighed. He flipped to a new page in his notebook, titling it HORWOOD in neat capitals. "Do you know Dr Marston?"

"Yes."

"Did you know Jonathan Briggs?"

"Yes."

"How well did you know him?"

"I met Jon when I was fourteen." He smirked. "Which

24

means I've known him for seventeen years. In that time, we've spoken or emailed at least every four to six weeks—unless he was away working, or I was."

"You knew what he did when you were fourteen?"

Jack thought about his response for an extra five seconds. Then he shrugged. "I'd just started working for the service."

Wynant narrowed his eyes, but asked nothing further. "I'm sorry."

Jack nodded. "Yeah. So am I. Not how I expected to lose him. I'm on your side here, Superintendent."

"Can you tell me what you do?"

"Here or in general?"

"In general."

"I'm an IT specialist." He grinned. "A hacker, if you must."

"With a doctorate?"

"Network security."

Wynant wrote that down before he regarded Jack once more. "Dr Marston said she asked you to look through Mr Briggs's notes and papers to see whether anything is missing."

"And to determine whether his death has anything to do with his work, yes." Jack liked the detective. He didn't rile against restraints he had no prospect of shifting and worked with what he had instead. And he'd let Jack ask questions first.

"I started with a survey of the house." Jack began a recital of his own activities. "No sign of forced entry. In fact, his security system was on when I entered. It's... extensive. No visible disturbance inside, either upstairs or down. Nothing was out of place inside, except for a rogue dishtowel."

"You knew him well enough to say that?"

"Jon practiced neatness like an art form. Every item had

25

its place. It's the only way to ensure your safety when you do the work he did, Superintendent."

"And the rogue dishtowel?"

Damn. The man had dimples. So not fair. Jack shook his head and felt coffee sloshing through his brain. He'd need food soon, or he'd drown.

"Dr Horwood?"

"Sorry. Dishtowel. Right. It draped the edge of the sink. Just tossed down, not hung up. Maybe he heard something and put it down to go outside and look. It can't have been urgent, though."

"How do you figure that?"

"He changed out of his slippers into gardening shoes. The slippers are sitting on the mat by the back door."

Wynant pounced on that. "Anything else?"

"He didn't take a coat." And yes, the man was as quick to rile as Gareth. "I've been going through his notes, starting with his journals. So far, there's nothing that jumps out at me. Jon was careful with his communications. If there is something, it may take me a while to find it."

"Will you tell me if you do?"

"I'm cleared to discuss anything pertaining to the case and I'll give you what I can, even if I have to redact details. I want this solved."

Wynant waited, and Jack gave him extra points for astuteness. It wasn't something he'd have shared before, but time with Gareth and the boys had bent his fences. Wynant needed to understand how serious Jack was about helping him.

"I owe Jon Briggs my life. I want to know who took his." He wanted more than *know* who'd killed Jon and the ferocity of that need knocked him sideways. He took the empty mugs to the sink and plonked the glass carafe back on the coffeemaker's warming plate, desperate for movement, for tasks to occupy his hands and mind. "If you need more on me, Dr Lisa Tyrrell will give me a reference. She's attached to the Met's Special Projects Unit, and we've worked together."

Wynant stood when Jack turned back around. "Thank you. Do you think you could do something else for me?"

"Such as?"

"You're here for a day or two, right? Do you think you could keep an ear out in the village?"

"You're short of men?"

"No. God, no. Not on this case, but everyone knows us. Two of my team even live here. Well, not in Holton Wick, but in the next village over. You have a chance to fly under the radar."

Jack felt his lips curl and didn't fight the amusement. "Won't I stick out even more? As an outsider, I mean."

"Of course you do. But you're not the police and—"

"I get it. And I'll keep my ear to the ground. After all, a man needs to eat. I hear there's decent food at the *Horseshoes*."

"And at the *Yarn Looters*, if you fancy cake and a cuppa." Wynant shrugged into his coat and buttoned it up. "Thank you."

They shook hands on the doorstep. The door closed. And Jack was once more alone with his memories and the sweet scent of pipe tobacco in the air.

THREE

J ack stepped out of the cottage's front door onto a short stretch of gravel path. On the Strand, his usual habitat during the working week, office workers on their lunch break would dodge tourists gawking at architecture amidst streams of traffic. Holton Wick, by comparison, showed few signs of life.

Wood smoke scented the air. Small houses—some thatched, some roofed with slate—lined the lane on both sides, the front gardens neat even in the middle of winter. Bare branches shivered in the breeze, but nothing else moved. He counted three parked cars, eight solar panels on a sloping slate roof, and zero people.

Did nobody live here? Was Holton Wick a commuter village, or did anyone with any sense stay inside?

Jack's stomach growled.

Pub.

Lunch.

Now.

Salt-laden slush slicked the narrow lane. Jack slipped and slithered and wished he'd brought walking boots. It had grown colder since the morning, and the rain had turned to snow once more. Everything in view—roofs, cars, gardens—sported a dusting of white. It made the village look even more remote than it had when he'd arrived.

The lane emptied onto the village green, which Jack

knew to be a lush, inviting space in the summer, with the church and the manor house on one side, and thatched cottages lining the other three. Right then, the frost-rimed grass didn't invite anyone to linger. The few people who were out and about—a stout woman with two chocolate Labradors and two builders who'd just climbed from their van—stopped what they were doing and stared at him as if he'd turned up wearing pink dreadlocks and a purple bunny onesie rather than serviceable jeans and a fleece top.

Yeah, villages were weird. He'd always thought so.

Jack nodded a greeting at his audience and made a beeline for the *Horseshoes*. The whitewashed, thatched building held a prime position in the village, and if Jack remembered correctly, it had a huge open fire in the tap. Just the thing in this weather.

There'd been two pubs in the village the first time Rio had brought him here, but *The Bull* hadn't survived the last recession. It had stood empty for a while until two enterprising ladies had bought the neglected old building and had turned it into a thriving teashop and bakery.

Or so Jon had said. Jack hadn't been to Holton Wick since before the teashop had opened, but he knew Jon had loved the place. Jack looked forward to checking it out. He wanted to find a new recipe for Daniel, and Jon had mentioned the local cheesecake more than once.

Food first, though. Flavoured with a touch of gentle snooping.

The pub's interior had changed little. The inglenook fireplace, big enough to spit roast a pig, was full of deep red coals, smouldering logs, and orange flames and the fire threw out enough heat to make the tap feel cosy.

To Jack's surprise, the room was moderately busy. By the time he'd closed the door and turned around, it was also dead silent. Every single patron had stopped talking, and they watched him as if he might order rat poison at the bar.

Jack didn't blame them. He'd been in the pub a handful of times over the years, and he'd done nothing to make himself memorable. No wonder the locals regarded him as they did any other stranger. It also wasn't every day the village lost one of its inhabitants to violence, so a healthy dose of suspicion was justified. Jack plastered on a vague smile, ignored the silence, and stepped up to the bar.

"What can I get you?"

Jack scanned the taps lining the bar and the specials board on the wall. "Pint of Old Hooky and a steak sandwich."

"Chips and salad?"

"Please."

"You're with the police, aren't you? Looking into Jon's death?" The landlord set a glass in front of Jack. He was big and beefy enough to deter arguments and break them up if they started. Jack remembered his face.

"I'm an IT specialist."

"Computers? Did Jon even know what they were?"

"Sure." Jack kept his face blank, not convinced he'd learn anything in this place when Jon had a houseful of electronics, and his neighbours hadn't known.

"Is that why he was murdered?" A woman called from the other end of the bar.

"I don't know why someone killed him. Or even that someone did," Jack said. "For all I know, it was an accident."

"He didn't bash in his own head. Doesn't that make it murder?"

"No, it doesn't," another voice cut in. "Murder needs intent."

"So if I bring a cricket bat to the pub, hit you over the head and kill you, it's murder, but if I just pick up the bat hanging on the wall behind the bar and do it it's not?"

"Something like that."

"Bollocks. Surely if—"

Jack claimed the barstool beside the wall and made himself comfortable. When his food arrived, he made quick work of it while listening to the voices in the taproom, where Jon's death got pushed aside in favour of a pointless argument.

Jack hated the callousness of it all, but he didn't move. He kept his head down, his face out of the light, and listened as the discussion he'd started went where it wanted to go.

Jon and Rio had taught him that intelligence gathering, whether face to face or on a computer, was about amassing tiny, random snippets of data, hoping to find missing puzzle pieces. It was a game of listening, of appraising, and of thinking sideways. Of following the facts where they led and making connections that didn't appear logical in the beginning. It was a game of patience, and Jack had that in spades.

His lunchtime sojourn in the *Horseshoes* left him with only a few bits of useful information. The villagers present had liked Jon. They'd thought him supportive and occasionally entertaining. Even when Jack had made himself darned near invisible, he'd heard nothing to help him find a murderer.

Nothing except the odd, broken-off sentence and sideways look, and a vague feeling that he was missing something.

Alex had cleared the last highlighted passages in Jon's journals when he returned from the pub. Jack removed the post-It notes and replaced the books on the shelves with genuine relief that Nigel Briggs would have his father's diaries.

He left the electronics and the maybe-bookmarks he'd found earlier on the kitchen table and made his way up to Jon's study, ready to explore the filing cabinets and deed boxes that lined the room.

His phone pinged before he had decided where to start.

How are you doing?

Gareth. Of course. Jack smiled, grateful he had the man. Left to himself right now... He dialled. "Hi."

"Hi yourself. How was your journey?"

"Damp. Chilly. Full of lorries. Did you go back to sleep after I left?"

"We went to the gym. But only because the ice rink doesn't open that early."

Jack chuckled. "It opens at seven." Nico and Daniel loved to go ice skating. Never mind that the indoor ice rink was open year-round, the two only wanted to go skating while the weather outside somewhat matched the temperature within.

Jack didn't mind and Gareth had learned to skate so he could join in. They raced each other around the oval and played tag and ice hockey. They'd even tried their hand at short-track speed skating one night. Jack had overcooked the tight bends with beautiful regularity and had spent more time on his arse than his skates, laughing his head off while the other three sprinted for the line.

Gareth's backside and the way he bent over to balance on his fingertips had been far too distracting. Jack didn't deny it. He was simply glad that none of the others noticed he never crashed when he was the one in front.

"It was a long way from seven when you left." Gareth recalled him to the ongoing conversation.

"I know. I'm sorry."

"It's hardly your fault now, is it? Any news?"

"No. The police suspect it wasn't an accident, but they're waiting for the results from the autopsy. The house is tidy. I don't think anyone but Jon's been in here. And I've met the Detective Super in charge."

"Is he okay with you being there?"

"Yeah, he gets it. He even asked me to help."

"Help? How?"

"Fly low. His guys are visible. I'm a little less so."

"Only a little less?"

"It's a village. I stick out whatever I do. Went to the pub for lunch—lovely steak sandwich, by the way—and the place went completely silent the moment I set foot in it."

"That's the effect you have on people, baby," Gareth crooned.

Jack rolled his eyes. "You know it. Wish I could turn it off, since I'm supposed to be sleuthing."

"I'm sure you made yourself invisible soon enough. How's the beer up there?"

"Hook Norton." Jack recited the name of the local brewery he'd memorised; sure it meant something to Gareth. "One I had was decent." He scanned one of Jon's number-dotted bookmarks as he spoke. It looked like a simple enough cipher and—Jack's sudden laugh was a pitiful one, the gasp at the end of it hastily swallowed before it turned into something much more embarrassing. Who wrote a shopping list and dinner recipe in code? Jon Briggs, that's who.

"Jack? What's wrong?"

"Nothing, nothing. Just…" He took a snapshot of the paper and sent it to Gareth's phone. "For Daniel and Nico," he said. "Tell them I want that when I get back."

"Excuse me."

Jack froze, keys in the door. He'd moved his bike off the lane and into the shelter of the carport after the police had cleared the area for his use. Police tape still roped off the garden, though everyone who'd been working the scene had called it a night. He took a step to the side as he turned, positioning his back to the wall and doorframe rather than the door.

In front of him stood a pixie of a woman holding a covered plate.

"I'm Jon's neighbour," she said. "I've been baking and wondered if you'd like a cake?"

Jack closed his mouth. Then he located a smile. "Cake?"

"I'm sorry. It sounds absurd, but I ... I found Jon last night."

"Mrs Rowntree, is it? Would you like to come inside?"

"Oh, I couldn't do that. Jon wouldn't like it. He is very particul—" And then it hit her that Jon was gone. Her eyes went wide, and her mouth fell open in something that started as a gasp and would end as a wail.

Jack had the door open in a blink, grabbed the woman's elbow, and pulled her inside, glad he hadn't armed Jon's security system when he'd stepped out to park his bike. He made tea while Mrs Rowntree huddled at the kitchen table, sobbing into a dishcloth.

"I'm so sorry."

Jack gave up telling her not to apologise. The woman reminded him of Daniel as she sat there, lost in her misery, and he knew he had to give her a little time to exhaust herself before she'd listen to anything.

"He was such a lovely man," she said, when half her

mug of tea was empty, and the torrent of tears had slowed to a trickle. "He always knew when someone needed cheering, you know? And just what to say."

Jack nodded. He craved his own moment of grief, but the person responsible for Jon's death was still out there, nameless and faceless and free to do as he damned well pleased.

That was unacceptable.

"Jon would have appreciated you coming to his aid," he said instead.

She gave him a little sniff in response, not convinced by his words or not sure he'd meant them. Jack didn't care. He wasn't in the business of consoling grieving women. He was here to help find the culprit.

"Did you notice anything unusual?" he asked. "When you stepped outside, I mean?"

"It was dark. The light by my back door reaches to the shed, but beyond that it was just dark." She twisted the dishcloth between her fingers. "When I came back from the shed, I noticed that his outside light was on."

"Is that unusual?"

"Of course, it's unusual! He has it on a sensor, doesn't he? It only comes on if something moves. Cats sometimes trip it, but I couldn't see a cat. Just his jumper. That old orange thing he knitted years ago? Such a vile colour, but he liked it."

"Where did you see the jumper?"

"In the vegetable patch. I thought maybe he'd fallen and couldn't get back up, but he didn't answer when I called, so I went through the little gate."

Jack didn't interrupt. He made more tea, sliced the cake, and settled back in his seat. Mrs Rowntree rambled on, moved from talking about Jon to talking about the neighbours and the village. Petty jealousies came spilling out alongside a few real disputes, but nothing serious enough to get a man killed in his own garden.

Jack memorised every word, intent on picking the facts apart later. And when Mrs Rowntree finally ran out of words and returned to her own home, Jack hoped she felt a little less bleak than when she'd arrived on his doorstep.

FOUR

C lunk. Squeak. Thud.

Jack jerked upright. His eyes darted around the unfamiliar room as he searched for threats amongst the shadows. Nothing was out of place, so what was the noise that had woken him? He listened for a repeat of the sounds, but he only heard the intermittent ticking of the radiators as they cooled and the creaking of the thatch above him.

Despite the 03:00 a.m. wake-up call, sleep hadn't come easy. He'd summarised his chat with Mrs Rowntree for Wynant, had talked to Gareth, Daniel, and Nico, and had planned how to tackle Jon's study before he finally stretched out on the bed in Jon's spare bedroom. Even then, he'd tossed and turned before his mind took the hint that it was bedtime.

And now he was awake, at half past friggin' four in the morning. Woken by monsters under the bed, no doubt.

Jack wished he was home. There, strange noises woke him at all hours. But once he'd made sure that Daniel and Nico were safe, and nothing was on fire, he could return to bed and drape himself over Gareth. With Gareth's heartbeat under his ear, he had no trouble drifting off to sleep again. He'd wondered whether a recording might help but had dismissed the idea as idiotic. It only ever occurred to him when he was awake at an ungodly hour somewhere Gareth wasn't.

Thunk. Thud.

Jack was out of bed now. He grabbed the flashlight from the bedside table and left the room, tiptoeing to the stairs.

Nothing moved, and no sounds came from downstairs.

Maybe the old house had mice?

No. The sound he'd heard had been a definite thud and mice didn't have that heavy a tread. Nor did they jump around. Had the sound come from the thatched roof? A squirrel jumping from a beam, or a bird that had fallen off his perch?

He really had no idea.

The stairs creaked a little as he came down, but the ground floor lay as silent the first floor. Jack made a quick survey of the kitchen and living room.

Nothing.

He checked the doors.

Bolted.

And the alarm was as he'd left it when he'd gone to bed: fully armed.

Jack was sure he hadn't dreamed the noise, but he couldn't account for it either. He grumbled his way back upstairs and buried himself in the pillows, not convinced it would do him any good.

Despite his misgivings, he woke three hours later to a milky twilight and a mist so thick he couldn't see the house backing onto the end of Jon's garden.

Jack loved misty mornings. The damp, cold, and visibility problems didn't bother him. He enjoyed the way the moisture clung to branches, cars, and signs, how it muffled sounds and kept people indoors. Some days he'd gone running in the early hours and had felt as if he was the only one awake in all of Kingston.

Maybe a run would help him shake the antsy feeling that made his neck crawl with imagined creepies.

His phone interrupted his thoughts, and he smiled at the image of their breakfast table at home, with his biggest coffee mug taking up his place at the table. No words accompanied the image, but it was unquestionably a reminder to eat breakfast.

Jack did as he was told, finishing the cake Mrs Rowntree had brought the previous evening.

When he found the corpse of a rabbit on his doorstep ten minutes later, he almost wished he hadn't.

This... was creepy.

It had snowed a little more during the night, and not a single footprint marred the pristine dusting of white covering the path from the gate to his front door. The bare flowerbed beside the path didn't show any prints either. Nothing but a little drag mark on the doorstep.

Who had deposited a dead rabbit at his door, leaving no footprints?

And why had someone *wanted* to leave a dead rabbit for him, anyway? He'd just arrived. His interaction in the village had been negligible. He'd spoken to the pub landlord, Mrs Rowntree, and the police officer who'd guarded the house the previous morning. There'd been no drama and no arguments. Nothing that warranted such a macabre gift.

The little thing was stiff as a board when he picked it up. It was intact, too. Not roadkill, then. Jack stepped back inside and closed the door in case someone was watching.

Ten minutes later, he left the house to go for a run.

He'd bagged the rabbit and disposed of it and had armed every single deterrent in Jon's security system. The lengthy list wasn't enough for him. A few quick keystrokes had paired the alarm with his phone, and after a moment's thought, he'd added Alex's phone number to the list.

Any security breach would sound as if World War Three had broken out and raise flags all over the place.

He fitted the headset into his ear while he walked to the end of the lane.

"Morning." Alex answered on the second ring.

"I'm going out." Jack said. "I've hooked your phone into Jon's security system alongside mine. If it goes off, someone is nosing who shouldn't."

"You found something?"

"No. Gut feeling. I need to get out of the house to think. It's too quiet without Jon there."

"I understand."

"Good. I call you when I'm back."

Between the fog, a bag of Towcester cheesecakes, and one enormous stack of ancient tech, the day dragged.

The long run along tiny lanes had done nothing to quell Jack's misgivings. He'd stopped in the *Yarn Looters* on the way and the reaction to his presence had been the same as in the pub: hastily aborted conversations and a slew of sideways glances. He hadn't even sat down, though the place looked inviting with its deep, cosy armchairs and small tables.

The *Yarn Looters* was a place for knowing looks and whispered confidences. Jack knew he'd be the topic of many such conversations as soon as he was out of earshot. The words already hovered over the handful of patrons like the fog hung over the village, hinting more strongly than the silence that had greeted his arrival that something was amiss.

Nothing he said or did would get him the answers he wanted. Instead of asking questions, he'd bought cheesecake and croissants and took them back to Jon's house and a study full of diskettes and cartridges that needed checking one by one.

Jack shivered while he sat in the silent study over his slow, painstaking work. The house was warm, the chill not physical. He was reacting to Jon's absence; to the walls staring accusations at him as the stack of disks by his side grew and grew.

At dusk, men arrived with packing crates and bags of shopping: coffee, milk, sugar, bread, beer, and takeaway curry. It was a relief to know that, as out of sorts as he felt, he could avoid the pub that night.

"You sound strange. What's up?"

They were twenty minutes into their Skype call, and Jack was curled up in bed in Jon's spare room. He had the tablet propped on the pillow beside him and listened to Gareth breathing. Without the call, he'd be working through the night, but Gareth knew him too well. He'd insist on an answer, too.

"Nothing in particular. Just... being here when Jon isn't. Wishing I knew what had happened."

"Have you talked to the villagers?"

"Hm. They're not saying much."

"That's villages for you, I suppose."

Jack kept quiet, and Gareth didn't make him wait.

"You think the villagers know who did it?"

"Not entirely." Jack tried to explain the strange vibe he'd got every time Jon's death had come up. "It's like... they have an idea, but won't say anything because... it would sound ludicrous?"

"Ludicrous." Gareth tasted the word on his tongue and Jack pictured his eyes narrowing and his brows creasing. "Unbelievable, you mean?"

"I don't know what I mean, Gareth. It's a vibe. Unbelievable, implausible, impossible... I've no idea."

"Have you talked to that detective fellow?"

"About a strange feeling I had in the pub? He'll suggest I had a drink too many. Or he'll tell me to stay away from the pickles."

"Maybe your villagers feel the same way."

"You've never lived in a village in your life. How do you know?"

"I know about people and people are predictable. If you're after the intricacies of village life, talk to Conrad. He grew up in a place so tiny it isn't even on the map. As he tells it, cows walked in the streets."

"Yeah, right. When did he tell you that?"

"We may have gone out drinking one night."

"That must have been a brief night. Man's a lightweight. If you really want to go drinking, go with Lisa. Though, come to think of it, you probably have, haven't you? Spill it, Flynn, who dragged whose arse home?"

"Jack. Look at me."

That was an order. Jack realised he'd rolled onto his back and lay staring at the ceiling. Realised, too, that he'd been rambling. He turned his head towards the tablet and saw Gareth frown. "I'm okay. I promise."

Gareth kept studying him. "No, you're not. But you'll do. For now." *Until I get you home* went unspoken.

Jack heard it anyway.

Talking to Gareth had helped. Jack woke with fresh determination early on Friday morning.

The dead rabbit on his doorstep the previous day, coming on top of feeling out of place in Jon's home without Jon around, had rattled his cage.

Finding an equally dead fish barely ruffled his composure.

The fish was dinner-sized, pale with dark splotches, and the pouty mouth and the whiskers suggested a carp or something similar. Like the rabbit, the fish was intact except for a few puncture marks that made Jack think of someone fishing with a barbecue fork.

And that made no sense at all.

Jack didn't let it bother him. He bagged the fish and put it in the fridge to deal with later. Then he went running, picked up another supply of cheesecakes, showered, made coffee, and settled down to work.

Raf interrupted him at lunchtime. "Hey. How's it going?"

"Slowly. Do you remember six-inch floppies?"

"You need a doctor?"

"You need to pick your teeth up from the floor?"

"You started it. What's a...?"

"Don't ask. They're old tech. Slow tech. And he had hundreds of the things. Different question."

"Shoot."

"What's the technical term for someone breaking into a place and leaving things?"

"What?"

"Yeah. Food. Or at least I hope it's meant as food. It made sense on the first day when Jon's neighbour brought

43

cake. I thought she was nosy, and it was an excellent cake. But now? Stuff turns up on the doorstep. There was a rabbit. And then a carp."

"Why don't you wait for them to drop off some vegetables and then ask Gareth to cook you dinner?"

"Hilarious."

"Not. Flynn said he's driving up to see you tomorrow. You know that, right?"

"I know that." Jack was looking forward to it. No. Scratch that. A visit was fine, and he *was* looking forward to it, but he wanted to be back home.

A long evening in the hot tub with music, a glass of red, and Gareth lounging in the water opposite him ... now there was motivation to finish going through Jon's notes.

"Have they found the bugger yet?"

"Not to my knowledge."

"And the villagers aren't cooperating, I guess."

"How do you know?"

"I haven't spent all my time in London," Raf said. "I did a two-year stint with Dorset CID, and I tell you one thing ... never again. When people have known each other since the year dot and families have lived in the same place for generations, the number of skeletons lying around for you to trip over is unbelievable. You get called to a simple break-in, and it turns out to be a family feud going back to the Great Depression. Gimme London any day. People move every few years and yes, they're nosy and spiteful, but at least they talk."

"Jon wasn't born here."

"Way I heard it, he's been living there for thirty years. That's practically local."

"I suppose."

"So why is someone leaving dead rabbits on your doorstep?"

"One. One dead rabbit," Jack said. "And I have no

idea."

"Don't you find it just a bit creepy?"

"I did. Do. But what do you expect me to do about it? Mount a camera over the door?"

"That would work. What about footprints?"

"That was the weird thing." Jack pulled the disk from the reader and tossed it into the packing crate he had open beside the desk before reaching for the next item on the stack. "There weren't any."

"At all?"

"Not that I saw. The path had a thin layer of snow. The flowerbed beside it was wet earth without. I'd have said that whoever left the thing must have brought it before it snowed, but there was a drag mark in the snow beside the rabbit. And then, of course, Jon's early warning system."

"Huh?"

"The gate squeaks. You don't sleep through that."

"Sounds as if you've landed yourself a proper little mystery." Raf said. "I wanted to ask your help with something, but you've got enough on your plate right there."

"You sure?"

"Yeah. It'll keep until you're back home."

"Thanks, Raf. I'll call you."

FIVE

"Do you think Jack is awake yet?" Nico asked as Gareth pulled the Range Rover into a space on the village green. "Or do you think he worked all night again?"

"He promised to go to bed after we talked." Gareth didn't think Jack had stopped working. They'd signed off not long after midnight, but Jack had been too keen to be done with his task, and Gareth had seen him immersed in work often enough to know that he rarely stopped once he got properly stuck in. "I'm thinking he needs breakfast."

Daniel's hands stilled on the open car door. "You want to go back into town?"

"No, no. Remember Jack talking about the teashop? We'll get cakes." He pointed towards the thatched, whitewashed cottage across the green with its understated black sign beside the door. "It looks as if it's open."

"Why's it called *Yarn Looters?*"

"Jack told us that," Daniel said. "It's a knitting shop and a cafe."

"I know he said that. But loot is something you've stolen, right? Why would you steal the wool? Or are they stealing sheep?"

"Rustling. Stealing sheep is called rustling," Gareth said.

"Why?"

46

"No idea. Put it on your research list."

"I'm sure Jack knows."

"We'll see him in a minute. Ask him."

The interior of the teashop was warm and cheerful. Cosy armchairs and sofas—each one with a basket beside it—huddled around small tables.

A rainbow display of colourful yarns took up one side of the room while on the opposite side were shelves filled with boxes of home-made biscuits, jars of jams and preserves, cakes, and artisan chocolates.

Pencil sketches and watercolours decorated the walls. The china on the tables matched, the furniture around the room did not, and Gareth recognised the low-ceilinged, oak-beamed space for what it was: someone's passion, each tiny detail chosen with care and put together with love. The vibe spilled out as it did in their home when Jack was around, and Gareth wondered whether Jack had noticed and what he thought of it.

Nico and Daniel grabbed a basket and made a beeline for the food. They'd need supervision before they bought the store and Jack complained he needed to go on a diet, but for a while he'd let them have their fun.

Gareth trundled after the two, stopping to examine a rather austere drawing of a graveyard in winter. The sketch took a hint of colour from the skeins of purple wool that lined the neighbouring shelf until the image reminded him of vestments and chant and, weirdly enough, an afternoon spent learning to use eyeliner.

It was the sort of place that Jack sought when he needed solitude, and as Gareth breathed the enticing scents of baking cake and cast an appraising glance over the extensive display of home-made food, he could picture Jack curled up in the corner, coffee by his side and a laptop on his knees.

"Good morning." A cheerful voice drew him from his

thoughts. "Welcome to the *Yarn Looters*."

"Bonjour." Gareth reacted to the sexy accent more than the words and replied in French before he'd thought or even turned.

The woman offering him a welcoming smile had dark eyes and that indefinable something only French ladies seemed able to pull off, whether they were out shopping, attending a soiree, or coming home from three days stuck in the mud. Gareth couldn't explain how it was done, or even what the "it" consisted of, but he was very much aware of it.

The lady presiding over the *Yarn Looters* was a case in point. A streak of flour marred her cheek, and her auburn hair was a messy twist held up with a pencil, but she looked more put together than any Englishwoman Gareth had ever met.

Cheered, he matched her friendly smile. "Comment allez-vous?"

"Very well, thank you," she replied in her mother tongue. "We've not seen you here before, have we?"

"No. First visit. It's a charming place you've got here. Jack said you restored it from a wreck." Gareth was pleased to find that his French didn't desert him. The flowing cadence suited the quiet charm of the colourful interior.

"Jack?"

To Gareth's delight, she pronounced it the French way, just as Rio did. It sounded sexy that way and a touch mysterious.

"Oh, Jon Briggs's friend—dark hair, green eyes, very... serious? Yes. He's a little right. It wasn't quite a wreck. A touch neglected, but perfect for what we wanted, you see?"

"Yes, I see. How long have you been open?"

"Three years next summer. Jon was one of our best customers. He used to spend a couple of hours here almost every day." The cheer faded from her eyes, and she was no longer smiling. "It's awful, losing him like that."

Gareth looked around the cosy shop and tried to reconcile her words with Jack's description of Jonathan Briggs. "Jon Briggs came here to... knit?"

"Why not? Have you seen the gorgeous yarns we stock? We dye our own, too." She smiled a little roguishly and Gareth felt his lips curl in response. "Knitting is relaxing. That's why people come here. It gets you out of the house if you're living by yourself, gets you the chance to chat with other people."

"And to eat your cakes, I imagine. You have something on the go that smells delicious. Gingerbread?"

"Almost right. They're honey cakes. Do you bake?"

"I do."

"And do you knit?"

Gareth laughed and shook his head. "I wouldn't know where to start. And then I'd be all thumbs."

"It's easy, really." She held out her hand. "I'm Aviva, by the way."

"Gareth. And the two looting your biscuit shelves are Daniel and Nico." The two had stacked a basket with more than breakfast for Jack, though Jack had been foremost in their minds.

"Look at this." Daniel waved a packet under Gareth's nose. "Morello cherry granola. He'd love that for his breakfast, right?"

"If you're talking about Jack, he also loves these little cheesecakes," Aviva said. "He bought them on Thursday and came back for another batch yesterday morning."

Daniel inspected the small cake Aviva handed to him. "They look like custard tarts."

"They're a local specialty." Aviva took a cheesecake from the plate and broke it in half to show Daniel. "See. It's a pastry case and curd cheese, mixed with currants."

Daniel chewed on the piece Aviva had given him. "Oh,

that's good. We'll take some, right?"

Gareth nodded. "Let's have a dozen."

"How is Jack getting on with Bagpuss?" Aviva asked when Gareth joined her by the till to pay for his purchases.

Nico and Daniel clearly thought that Jack hadn't eaten in a week. Or that he shared the house with a horde of starving Vikings. "Getting on with whom?"

"Jon's cat?"

"He has a cat?"

"Oh, mais oui bien sûr. A lovely Russian Blue Jon rescued a couple of years ago. Big old softie, that boy. And a formidable hunter, or so Jon's neighbour keeps saying, even though Jon always denied it."

Gareth wanted to continue that conversation, wanted to understand why Jack hadn't mentioned sharing Jon's house with a cat, but the bell over the door jangled as a middle-aged couple came into the shop and settled themselves at a table. Aviva would be busy looking after them, so Gareth gave up on his plans and followed Nico and Daniel out into the village.

"Gareth was flirting with the lady in the tea shop," Nico snitched as soon as they had finished the greetings.

"Was he? Which one?"

"The French lady."

"Oh, Aviva. She's nice."

"And you know that ... how? You've been in the *Yarn Looters* twice to buy cheesecake."

"Hey. I used to be a spy. I have skills," Jack said, mock-serious. The air force blue rollneck made Gareth's eyes pop and was tight enough to make Jack's mouth water. He hugged that thought to himself until they had a moment alone. Was it weird that seeing Gareth still did it for him, even after being together for over two years?

"Her hair is cool."

Daniel's comment distracted him from thoughts of Gareth in fitted clothing. "It's chestnut. What's cool about it?"

"It has purple in it. And pink. And... and you're never sure if you've really seen the colours. They're sort of... underneath? I have to tell Jess about that."

"I didn't see any purple."

"Maybe she just had it done yesterday."

That was Gareth. Voice of reason and unrepentant flirt. He held Jack's gaze when Jack looked up, but the hint of colour in his cheeks said Nico had it right and Gareth had been looking.

Jack smiled. Nothing wrong with window shopping as far as he was concerned. And it was nice to have the three of them here. "Learn anything useful? In the teashop, I mean."

"Jon could knit."

"I know." Jack waved at the colourful cushions and rugs that decorated the chairs and window seat. "He taught himself after he came out of prison."

"He was in prison?" Nico squeaked. "For what?"

"For being a spy. In East Germany. They had him for eighteen months before they exchanged him for one of theirs that we caught."

"Did they ... hurt him?" Nico's voice was whisper soft as he remembered something he'd read.

Jack shrugged. "I don't know. He didn't talk about it. Not to me. I know he didn't sleep well when he came home. He read somewhere that knitting was relaxing, so he bought some needles and wool and taught himself."

"He didn't go to the shop for help?"

"The shop wasn't there, back then. Or rather it was, but it was just another pub."

"Now it's really cosy," Nico said. "I like the armchairs."

"The cakes are great, too. We bought honey cake for you. It's Dutch. And cheesecakes."

"Are you trying to fatten me up? The lady next door brings cake, someone's left a rabbit on the doorstep the other day, and yesterday morning I got a fish. It's huge."

"Why so grumpy? Shouldn't you be pleased they're looking after you?"

"Nosy so-and-sos, that's what they are. There's a perfectly decent pub in the village. And the teashop. No need to leave me food as if ... hey, do you think someone has a guilty conscience?"

Gareth's eyebrows drew together. "That's an interesting idea. It would mean the murderer is a villager, though."

"What kind of fish is that?" Daniel breezed back into the living room, holding the latest of the offerings left for Jack. "We've not cooked one like that before."

"I should hope not. That's a hugely expensive koi. Look at the size of that thing. It must be ancient."

"What?"

"Koi? Ornamental fish you keep in a pond?" Gareth took the fish and turned it this way and that. Then he went still.

"What?" Jack asked again, suspicious now.

"That rabbit someone left you... was it dressed?"

"No. Just dead. Why?"

"Because this carp... I wonder... Where is Bagpuss?"

"Where is what?"

"Jon's cat."

"He doesn't have a cat."

"Your lady Aviva told me he rescued one a couple of years ago. You've been here four days. You must have seen it."

"No."

Gareth took the carp back to the kitchen while Nico sidled up to Jack and tugged on his sleeve. "There should be a bed for Bagpuss. And dishes and cat food and—"

"There's not even a cat flap. And I've been here most of the time. Unless it's an invisible one, there's no cat here."

Gareth considered the packing crates in the corner of the living room, the pile of notes, and the neat stack of files covering one end of the long dining table. "How far along are you?"

"Almost done. Couple more hours."

"You mean you can come home with us?"

"All going well. Yes."

"Then why don't you finish your stuff while we look for the cat? Anywhere sensitive we shouldn't go?"

Jack shook his head. "Ignore the boxes with the red tape around them and don't cross the police tape. They're not done in the garden yet."

"That's cat food, right?" Daniel stood on a chair and inspected the contents of the cupboard in the utility room. "It has a cat on the front, but it looks like... I dunno... breakfast cereal. Do cats eat cornflakes?"

"They eat dry food that looks like those grape nut things you broke your tooth on," Nico said. "Not cornflakes. They also have meat or fish in sauce."

"Like these?" Daniel held out a box of food packets.

"Yeah, that looks right. My mum used to buy Whiskas. Ours came in tins, but it was Whiskas. Did you know cats can't chew?"

"No way. How do they eat mice and rabbits if they don't chew?"

"They tear out chunks that are small enough to swallow."

"Yeah, sure."

"Nico's right," Gareth said from the door. "You've found the cat food?"

"There's dishes here, too." Daniel held up a couple of white ceramic bowls that had black cat silhouettes at the bottom. "Why didn't Jack see these?"

"Alex asked him to look through Jon's papers. He'd find that tough enough. I imagine he didn't want to dig around in Jon's personal stuff more than he had to."

Daniel nodded. Jack was like that. He always knocked before he came into their room, and while he told him and Nico to tidy up, he touched none of their things unless they said so. He and Gareth weren't like some of their school friends' parents, who read letters, diaries, and school reports without ever asking.

"If there's cat food and dishes, where's the cat?" Daniel jumped down from his chair. "And where does it sleep?"

"Jack!"

The scream—and it *was* a scream—sent ice down Jack's back. He dropped what he was doing and flew down the stairs so fast the hallway blurred around him.

Nothing was on fire. But in the living room he found Gareth leaning against the door as if he was guarding it, while Daniel, white as a sheet, held a poker, and Nico struggled to stay still.

"Your friend really was a spy! He's got a secret room!"

"What?"

"Look!" Nico pointed and then Jack saw it. One side of Jon's large bookcase wasn't fixed to the wall as he'd thought. Instead, it *was* the wall. Or rather—a door.

"I only meant to tidy the poker away with the other tools," Daniel said. "I picked it up and there was a noise and..." He waved his hand at the bookcase.

"Have you looked inside?"

"We thought we'd leave that to you," Gareth said. "Just in case it's full of dead bodies. Or spy stuff."

"Good thinking." Jack ignored the possibility of dead bodies and Gareth yanking his chain. He stepped past Daniel and reached for the moving section of the bookcase. What he found behind the hidden door explained the upstairs study full of low roof beams and strange, out-of-date electronics.

Here was Jon's proper study, a room that ran the full length of the house, the place where he kept the sensitive data, his computers, and the files that mattered. Everything else in Jon's house was a decoy, designed to protect what he kept in this hidden room.

And Jack should have done more than wonder why a man of six feet five chose a room with low beams to work in.

Jack returned to the living room. "Well done, you. How did you find it?"

"I didn't even look for it." Colour was returning to Daniel's cheeks. "I picked up the poker to put it back in the rack."

Gareth's arms sneaked around Jack's waist. Jack turned his head and grinned at him, knowing what was coming. "How did you *not* find that?"

"I might be off my game. Then again ... I wasn't looking, either. I had no incentive to find it."

"And the poker leaning against the bookcase in an

otherwise painfully tidy room didn't bother you?"

"The poker's been sitting in that corner for as long as I've been visiting here. I thought Jon does what I do—stash weapons all over the house."

"Did you see a cat in there?"

Jack hadn't. "Shouldn't it have said something if it was there?"

"Not if Bagpuss is sleeping," Nico said. "Not if he feels safe."

"How do you know about cats?"

"We had two. We got them as kittens when I started school. I wanted to call them Bangers and Mash, but I lost against my mum and Tina and the two ended up being Roobarb and Custard."

"How is that any more logical than Bangers and Mash?" Jack asked, only to have Gareth chuckle in his ear. "Children's TV show characters. Even though I believe Roobarb was a dog."

"Yeah, a green one who kept getting beaten up by a pink cat. Which is why it was so stupid."

The matter clearly still bothered Nico years later. Jack decided on a distraction. "How do we find Bagpuss if he's hidden away and asleep?"

"Can we look?" Nico turned toward Jon's study.

"As long as you don't look with your fingers. Jon hid this room, so there could be traps."

"No touching. Understood."

"Yell if you see anything."

Daniel and Nico disappeared through the door, and Gareth's arms tightened around Jack's waist. "You really think he booby-trapped his study?"

"No idea, but I won't put it past him. Did I tell you that his alarm system nearly took me out the morning I got here?"

"Then maybe we should supervise the search party."

"You're not expecting to find a cat in there, do you?"

"I'm keeping an open mind," Gareth said. "There's cat food in the house, and dishes, and just as Daniel yelled, I found a cat basket. On evidence, I'd say Jon had a cat. But it's obviously not a house cat, or you'd have tripped over it already."

"We found a cat flap!"

"There you go."

Gareth let go of Jack and Jack minded losing Gareth's warmth and the comfort of his touch. He couldn't get home fast enough. Though going home today had just turned into a pipe dream.

At least he'd found Jon's other study. Or Daniel had. It saved him the embarrassment of telling Alex he'd done as she asked, only to be proved wrong three days later.

They joined the two boys in the study. The patio door, half covered on the garden side by an out-of-control shrub, had a cat flap. And since the garden was still a crime scene, it was no wonder Jack hadn't spotted the hidden room.

He turned away from the expanse of glass and looked over the room that—in its configuration of half study, half workshop—looked eerily similar to his own. If a cat needed a hiding space, it had plenty to choose from.

Fortunately, Nico and Daniel were as good as their word. They were on their hands and knees, peering into corners and under stacks of gear, careful not to touch a thing.

It was Gareth who eventually found the cat, curled up asleep in a large canvas bag on the bottom shelf of the bookcase.

"He *is* Bagpuss," Nico crowed and reached into the bag to pick up the furry bundle. "And he's *blue*."

The cat's fur was an unusual shade of blueish grey. Only its face and the tips of its ears were darker.

Jack's limited experience with cats included hisses and

claws, but Bagpuss didn't mind when Nico picked him up. He blinked his large green eyes and sniffed at Nico's fingers. Then he curled into Nico's arm and when Nico rubbed under his chin, Bagpuss purred loud enough for Jack to hear.

"Look how nice he is. He likes this. He's been feeling left out since you didn't even realise he was here."

Jack remembered being woken by strange sounds during his first night. He narrowed his eyes. "I was about to start a mouse hunt," he told the cat. "You could have said something."

Bagpuss ignored him and purred louder when Nico rubbed his chops.

"Come on, Bagpuss. Jack's neglected you all week. You had to hunt your own food, didn't you? I'm sure you'd love some dinner, right?" And then he marched right out of the room, cat still cradled in his arms.

"Did we just lose Nico to a cat?" Jack asked into the sudden stunned silence.

"Looks like," Gareth said. "You'd better tell him."

"Coward."

"What? Why?" Daniel looked confused.

Jack took a deep breath. "Nico looks as if he wants to take that cat home with us."

"Yeah, sure."

"It's Jon's cat," Jack reminded. "So, legally, it now belongs to Jon's son, Nigel."

"But he lives in Canada. Can he even take a cat from England to Canada?"

"I have no idea. But that is his choice to make, not ours."

"But at least we can take Bagpuss home with us, right? Just for the moment," Nico said from the doorway. "When you're done sorting out Jon's papers, there's nobody here to look after him, and we don't know when Jon's son will get here. I say we look after Bagpuss in the meantime, and then, when Nigel realises he can't take him back to Canada, Bagpuss will already have a new home and won't need to go to a rescue place."

"Nico. You've found this cat five minutes ago and you're already... well... like this." Jack waved his hands, wishing Gareth would step in and take over. Only the damned man didn't. If his face was anything to go by, Gareth was just as unequipped to handle this as Jack and Daniel. "What if Nigel wants Bagpuss?"

"Then we'll give him back. I just don't want him to be alone. Don't you think he misses your friend, too?"

Jack had nothing to say to that. He looked from Daniel to Gareth. "Any objections to offering a homeless cat a place to sleep?"

Six

"We're home," Daniel told him a few hours later over Skype. Jack had finished with the ancient tech upstairs and was now ensconced in Jon's proper study, assessing the documents there.

"How is Bagpuss?"

"He's fine. It's Nico who can't move. He sat the whole way with the cat carrier on his lap and his fingers threaded through the bars, so Bagpuss had something familiar close to him."

"I thought you took the blanket from Jon's armchair to keep him calm?"

"We did, and Bagpuss wasn't worried. He curled up in the basket, put his chin on Nico's fingers, and went to sleep. He only woke up when we were home and wanted to let him out."

"Make sure Nico stretches his back out before he goes to bed, or he'll be in agony tomorrow morning."

Both boys carried a raft of scars from the beatings they'd endured at Goran Mitrovic's hands. As they grew, abused muscles and scar tissue caused trouble, especially when they had to sit still for long periods. Jack and Gareth had worked with an osteopath and a physiotherapist to design the exercise schedules for the two, intent on reversing as much of the damage as possible. Stretching was key, and

60

while Jack didn't fuss about chores, bedtimes, homework, and sleepovers, he was an immovable object when it came to stretching and exercise.

"Gareth already told him," Daniel said. "We looked up what to do for Bagpuss and it said we need to let him explore each room and not disturb him. He makes a map in his head, so he knows where everything is and that it's not dangerous. Nico's following him around with the catcam."

"What?" Jack lifted the cover off an old desktop PC to check for surprises inside the case. Let nobody say he wasn't thorough.

"Jack, are you even listening?"

"Yes. Mostly. Why do we need to film the cat?"

"So we know what he's doing. Gareth said I can go into town tomorrow morning for cables and stuff. We need to go shopping anyway to get a cat flap and a bed and—" Daniel took a couple of deep breaths. "Nico's made a list."

"I'm sure he has." Jack wanted to be home. But on some level, he was also grateful he was stuck in Jon's study for a few more days. He felt profoundly sorry for Bagpuss. "There's cable in my workroom upstairs," he offered instead of criticism. "I think there's enough for what you need. Wireless would be easier, though."

Daniel chewed on his lower lip, thinking through his plan. "Nico wants him to sleep with us, so I'll set up a camera in our room first. And one downstairs. Maybe we can do the others when you come back." A shout from somewhere off camera distracted him and before Jack could ask anything else, Daniel tossed him a brief "talk to you later" and disconnected the call.

"Outclassed by a cat," he said when Gareth checked in much later that evening. "Are they okay?"

"Yep. All three fed, washed, and fast asleep. Bagpuss has claimed Daniel's pillow for his bed. You should have seen

Nico's face! You know, I think you were right about him. He's very like you."

"You saw it too, didn't you?"

"We all saw it, Jack. And I wasn't complaining. It's not a bad thing, the stuff you do."

"No, I know. It doesn't bother me when I'm doing it. But thinking of Nico like that— Don't say it, Flynn."

"I don't need to."

He didn't. Jack had returned to helping Baxter and Lisa in his spare time to ease the guilty feeling, only to find that he was taking greater care when picking his cases, which added a different kind of guilt.

There was no winning that one. Just as he couldn't make Nico's choices.

Gareth knew it, too. His smile was a little lopsided. "He may still change his mind, you know? Not completely. I don't think that will happen, but by the time he's old enough, he'll have choices we can't even imagine yet. It's not as if he has to go pimp hunting with you."

"I'm gonna kill anyone who suggests that to him." Jack's gut clenched at the thought of Nico playing bait in bars and clubs, dressing up like an underage rent boy, as Jack had done, to hunt men who bought children for sex.

Jack was older now, and even with makeup and costume tricks, he no longer looked half his age. He'd adapted the way he worked, but looking as if he wasn't old enough to vote had produced swift results. And enough people wanted those results and didn't count the cost.

"We'll talk to him about it when it comes up," Gareth said, reasonable and steadfast. "Let's not suffer the consequences before there's need."

Jack wanted to lean into Gareth's strength and remembered that he could. They were a team. They looked out for each other. "Thanks for driving up to see me. I needed that. Even finding the cat."

"Even when finding the cat meant you had to stay behind?"

"Yeah."

"Any idea how long you'll be? That room looked like a heap of work."

"It's not too bad. I'm getting through it faster than I got through the rest of the house."

"Why? Because everything is classified?"

"Nah. Because Jon has everything tagged, so picking out what's sensitive is easier. It helps that he trained Rio and Rio trained me ... so the tags we're using to index stuff are similar."

"Doesn't that defeat the object of keeping things secret?"

"Rio only ever trained me. And I don't think Jon had many people he trusted that much. It isn't so much about secrecy, either. It's more about making sure the right people can find the information they need."

"If you say so."

"I do."

"So ... timeframe?"

"I'm hoping to get it done by tomorrow night. Monday morning at the latest. Can't wait to sleep in my own bed again."

"Can't wait to have you there."

Jack wanted to roll his eyes, wanted to say something snarky in response to the clumsy innuendo, but it was too late. Gareth's voice had dropped half an octave, and the tone washed like honey over Jack's skin. He had met the man when he was seventeen, and fourteen years later the sound of Gareth's voice still gave him butterflies. So, who was the sappy one in that scenario?

"He's cute when he washes behind his ears." Nico held up Bagpuss in front of the camera and made him wave a paw while Daniel rolled his eyes. They were in the kitchen, having just finished lunch, and decided to Skype on the big screen Jack had fixed to the wall.

Jack wished he were right there.

Exhaustion pounded in his temples. He'd worked through the night, stopping for a couple of hours sleep around six, and continuing after a quick shower to wash away the cobwebs. He had a fridge full of food, thanks to Gareth's need to look after people. A stack of beef pasties and a dish of shepherd's pie had provided dinner and supper. The cake Gareth and the boys had brought from the *Yarn Looters* made a decent breakfast. And now Daniel, Nico, and Bagpuss helped him stay awake.

"He may be cute when he washes his ears." Daniel didn't sound convinced. "But he also licks his balls. How gross is that? And then he goes and snuggles with Nico..."

"You're just jealous he didn't snuggle with you."

Daniel stayed suspiciously silent.

"You could bribe him with food," Jack suggested. "Show him you like him."

"Cat food smells disgusting. And Nico always feeds him."

"You could offer him a bit of the chicken you cooked for dinner. He's bound to like that."

Daniel's sudden, arrested look was a sight to behold. When he got up from the table and disappeared from Jack's field of view, Jack bet he was making for the roasting tray and the chicken carcass, leaving Jack and Gareth to smile helplessly at each other.

"Do you have any idea how much gear one cat needs?"

"Nope. Blissfully ignorant."

"Yeah. I wish I was too. I'm sure the shop assistant saw us coming." Gareth grumbled, but Jack knew he really didn't mind. "You might think this house has enough comfy nooks for a cat to sleep, but you'd be mistaken. Bagpuss now has his own bed, not that he's taken any notice of the thing since we brought it in. We've also bought a cat flap."

"Which is still in the box, I assume?"

"You weren't expecting me to saw holes in the back door, were you? I'm leaving that sort of DIY to you."

"You'd better. I'm in no mood to go shopping for a new door." Not after he'd just replaced all the small glass panes in the old one for the second time. "How big is that cat flap?"

Gareth shrugged. "Big enough for Bagpuss?"

"Yes, thank you, Captain Obvious. Will it fit between the panes, or do I need to deconstruct the whole door?" Jack could guess the answer from Gareth's blank look. He and the boys had probably argued over the design and colour of the cat flap. None of them had given a thought to the back door. "And don't pout. 'S not as if I can do anything about that from here."

"Cranky Jack is cranky."

"And that grin you're sporting is illegal."

"Did you sleep at all?"

Damn man knew him far too well. And Jack didn't want to have it any other way. "Two hours," he said just as the doorbell chimed.

Gareth heard it too, and he smiled. "Go do your stuff. Call me later."

SEVEN

Detective Superintendent Peter Wynant wasn't his elegant self. The three-piece suit was gone, replaced by a woollen jumper and heavy coat. Mud spattered his boots and the bottom of his jeans, and his shadowed jaw and the dark circles under his eyes made him appear as tired as Jack felt.

Losing Jon Briggs wasn't personal for the detective, not in the way it was for Jack, so for Wynant to look like he did, there had to be a lot of pressure on the man. It didn't erase the hurt Jack felt, but it eased it a little. Jack held the door wide. "Come on in. Coffee or tea?"

"Tea, please. I've had far too much coffee in the last week." He followed Jack to the kitchen, cataloguing the rows of packing crates everywhere. "Once the crates are gone, nobody will know you've been through the house," he said, peeking into the living room. "Any particular reason?"

"Jon's son. We didn't want him to walk into a place that looks as if it's been ransacked."

"So instead of packing up anything that looked like paper or electronics, they sent you."

"You've got it."

"You've certainly been busy."

"I'm also almost done, so once we've had tea, I'll give you the tour."

"I need a tour?"

"I'm not here in any official capacity. Unless Nigel turns up in the next six hours, someone will need to..."

"I see."

"I'm sure you do. No news, I assume?"

"Not from our end. It sounds ludicrous given the life he lived, but he doesn't seem to have had any enemies. Not locally, at any rate. I was hoping you might have something for me."

Jack wished he had better news. "Nothing in his notes and papers that anyone might want to kill him for. He was far too canny for that. I think the villagers have a fairly good idea of what happened."

"Interesting. Kingsley, my partner, tells me the same thing. Anything to back it up? Any detail?"

"I wish. It's a feeling more than anything. Silences and sidelong glances."

Peter Wynant's tired gazed sharpened a little. "Why do you think they aren't talking? Are they protecting someone?"

"See? That's the exact impression I *didn't* get, and it's been bugging me since I set foot in the pub. It didn't feel protective. More like someone was afraid they'd not be believed. Or worse."

"Accused?"

"No." Jack tried to verbalise his impression. "Ridiculed."

"Ridiculed? How extraordinary."

"I know. Alien abductions are not common around here, right? I mean, what else can it be? Religious cult who leaves dead rabbits on people's doorsteps?"

"What?"

"Yeah. Just one strangeness of village life."

"Hang on. Someone left a dead *rabbit* on your doorstep?"

"And a dead carp." The words zinged through him as he spoke, reminded him of Gareth turning the fish over and over in his hands and— "I just had an idea. How far along are you with the garden?"

"That's what I came to tell you: the crime scene guys are done. They've packed up the last of their stuff."

"Then, after I've given you the tour of the house, could you give me one of the outside?"

"Sure."

The detective was damned good at his job. Despite knowing that something had caught Jack's interest, he didn't push or badger. He didn't demand answers Jack wasn't ready to give yet. He simply finished his tea and followed Jack through the house.

"Alex Marston will have the crates collected as soon as I tell her I'm done," Jack said. "If she doesn't, or Nigel gets here first—"

"I'll make sure nobody goes near them. Is any of it dangerous?"

"Not physically, no. And not in the metaphorical sense either. Wouldn't matter if we let the villagers have a read. But even the seemingly harmless can cause trouble if the wrong people get hold of it. Now let me show you the pièce de résistance."

He clattered back downstairs and crossed the living room. The door to the hidden study popped open before Wynant was close enough to see what Jack was doing.

"Right." Wynant's voice was like a quieter version of Nico's. "Now I believe he was a spy."

Jack rolled his eyes and led the way inside. "If a hidden study is all that's needed ... I've packed and labelled everything that needs to go into safe storage. As before, if Nigel gets here first—"

"I'll make sure it's out of the way. Are you contactable if there are questions?"

"Sure. I'll be back at work tomorrow, but I can answer a phone. Now, wanna show me around the garden?"

The light was fading as they stepped out of the back door into Jon's garden, a space as bare as befitted the end of January. A few evergreens grew between leafless shrubs, and the flower borders showed nothing but turned earth. The lawn was a ruin of muddy patches and trampled clumps of tired green. It would recover, given time and warmer weather, but for the moment, it reminded Jack of a battlefield.

A hint of wood smoke hung in the air, hinting at open fires in the neighbouring houses and reminding Jack of home. He hadn't bothered lighting a fire while he stayed at Jon's house, and now he wondered how Bagpuss was settling in. So far, the cat had taken everything in stride: a bunch of strangers clustering around him when Jon, the human whose company he was used to, hadn't been there for days. Being picked up, followed around the room, and shoved in a basket. And being in a car for a couple of hours before emerging in a strange place full of unexpected smells.

Jack hadn't thought that cats were so malleable. Maybe Bagpuss bided his time, hid claws and attitude until he knew what was happening, like a prisoner pretending to be unconscious or docile while hatching escape plans.

"Points of interest," Wynant began, and Jack peeked at the sketches that covered the pages in his notebook. Distances and angles, notes, and names. "Mrs Rowntree's house and garden to the right, Mrs Fergusson on the left. The end of the garden backs onto the lane." He moved towards the left-hand side of the garden. "The vic— Jon was found here."

Jack had seen the opaque gazebo over the space when he arrived and had known it marked the spot where Jon had died. With the forensic team gone, nothing hinted at the tragedy. No chalk outlines, no little yellow markers, no bits of string and no police tape.

Jack stopped for only a moment.

He hadn't come out here to see where Jon had died.

He'd come to connect the dots that floated loose in his mind, and it didn't take him long to find what he sought.

Lines of picket fencing, four feet tall with a gate near one end, separated Jon's garden from Mrs Rowntree's on the right and Mrs Fergusson's on the left. "I'd have expected a little more privacy."

"You mean the gates? That's an ancient public right of way. The council redirected the path to the bottom of the lane years ago. I'm told nobody but the residents ever use the gates nowadays."

"Did your crime scene people find any footprints near Jon's body?"

"Jon's garden shoes, Mrs Rowntree's slippers, and another unidentified set. Something with a smooth sole and soft edges. A second pair of slippers, or maybe overshoes."

"A third person?"

"They think so, yes. Broader than Mrs Rowntree's and deeper."

"That's no challenge. I'm surprised the woman leaves any footprints, tiny as she is." He scanned the fence, noted that the only sizeable gap in the row of pickets was right beside the gate, and then stepped closer.

Mrs Fergusson's garden reminded Jack of his travels in Japan: a pond, complete with rocky stream and tiny waterfall. Miniature maples and bamboo plants growing in glazed pots. A sculpted wilderness of shrubs and winding gravel paths. It was a garden made for contemplation and meticulously cared for.

"You like manicured gardens?" Wynant's voice came from beside him.

Jack thought of his own piece of wilderness, which Gareth was busy taming while Jack gave the house an overhaul. He considered the carefully placed rocks and flawless gravel and remembered a tranquil oasis in the middle of buzzing Tokyo. "It's ... pleasant. But it feels a little like a fish out of water in these parts," he said, not surprised to see an older lady approach the fence from the other side. She wasn't much taller than Mrs Rowntree, but wider and sturdy. And she moved around the ornamental rocks without looking where she was going, aware where each one was.

"When are you going to turn those bright lights off?" Her voice was sharp and querulous. "You've had them on at all hours. They disturb the fish."

"You should be alright now, Mrs Fergusson." Wynant's tone was apologetic. "Our team finished this afternoon. They've disconnected the floodlights, as you can see."

"About time. I hope someone put that horrid cat down, too."

"I beg your pardon?" For a heartbeat Jack thought he'd misheard, but the woman promptly disabused him of that notion. She knelt beside the gate and waved him over.

"Look at this. Just look at it, young man! These are scales from my prize-winning koi carp. That ruddy cat ... He steals my fish and molests my chickens, and I'm sure I had tuna in the fridge the other day, but when I looked it was suddenly gone and—"

Jack shot a glance at Wynant. Judging by the crease between his brows, his thoughts weren't any more pleasant than Jack's. Here, finally, *was* someone with a grudge. A belligerent someone with a temper. And she was talking to him.

Jack took a breath.

Let it out.

"Bagpuss stole tuna from your fridge?"

"How do you know the name of that blue devil?"

"Jon was a friend."

"Well. Then you should have visited him sooner, young man. You should have told him to put that murdering cat down. Besotted with that animal, he was. Wouldn't hear a word against it. He laughed when I told him it had stolen my carp. Told me a cat couldn't carry a fish as large as that, when I'd seen it with my own eyes and found the fish scales the next morning. He didn't listen. And he laughed." She turned to Jack and almost poked his eye out as she pointed a finger at him, shaking with anger. "You should have come sooner. *Someone* should have made him listen. If he'd not laughed at me, I wouldn't have hit him."

"You hit him?"

"Yes."

"What did you hit him with?"

She pointed towards the pond. "With the metal rod I use to pull the netting across to keep leaves out."

"If the pond had netting, how did the cat steal your fish?" Jack spoke the way he'd have talked Daniel out of a nightmare, calmly and quietly. He didn't display any emotion, but inside he was shaking apart.

"It's broken, isn't it?" She shouted now, spittle flying. Even that small sign of disagreement from Jack had set her temper blazing. "I had it put in just after Jon brought that horrid cat home. I kept catching him in the garden. Messing up the gravel and stalking my fish. And then, just before Christmas, the mechanism broke, and just as I'd expected, my carp started to disappear."

Jack nodded, but then he fixed his gaze on her. "You

know you can't have hit Jon. He was well over six feet tall. You're maybe five two. You couldn't have struck a blow that hit his head."

"I did. He knelt right there, fussing over that cat. I was speaking to him, and he ignored me. And he was *laughing*. I hit him. Twice. And he pitched forward and stayed there. I tried to get the cat, too, but he was already gone when I turned around. Horrid thing."

Until then, horror and compassion had balanced themselves out, but at the venomous satisfaction in Mrs Fergusson's voice, Jack went cold. His gaze met Wynant's over the woman's bowed head. The detective reached for the phone he carried holstered at his hip and pointed first at Jack and then at Mrs Fergusson's house.

Jack took the woman's arm. "The police are done with their work now, so there won't be any lights to disturb your carp," he said. "But you're shivering. Can we talk inside? Over a cup of tea, perhaps? You must be cold."

He steered her deftly towards her backdoor and inside to await the police.

EIGHT

"I'll find a car to drive you back to Jon's house," Wynant said four hours later. After he'd called in their news and asked the forensics crew to return—this time to go over the neighbouring garden—he'd arrested Mrs Fergusson. She'd been docile after her confession, and she'd moved like an automaton when Wynant and Jack had bundled her into the backseat of Wynant's jeep for the short drive to the police station, where Alex had joined them not long after.

Jack hadn't been interested in observing the interview. He'd spent the next two hours giving verbal and written statements of everything that had happened in a separate room from where Wynant was writing his own notes. Now everything had been typed, read to him, and signed, he wanted out of the place, keen to return to Jon's house and finish the task Alex had set him.

He didn't want to wait for a car, didn't want to talk, or be anywhere near people. Not with the rage boiling inside him. Jack shrugged into his leather jacket and rammed his fists into the pockets. "No need. I'll walk."

"It's five miles in the dark. In case you hadn't noticed, the villages don't have streetlights."

"Not as if I can get lost, now, is it? Straight up the A5, turn right at the roundabout and follow the road until I'm there. I might even find a pub along the way."

"I'll drive you," Alex said from behind his shoulder, and she sounded so like Lisa in that moment, or Gareth at his most bossy, that Jack didn't even think of arguing. He followed her out of the police station and into her car, hoping that she didn't expect him to make conversation.

She didn't, of course. She knew him better than that.

His phone was a welcome distraction. He had six missed calls—three each from Nico and Daniel—and one text message. The text was from Gareth.

Let me know you're okay.

It was as good as an order, and Jack wondered how to respond. His first inclination was to send a quick *I'm fine*, but it would be a deflection, a lie.

He didn't want to lie.

He didn't want to talk, either. Not even to Gareth. Not yet.

Jack stared at his phone; indecision writ large.

"It's Gareth. He knows you," Alex said from beside him, demonstrating once more that she knew him, too. And that some days, she read his mind.

Gareth knew him. Jack had gone to some lengths to let it happen. He shouldn't question it now.

Going to sit in the shower with a bottle, he typed, knowing Gareth would understand exactly what he meant.

He didn't send the text. It was too revealing.

Undamaged. Not okay, he texted in the end, just as the car stopped outside Jon's house.

Jack unbuckled his seatbelt. "Send your guys 'round tomorrow morning to pick up the crates and clear out the study. I only have the safe to go through. Then I'll write up summary notes for you."

"Anything we need to be concerned about?"

"No. He was too conscientious for that. Couple of minor things that might grow hot in time."

He reached for the door handle when Alex pulled a

metal flask from her coat pocket and held it out to him, not moving until he took it. "It's Islay Malt."

"Fitting."

Two heads popped over the edge of the sofa like curious otters when Gareth's phone chirped with a text message. It had grown late, but neither boy made any move to go to bed as they waited for Jack to call.

They'd all been on tenterhooks after Nico and Daniel's failed attempts to speak to Jack at dinnertime. Gareth suspected there'd been a break in the case. It was the only thing that would stop Jack from replying to a text message. They'd come this far, at least.

He swiped the screen to life and read the words. *Undamaged. Not okay.*

"He's not hurt, but he's not okay either," he told the two boys.

"Maybe he found out who killed his friend. He wouldn't be okay then," Nico said.

Gareth hadn't put his phone down yet when it started ringing. The tune it belted out wasn't *Rusty Nail*. Instead, a quiet piano melody sang through the room until Gareth answered.

"Hi Alex. Is Jack okay?"

"Physically he's fine. He and Wynant arrested the neighbour, and Jack's been at the station giving statements. I've just dropped him off at Jon's house. He insisted on finishing up, so he can leave tomorrow."

Gareth appreciated the details, but Alex hadn't told him yet what he really wanted to know. "How is he, Alex?"

"Quiet. Brittle. He and Wynant both look as if they

haven't slept in days, but I don't think it's physical exhaustion. Jack wanted to walk back from the police station. Five miles in the dark."

"I see." And he did. When life hit him with a low blow, he'd hide in the shower with a bottle of hooch. Jack needed action, motion, needed to walk or run or hit a bag.

"The neighbour, did she do it?"

"It looks like it. Whether she's entirely sane and responsible is another matter. She objected to Jon's cat robbing the prize-winning koi carp from her pond. Jon didn't believe a cat could snag a fish that big and she hit him over the head during an argument."

"Oh, dear." Gareth had seen death. Violent death and slow death and a couple of accidental deaths he still remembered in vivid detail years later. This, though ... of all the stupid ways to go... "You think Jack will be home tomorrow?" he asked instead of sharing any of the thoughts that swirled in his mind and crowded at the edge of his tongue.

"He told me to collect the crates tomorrow morning."

Alex knew what he'd been asking. Her non-answer told him she had no way to predict Jack's actions, either.

Jack pulled the carpet back and lifted the loose floorboard. Apprehension sliced through him when he saw what lay beneath, just as it had early that morning when he'd found the safe. He knew he needed to get inside to check it out. But safe breaking wasn't part of his skill set.

He could pick locks. He loved ciphers of all kinds ... and he needed a tricky challenge to occupy his mind. If he let himself dwell on the reasons why Jon had died, he'd implode.

Three deep breaths later, Jack fished his phone from his pocket. He snapped a photo of the front of the safe and sent it to Raf. Then he unscrewed the flask Alex had handed him and took a swig. The alcohol burned down his throat and spread warmth through his belly. Not relaxing him but softening the ragged edges. He contemplated a second sip when his phone rang.

"That your Sunday challenge?"

"I'm still working."

"Clearly not, or you'd have it open already."

"Oh, shut the fuck up, Gallant. Or rather, don't. Tell me how to get into this thing."

"Cut the back open?"

"It's in the floor. I'd need a JCB to get it out."

Raf hummed thoughtfully.

Jack let him think.

"Okay, listen up. I think you can do this. The lock's a six-digit combination with a clutch-driver and you're not up to manipulate that. If you can't get at the back, your best chance is to guess the combination. Normally I'd say you'd be there 'til Doomsday, but you knew the man whose safe this is. That gives you a fighting chance."

The second swig of malt was welcome. It also gave him an idea. Jack waited until the burn had dulled to embers before he spoke. "Thanks, Gallant. I'll keep the JCB in reserve."

Jack didn't entertain visitors while he worked. He'd rarely ever entertained visitors, period. But while he'd been fitting out his turret, he had added a sofa to his workroom, true to the deal he'd struck with the boys. Daniel often sprawled there, quietly doing his homework while Jack followed trails of his own. Nico visited more often since Jack had resumed his hunt for pimps and paedophiles. He never asked questions, but being with Jack while Jack worked seemed to give him a measure of comfort.

Now, curled into a corner of the small sofa in Jon's office, drawing squiggles on the notepad he had on his lap, Jack wondered who'd kept Jon company. Was this why he'd rescued Bagpuss? To have someone there with him while he worked? After finding the cat asleep in the tote, Jack could imagine him curled on the sofa beside Jon, snoring softly. Did cats snore? He realised he didn't know. He'd never really watched one sleep.

Maybe he'd remedy that soon. Maybe Bagpuss would sleep on his sofa now and then and keep him company.

The shapes on the notepad grew ever more fantastic while Jack let his mind wander. He was ace at patterns. What seemed random to many had shape and repetition to him. Jon hadn't been wired that way. He'd earned his spurs in the Sixties, at the height of the Cold War, and he had a knack for hiding information in ways that searchers would disregard as too obvious.

Had he done that here? Had Jon used an obvious number as his six-digit combination? Something like a date, maybe?

Of course, there were layers of obviousness.

Jon's date of birth was out of the question, as were those of his wife or son. He'd not used his wedding date, nor the date he lost his wife.

These dates were in the public domain and far too easily traced. If it *was* a date, it had to be one not automatically connected to Jon Briggs. The date of the Queen's coronation or some important cricketing milestone?

The church clock had chimed midnight when Jack

knelt beside the safe and carefully turned the dial. He selected number after number, and when the latch gave with a satisfying snick, he was grateful for his magpie mind.

Tiny pink baby shoes were the first thing he saw when the door swung back—not that he needed the confirmation.

The combination that opened the safe was the date Jon had lost his only grandchild. And Jack felt like an intruder.

The safe held a deed box with Nigel's name and address on the label. A folder for Rio. And a letter addressed to Jack.

Jack stared at the envelope for a long time. Why write to him? He and Jon spoke every few weeks. They didn't have any unresolved issues between them. Neither could Jon have predicted that his neighbour would lose her temper over a dead fish and brain him with a metal pole.

That thought burned like acid as it had earlier and every time since.

Jack took another swig of Islay malt. Needing liquid courage to open an envelope was ludicrous. He'd never given a toss what anyone thought of him.

Except for Rio, and Gareth, and Jon, of course.

He tore the envelope open with a huff. The letter inside was dated 23rd May 2012.

The day Jack had resigned from MI6.

Hi Jack,

Gandalf's been wailing in my ear for the last hour, bemoaning the fact that you've finally called it a day.

He also told me why.

I'm glad you went after those kids. Houseman was a mess when they got to him, but he'll live and he'll heal. He'd never do that knowing you'd rescued him at the expense of his children. I'm glad you saw this and didn't let Gatting dissuade you.

I'm glad about the choice you made, too. You may not be. But then again, you've taken a long time to think about it, so I hope you have that calm, still look that says you're at peace with yourself. I wish nothing more for you.

You've given the service the best of yourself for almost fifteen years. There's no shame in walking away before it kills you. Though I think the being killed was never the issue. You'd have taken that without complaint. But they were twisting you up inside and you don't need or deserve that.

I left you a message. I know you won't answer it. Not now. Not until you've decided what you're going to do next. I hope you'll take your time with that decision. As much time as you took deciding to leave.

I assume Rio is abroad because he hasn't called me yet. If you're worried he'll try to dissuade you, don't be. He'll want to keep you close and cooperating, but he won't keep you in against your will. That's not how Rio works, and I'm sure you know that.

Don't grab the first job that comes your way, Jack. I know you don't need the money and you deserve time to decide what's important. You've changed so much since we first met. But you still believe that you don't deserve to be happy.

Let me tell you for the million and seventh time: you're wrong.

For all the good you've done over the years, you deserve tenfold in return. And a bunch of us are ready to bargain with hell to make sure you get it. Give yourself time and if you need help, pick up the phone and ask. You know whom to call and none of us will turn you down.

Remember the day our little girl died? You were what? Fifteen? You could barely tolerate being in the same room with strangers, and you certainly didn't go out of your way to talk to anyone. That day, when you came up with Rio, you talked to me. You were looking at me, always so serious, and you said: I'm sorry you're hurting. Just remember that she isn't.

That's what I wish for you, Jack.

Stop hurting. Stop being the oyster ashamed of the piece of grit that got inside its shell when it was tiny. Because I can tell you

one thing, Jack: the pearl you fashioned from that grit, the one
you're hiding inside yourself ... it is glorious.

And nothing to be ashamed of.

Jon

Jack stared at the words, read them a second and then a third time. They brought back so many memories. Some that had already been close to the surface, some that he'd buried deep. He regretted none of his choices, though the way Jon had seen him startled him.

Gareth had accused him more than once of hiding himself away. Had he truly been that closed off, convinced he didn't deserve happiness?

Jack couldn't credit the thought, but he didn't dismiss it either. He filed it away to examine later, when grief didn't edge his thoughts and he wasn't raging at fate and batty neighbours.

For the rest of the night, he stayed curled up on the sofa, scrolling through the pictures of Gareth, Nico, and Daniel he had on his phone.

It helped.

NINE

B y nine thirty, the news was all over the village. Instead of the silence and stares he'd grown used to since his arrival, villagers nodded and murmured greetings as he followed the lane and crossed the green to the *Yarn Looters*. He couldn't face the silent house now his work was done, and Jon's killer had been caught.

He'd gone up to the church in the early hours and wandered between the graves for a while. They were the usual mixed bunch one found in any cemetery: some old, some not so old, some neglected, and some well-tended. He didn't know if Jon had planned to be buried in the village or if he'd left it to Nigel to choose his father's last resting place. He only knew there was a funeral in his future filled with ghosts and memories and people he'd never wanted to meet again.

The content of Jon's letter swirled through his mind. Jack didn't know why Jon hadn't sent it, and asking was impossible. All he could do was speculate and that, like nothing else before, finally brought it home that Jon was gone.

Remaining in Jon's house was not an option.

He was the *Yarn Looter's* first customer that morning, which had to be the reason Aviva threw her arms around him and hugged him as soon as he stepped through the door.

"Thank you for working it out," she said as she led him to a table in the far corner. "We were all so worried we'd never know what happened to him. Jon didn't deserve that."

Jack was too stunned to reply. He fell into the comfortable chair and when Aviva set a pot of coffee and a plate of warm cheesecakes in front of him, he dug in. It wasn't until later that he found his voice. And words.

"You could have told me about Bagpuss," he said, hands wrapped around the delicate china mug to soak up some warmth. He'd not felt warm since the scene in the garden.

"You didn't know Jon had rescued Bagpuss?"

"No. He never mentioned it. And Bagpuss stayed out of the way. He must have come home at night and hidden himself, because I tell you ... that first night... I almost started a mouse hunt."

Aviva had a lovely laugh. Jack wasn't surprised Gareth had been flirting.

"What's going to happen to Bagpuss? Does someone need to feed him?"

"No. Nico sort of fell in love and adopted him on the spot. They took him home with them on Saturday. I think they're even setting up video surveillance." He pulled his phone out and showed her the pictures the boys had sent him.

"Bagpuss seems to enjoy being there," Aviva said once she'd scrutinised them. "Jon said he's a very relaxed cat. He would have loved knowing Bagpuss has a new home."

Jack hoped she was right. He caught a flash of pink when she moved her head, and that reminded him of something else. "Can I ask you something ... personal?"

Aviva narrowed her eyes at him. "You can ask."

"That colour you have in your hair, the pink, and

purple ... why do you hide it?"

She smiled. "I'm not hiding it. I'm just not advertising." She shrugged one shoulder. "Many of our customers are very traditional. Body art might put them off coming. Crazy hair colour, too, I imagine. But I've always wanted to colour my hair, so Lydia suggested I'll do it this way. It's subtle, no?"

"Very. Daniel loved it, which is why seeing it reminded me. His girlfriend's a bit like you. She'd love to have colours, but she works in a GP surgery evenings and weekends and doesn't want to upset the patients."

"These colours wash out," Aviva said. "And they're only very fine strands. She needs to bleach first, I think. It makes the colour stick. If she goes to a good hairdresser..."

"Thanks. I know whom to ask if she wants to give this a go." Jack set his empty mug down and rose. He had to pack, make sure the crates were secure, and drop the contents of the safe and his notes at the police station before he went home.

Until this moment, he hadn't been sure of his plans. Talking about domestic things like Bagpuss and the boys had pushed going home to the top of his list.

"We'll not see you again, will we?" She waved him off when he tried to pay for his breakfast and accompanied him to the door.

"Not for a while. But maybe one day we'll all come back for your cheesecake."

Jack had never been so glad to see his home. Finding Gareth's Range Rover parked in the driveway when he pulled up only added to the feeling. Wynant had called him before he left Holton Wick to thank him for his help. When he'd dropped in at the station a while later, he'd learned that Mrs Fergusson had repeated her confession with both a solicitor and counsellor present and was being assessed for mental issues. Until that moment, Jack had kept his thoughts at bay. After that...

Jon Briggs hadn't deserved to die like this.

Grateful to be out of the nightmare traffic snarl that was the M25, he walked through the front door, straight into two tight hugs and a wave of giggles.

"Yeesh, you're cold." Nico jumped back as if Jack's leathers were pure ice.

"Bagpuss is sleeping on Nico's pillow," Daniel said. "You can feed him when he wakes up. He gives you a high-five when he wants food. Did we tell you?"

"He likes Daniel's roast chicken. When you put bits on the kitchen counter, he stands up on his back legs and nicks it. He drinks cream from a saucer, too. And he eats raw liver!"

"Does he eat any cat food?"

"Oh, sure. Beef in tomato sauce. How weird is that? He likes cheese, too. And scrambled eggs and—"

"Give him a chance to get out of his leathers before you prattle his ear off."

Gareth's voice boomed off the ceiling, and Jack heaved a sigh. Never mind the boys' chatter. His ears rang from almost three hours on the bike, and he struggled to take in all the details that came flying at his head. He couldn't decide whether Nico and Daniel were just sharing news or whether they had need of him, and that alone told him how worn out he was after two nights of little sleep and hours of veering between grief and rage.

A car horn blaring outside started a scramble in the hallway.

"Don't rush," Gareth barked. "He's not going

anywhere."

Now that the boys were past him, rushing into coats and boots, Jack saw Gareth held their duffel bags and school bags. He recalled nothing in their schedule saying the two wouldn't be home. "Where are you off to?"

"Aidan's."

"What for?"

Daniel turned back and hugged him. "Gareth said you're bound to be angry over the way your friend died."

The comment went like ice down Jack's back. "You're going to stay with Aidan, because I might be ... angry?"

"Not like that," Nico said from his other side. "You'd never yell when we're here, even if you wanted to, and maybe you need yell to get it all out. Gareth doesn't mind. We're going skating with Aidan, and then we'll eat pizza and ... and we'll be back tomorrow."

"Before you ask, they cooked that one up themselves," Gareth said as they stood on the doorstep and watched Aidan's Jaguar disappear down the driveway. "They'd skyped with Aidan, and had it sorted out before they told me." He pulled Jack back into the hallway and closed the door.

"Gave me a bad moment or two," Jack admitted while he finished shedding his riding gear and hanging the damp leather up to dry.

"They're not afraid of you, Jack. They never have been."

"Yeah, I know." Exhaustion swept over him. "Just feeling stupid."

Gareth pulled him close and wrapped him in a hug. Gareth's palm moulded to his nape, and Jack shivered even as he felt safe and cherished. "Do we have to be anywhere?"

"Not if you don't want to be." Gareth's breath stirred the hair at Jack's temple. "If you need a distraction ... there's a play at the Orange Tree that sounds interesting. Or we can go out to dinner."

Jack decided that people and noise would rile him to violence. "I need a shower," he said. "And if you don't mind, I'd rather stay in and watch you cook."

"Do you now?"

Jack braced his hands on the tile while streams of hot water pounded his neck and shoulders. It didn't relax him, only made him think of the open-air showers in the middle of a cold German winter Jon had told him about. How they'd had to slither over ice-filmed cobbles in bare feet, and how the water had stung like a deluge of tiny sharp needles.

It had been one of the very few times he'd ever seen Jon Briggs drunk.

Even if he had barely seen him at all.

It had been late one night when Jack had skyped him with a request for information. He couldn't remember what he'd needed, but his quick query had turned into four hours of talk. The sort of talk he'd never had with anyone before. Wouldn't have had with Jon had they been face to face in the same room together. They'd spoken about the price they each paid for the secrets they kept and whether they were better or worse off keeping those secrets. It was the kind of conversation that left Jack stripped bare and feeling as if someone had put him on display, even as he knew Jon wouldn't breathe a syllable of their discussion to anyone.

Jack had answered some of the questions their talk had raised for himself. He'd left the service that was twisting his sense of wrong and right into increasingly meaningless shapes and had made peace with parts of his past. He'd even chosen to make a family for himself. And while Jon knew about Jack's new job at Nancarrow Mining, Jack had never really told him about Gareth, Nico, and Daniel, and his new life. When Jon was one of the few people who had deserved to know.

Cool air stung his back, reminded him once more of cold and ice and the stupid ways men punished each other for their convictions. Then Gareth shut the shower door and warmth returned. Firm hands slid up his sides and along his tight shoulders. Gareth's fingertips dug into tense muscles and Jack let himself relax with a groan.

"Thank god we had the combi boiler fitted." Gareth spoke in his ear to be heard over the water. "Otherwise, you'd be freezing your nuts off."

"I think I'd have noticed the water running cold."

"Of course. Along with the squadron of flying pigs over there."

Gareth's hands came back, slippery with soap. They slid into Jack's hair, massaging his scalp until Jack was putty in Gareth's hands. "Gods, I've missed you doing that."

"Serves you right for running off to solve murders in the Home Counties."

"Murder, singular. And that's not what I went for."

"You solved it, anyway."

"And what good did it do? Jon's still dead, and to know he died because of a stupid fish—" Jack's fist hit the tile and he flinched at the sting. This was what hurt the most. That a man who'd offered his life for the greater good over and over, who'd bled and sacrificed and suffered, should die like this, so... pointlessly.

"Needlessly," Gareth corrected, as if Jack had spoken his thoughts out loud. "He didn't choose what happened to him, that's true, but Jack—most of us don't. He could have died on the roads or fallen off a ladder. Or he could have died slowly and painfully of cancer. Just because he spent years choosing the risks he took doesn't mean he wouldn't be subject to fate. Rather than focus on the manner of his death, remember how he lived. That's a better tribute."

Gareth was right. Jack knew it. He also knew acceptance would come in time. He just wasn't ready for it yet. Wouldn't be ready for a while.

In the end, he did what he always did: he found distractions. He took pleasure from the steam that wound around them, locking the world out. He relished the hot water that took the chill from his bones, and he savoured every slip and slide of Gareth's hands, every touch and caress, until the anticipation grew too strong to bear. That's when he turned and wrapped his arms around Gareth's waist.

"Bed," he requested, leaning forward to tug at the ring in Gareth's nipple with his teeth. "Help me take my mind off stuff for a while."

And Gareth was magic. He did just that.

Gareth set dinner on the low coffee table in front of the fire. It seemed fitting.

While Jack, content and quiet, had curled up in the window seat and watched, Gareth had assembled a platter of sushi and sashimi. He had boiled edamame in their pods, made hotpot, and stewed radish in mirin and soy. He'd made chicken yakitori, fried tofu with honey and sesame seeds, and mixed wasabi paste.

The result was a meal to linger over; talking food to go with the beer, plum wine, and sake he set out beside their feast.

"You know me so damned well." Jack settled in seiza

and reached for his chopsticks.

"Why? Because I can imagine that after subsisting on cake and pub food for a week, you'd be in the mood for something different?"

"Because you knew what I needed before I did. You usually do."

"Yeah, right. I know you so well, I couldn't even predict whether you'd be home or whether you'd go off and hide for a few days."

"I wanted to," Jack admitted. "I was thinking of taking the bike into Wales. Just ride around where there aren't many people." He swallowed a sliver of smoked eel and gasped when the bite of the wasabi hit his sinuses. "Damn, that's good!" He sniffled and took a sip of beer. "Then I remembered I had you to come home to."

"That brat's scary."

"What?"

"Daniel. He said exactly that. That you'd want to be alone, and then you'd remember that you didn't need to be. You taught them well, you know?"

"So did you."

"No. Fucking. Way." Jack stood in the doorway, scowling at the fur ball curled on the couch beside Gareth. The cat looked as if it had settled in for the night. That was unacceptable.

"That's my space," he addressed Bagpuss, "get your furry butt out of there."

"Jack. It's a cat."

"He has ears. He also has a brand-new, luxury bed of his own. And he slept all night and most of the day on Nico's

91

pillow, or so you've told me. Why does he have to be here?"

"Maybe he fancied a change of scenery. Maybe he's lonely? This is new for him. And Briggs was retired. He was at home. We're not."

Lonely. That was ... feasible.

Jack hadn't thought of it that way. He'd wanted to reclaim his customary place, the chance to flop sideways, let his head rest on Gareth's thigh and concentrate on the fingers carding through his hair and rubbing his scalp until the day's stress evaporated like mist.

But ... lonely.

"Come on then, fur ball, share." He scooped the cat from the sofa and claimed his space, close enough to stretch out his legs on the couch cushions, to lean against Gareth and feel the man's warmth through his T-shirt. Bagpuss didn't mind being moved. He lay pliant in Jack's arms while Jack manoeuvred himself into position and when Jack finally settled him onto his lap, he curled up, closed his eyes, and purred.

Fine. That worked.

A VERY
Bagpuss
CHRISTMAS

ONE

J ack heard the muted thump the moment he opened the front door. By the time he was inside and had turned off the alarm, Bagpuss was twining around his ankles. Jack sidestepped and pirouetted, shedding his damp riding gear to a symphony of cat sounds. Bagpuss wouldn't stop yelling and head-butting his shins until Jack picked him up and cuddled him, and then he'd rub his little face against Jack's stubble and chatter as if he had a day's worth of excitement and news to share.

Today was no different.

Jack set his boots on the rack and gathered the cat into his arms. "Hiya Bagpuss. Sounds like you had an interesting day. What have you been doing with yourself?"

Bagpuss chirruped, snuggling close, while Jack buried his hands in the thick, shadowy fur.

He had no idea how he'd become the cat's favourite.

Or why.

Of the four of them, he was the one who didn't continually check what Bagpuss was doing. He didn't pick him up and cuddle him unless Bagpuss asked for cuddles or jumped into his lap. Neither did he talk to him the way Nico and Daniel did or sneak him treats, as Gareth was wont to do.

Yet Bagpuss sought him out any chance he got.

"You can't possibly be hungry." Jack carried the fur ball

95

to the kitchen, not surprised to find his dishes bare. "I've seen the dismembered corpses in the garden, so I know you don't really need us to feed you." The thought caused his stomach to clench, and not in joyful appreciation. Just because he *could* find his own food ... Yeah. Maybe not go there. He focussed on their cheerful kitchen, where Gareth—and now Daniel—made sure that nobody went hungry until Bagpuss rubbed his nose against his chin and chirruped when he laughed. "I wish I spoke cat. It'd be so much easier to work out what you need."

He had no such concerns about Nico and Daniel. After two years of being the objects of care and protection, the two had thrown themselves hearts-first into caring for Bagpuss.

Jack understood the need for a measure of control and encouraged it, from letting the boys choose their after-school jobs to following Nico's edicts about how to treat Bagpuss. Now he scanned the kitchen counter for the plastic container Daniel left out each morning, because heaven forbid that Bagpuss should eat his afternoon treat cold from the fridge!

The chicken was in its expected place. Jack cut it into slivers and then sat cross-legged on the tiles, offering Bagpuss his treat one small piece at a time, a strange kind of ritual they'd developed between them and something that nobody else ever saw.

Bagpuss possessed only a limited amount of patience. He waited for Jack to settle on the floor and to offer him a piece of chicken. But after he'd snaffled the first of his treats, he demanded the others in quick succession, coming closer and closer until his front paws rested on Jack's knee and his little face brushed against Jack's palms.

When the dish was empty and Bagpuss had assured himself that no more treats were forthcoming, he climbed fully into Jack's lap and curled up, purring like an engine.

And Jack leaned against the cupboard door and let his head fall back.

Nico had told them that the mix of sound and vibration that was Bagpuss's purr was a powerful stress reliever. Jack disagreed. He considered it a danger to his peace of mind because every time they sat like this and Bagpuss purred, Jack remembered Jon Briggs.

Ten months after Jon had died, those memories still hurt.

"You know I didn't mean to neglect you when I came to Jon's house, right?" he murmured, rubbing the cat's silky ears. He'd arrived in Holton Wick only hours after Jon's death, locking away his shock and grief to deal with the task Alex had given him.

And he'd made a hash of it.

He hadn't known that Jon had adopted a cat, or that he kept his most sensitive papers in a hidden study. And while he'd found Jon's killer, he'd missed so much that had been right in front of his face.

Gareth had reasoned that grief had impaired his logic, and maybe he was right. But should grief not ease as the months passed? And what about the rage that grabbed Jack by the throat every time he held Bagpuss in his lap and remembered how Jon had died? Shouldn't that rage fade too?

So far, it hadn't diminished one bit, and Jack fought to keep his emotions under wraps and away from his family. The boys had been through enough. They didn't need to deal with his shit, too. As for Gareth ... The man had broad shoulders and was happy to let Jack lean on him, but Jack refused to be a liability. He wanted to stand as Gareth's equal.

Bagpuss shifted in his lap, jolting Jack's thoughts into a new direction.

Was it the cat's presence in their lives that kept his grief and anger fresh? Might distance help?

If he took a trip, filled his days with unfamiliar sights and new experiences, would memories of Jon's death stop hurting quite so much?

Jack sat a little straighter as his mind conjured a familiar image: a wooden training hall at the centre of a meticulously cared-for garden. Gravel swirls and trickling water. Tranquillity at the heart of a teeming city.

He didn't just see himself there, either. He pictured the four of them.

A holiday.

Christmas and New Year in Tokyo.

And why not? His New Year's surprise trip to Norfolk had worked a treat. What if he did it again? Organised time away for them.

Gareth, Nico, and Daniel would love Tokyo, Jack was sure of it. They'd go wide-eyed exploring the markets and restaurants, adore the tech and the temples. Jack imagined them visiting Asimo and Jack's favourite Gundam, stopping for fried onigiri and chicken skewers, and spending their evenings cooking pancakes on a griddle. It was a chance for Gareth to continue his love affair with Japanese whisky, and for Jack to treat himself to the finest sashimi on the planet. They could explore for days without a reminder that an exceptional man had died for … nothing.

"What did Jon do with you when he went away?" Jack smoothed the cat's soft fur and contemplated a problem he'd not encountered before. "He wouldn't have let you fend for yourself, even though you can. Did he ask his neighbour to feed you?" Jack remembered Jonathan Briggs's extensive security system and shook his head. "I can't picture that. How about a posh cat hotel? Cat spa?"

The sound of moped engines and the crunch of tyres on gravel had Jack scrambling to his feet. Bagpuss clutched to his chest, he headed for the hallway to greet Nico and Daniel, resolving to research luxurious, temporary Bagpuss accommodation and flights to Tokyo later that night.

Two weeks later

Finding hotel rooms in Tokyo wasn't an issue. Neither were flights for the four of them. What caused Jack headaches was ... finding a place for Bagpuss.

The owner of the first cattery he'd called had been scathing when he'd asked to book a space. "You realise it's the middle of November, yes? If you'd called six months ago, I might have been able to find you a space. Want me to pencil you in for next year?"

Jack had hung up, crossed the cattery off his list, and dialled again. This time, he'd started by asking about vacancies over Christmas and the New Year.

The answer had been the same.

After sixteen calls, extending his list, and calling another eleven catteries, Jack conceded defeat. "I get it. I get it. No room at the inn. Damn it!"

He stared at his sheets of notes, his lists of places to see, his careful plans for days out in Tokyo. Now what was he to do?

A tiny snort brought his head around. Bagpuss had snuck in while he'd been making phone calls and had taken up residence on his sofa. He sat upright on the cushion, tail neatly wrapped around his feet, eyes never leaving Jack.

"Don't you dare laugh at me." Jack stared right back. "I've wanted to find you a top-class cat spa, five-star accommodation with silk sheets, daily brushes, and hot and cold running ... what is it this week? Tuna? But someone's gone and jinxed it." He patted his lap and Bagpuss jumped the gap, digging in his claws as he landed. Jack winced, but he lifted the cat into his arms and stroked his fur. "Seems we're staying home for Christmas."

And if he didn't want to ruin it for everyone, he'd better get his shit together.

TWO

The one thing Gareth Flynn loved more than Christmas itself were the weeks leading up to it, when he spent a large part of his free time in the kitchen surrounded by mincemeat and relish, pies and puddings, cakes, and savouries. Not for him the last-minute panic over what to serve between early December Christmas parties and New Year's Day. Any guests stepping over his threshold could expect tasty fare.

Acquiring a family had only increased his enjoyment of the season. This year, Daniel had joined Gareth at the stove, with Nico supplying music and keeping them entertained while they cooked.

Jack was avoiding the cheerful chaos. He didn't spend afternoons sitting in the window seat with his guitar and a glass of wine, nor did he peek into pots or taste their creations. He ran errands when Gareth asked him to, but the season's cheer passed him by, and his smile had gone missing. Had it been anyone other than Jack, Gareth would have diagnosed a case of the sulks, but Jack didn't sulk. He identified what bothered him and then went and fixed it. That he wasn't doing so this time was ... worrisome.

Gareth decided to pay attention to the weather forecast.

Two days later, the alarm blared at an ungodly hour, loud and insistent in the darkness of their bedroom.

"What?" Jack shot out of bed—old habits dying hard

and all that—and stood blinking owlishly when Gareth turned on the bedside light.

"Good morning," Gareth purred and rolled from under the duvet. "I thought we should go for a run."

The thick mist outside the window produced the first smile in a week. Jack changed into running gear and they stretched on the doorstep before setting off into the moisture-laden dark.

Haloed streetlights guided their steps, and only the slap of their soles on damp pavement and the huff of their breaths marred the stillness of the morning. For a little while—until the early commuters took to their cars and the traffic on the main road grew busy enough for the sounds to cut through the blanket of fog—they could have been the only ones awake.

Gareth let Jack take the lead, content to watch his lover work the tension from his frame. He hated seeing Jack disheartened. Hated it even more when Jack didn't sleep, and his weight took a nosedive. Jack struggling during the Christmas season wasn't new, but Gareth had thought they'd put the worst of those ghosts to rest their first year together.

They followed the path up to the Common in the pre-dawn, keeping pace with each other until Jack slowed when they reached the benches by the pond. He braced himself on the back of one and let his head drop.

Sweat gathered on Gareth's neck, trickled in a chilly runnel down his spine. The sensation wasn't unlike fear, and Gareth had reason to feel it. Here was Jack, stripped of the determination and defiance he wore like armour. This was Jack ... naked. Vulnerable. Defeated.

Or as near to it as he let Gareth see.

His fingers itched to pull Jack close and wrap him in a hug. Gareth fought the urge. If he made a move, if he so much as breathed too loudly, Jack would snap his armour back into place and pretend that all was as it should be. Gareth locked his knees and stood unmoving, ignoring the chill drawing his damp skin into goosebumps.

"Am I being obvious?" Jack asked finally.

"No. I'm paying attention and learning my way around that busy brain of yours. This problem ... is it something I can fix?"

"I thought we could go away. Take a proper holiday for the whole of Christmas and New Year."

Gareth didn't mention the mountain of food they'd already prepared for the parties, the Christmas Day Open House, and the days filled with visits from friends that followed. He just waited.

"I wanted to take you all to Tokyo."

"Tokyo? As in Japan?"

"You'd love it."

"I'm sure. Tell me why." Because Jack wouldn't plan something like this without reason.

"I ... I keep remembering Jon, the senseless way he died. I can't seem to—"

Gareth waited for more, but Jack didn't continue. "You haven't mentioned Jon Briggs in months. Not since you first came back from Holton Wick."

"It's hardly a cheerful topic. And I should be able to deal."

Jack's capacity to inflict pain on himself caught Gareth out yet again. He clenched his fists and forced himself to breathe, so that he at least sounded calm when he spoke. "Do you really believe that there's no space for your memories and your worries in our lives? In our family? Do you consider us so fragile?"

"No, of course not." Jack's answer came too quickly. He realised it a moment later and sighed. "It's more than the memories. Every time I remember Jon I get ... So. Fucking. Angry. None of you need *that* in your lives."

He turned away and Gareth realised that it wasn't the cold, but shame that coloured Jack's cheeks.

Shame that he'd let his armour crack.

That he'd let Gareth see his pain.

He caught up to Jack and drew him against his body. "I know it makes you uncomfortable, but I appreciate you telling me. For what it's worth, processing grief takes time. And I think you've never given yourself permission to grieve properly for Jon in the first place. You've been too busy protecting us all."

A rush of frigid air ruffled the bushes and made them shiver. Jack let himself lean for a heartbeat or two and then he straightened and put space between them. "Let's head back before we freeze to the pavement," he said. "Talk over coffee?"

Gareth narrowed his eyes, then nodded. "Fine by me. As long as we talk."

Their discussion had to wait. When they arrived home, they found Nico laying the table and Daniel cooking breakfast, and Jack realised with a start that it was Saturday morning. The boys were about to head off to work. Jack had an MOT and a trip to Borough Market on his list of chores, and Gareth ... Gareth had plans to spend the day in the kitchen, cudgelling his brain for a solution to Jack's problem.

"Why did you change your mind about going to Japan?" Gareth asked while they showered and dressed.

Jack realised he'd never explained that part. "Bagpuss. Cat spas book out faster than holiday flights. The best ones are already taking provisional bookings for next

Christmas."

"Good intel for the next time we're planning holidays."

"It is. But it doesn't help me right now."

"That's because it wasn't meant to." Gareth buckled his belt and shoved his feet into his slippers. "Running is never an acceptable problem-solving technique."

"I wasn't running," Jack said.

But Gareth had already left the bedroom.

Gareth's comments looped through Jack's mind while he took the car for its MOT, while he went from stall to stall at Borough Market, working down his lengthy shopping list. He thought about grieving and running and protecting while he fought his way back to Kingston Hill through the thick traffic, and while he unloaded the car.

Bagpuss came to greet him, and Jack picked up the cat and took him upstairs to his den, not yet ready to talk.

Nico sought him out first, bringing a dewy bottle of Asahi. "Can I come in?"

"Sure." Jack accepted the bottle and took a sip while Nico settled himself on the sofa, careful not to jostle the cushion where Bagpuss slept.

"Did you really plan to dump Bagpuss over Christmas?"

"What? No!" Jack felt his face heat. "I was planning a family trip. Including a stay in a nice cat hotel for Bagpuss."

"But Jack ... with none of us there, he'd feel abandoned. That's hardly fair when he's barely settled in."

"He's been here almost a year, Nico."

"And? We've never even left him alone overnight, and you wanted to go away for two weeks!"

Jack rubbed his forehead, unsure what Nico needed to

hear. "I thought you'd enjoy Tokyo."

"We'd be worried about Bagpuss."

Nico spoke as if the cat was a member of their family. Jack hadn't considered that. "Does that mean you'd never want to go on holiday?"

"In a while, sure. We'll sort something out. Prepare for it, you know?" Nico shrugged. "Gareth said seeing Bagpuss reminds you of Jon Briggs."

Of course, Gareth had shared what he'd learned. Drat the man for believing in teamwork! "Yes," he said. "I think about Jon." *I also want to go inflict damage, not that I'm going to tell you about that.* "I think about him a lot."

"But that's good, right?"

Jack blinked. Wondered what conversation he was having with whom. "You think it's good to remember Jon?"

"Of course. You said ... when we came to see you at his house... you said Jon Briggs was a good man."

"He was."

"Then you should remember him." Nico turned his face away, but not before Jack noticed the colour in his cheeks. "My dad used to say that if someone remembers you, you're never really gone. That's why I say his name. His and mum's, even if it hurts to remember."

"I think I never had that lesson."

"Then why don't we have a party for Jon Briggs on Christmas Eve? You can tell us about him. And Bagpuss will be there and hear it, too."

"What?"

Nico rolled his eyes. "Cats are intelligent. I told you."

"I know you keep saying that."

"And you don't believe it. You don't have to. But have you never thought that he likes you best because you came to find out what had happened to his human?"

Jack wanted to argue that, but ... He knew nothing about cats. And Bagpuss had sought him out from the day he'd come home after finding Jon's killer. Maybe Bagpuss *did* know, and stuck to him because he'd known Jon. "That's a little bit out there."

"Maybe." Nico stood and stretched. "Gareth has invited Rio over for Christmas Eve. He said he'd come."

Jack turned away from the sofa and towards his screens, embarrassed as his eyes grew hot. He'd worked so hard to keep the hurt and confusion to himself, but Gareth had sensed that something bothered him. And once he'd winkled it out of Jack, he'd worked to help. "You know the work Jon did was—"

"Oh, come off it, Jack! Nobody's asking you to spill state secrets. We want to hear what kind of man Jon Briggs was. Surely that's allowed!"

THREE

B etween stringing lights, decorating trees, chopping firewood, and evading parties at work, Christmas Eve came faster than Jack had expected. And Nico's belief that Bagpuss recognised people proved spot on.

The moment he heard Rio's lilt, the cat launched himself across the hallway, twining through Rio's ankles and purring like an engine. Rio, familiar with the manoeuvre, stood unmoving, arms filled with a tower of plastic containers and the fingers of one hand clenched tight around a bottle.

"Grab the booze before Ah drop it, will ya?" he chivvied Jack into action.

Jack rescued the rum. "Why the stack of Tupperware? We're not short of food in this house."

"Ah promised your Daniel some Jamaican treats."

"You've *probably* gone a little overboard there."

"Ah'm not arguin'." He shrugged. "Though a lot of it is spice mixes."

He handed over half the containers, and Jack peered at the top one. "That doesn't look like spices. This looks like—"

"Mine! I asked for them. I get to taste them first." Daniel swooped in like an irate dragon, snatching the containers from Jack's grasp, and retreating into the kitchen.

Jack laughed. Rio had offered him plenty of Jamaican specialities to taste while Jack lived in his house. "Bammy," he said. "That was bammy in the top one."

Rio's teeth gleamed white in his face. "Righ'." He pointed to another container. "And here's your favourite. Or wha' used to be."

"Solomon Gundy. Oh, man! I want crackers." Jack took the remaining containers and made for the kitchen.

Rio picked up Bagpuss and followed, cuddling the cat. "From what Ah'm hearin', we need to have a wake."

Jack stopped him in the hallway. "What did Gareth tell you?"

"Tha' you're grievin'. Or maybe... not grievin'. You know there's nothin' wrong with rememberin'."

Did he? Maybe he'd forgotten and Rio had come to remind him. He'd needed to do that a lot over the years. "It's just ... I'm dragging my personal shit home and—"

"Ah see."

Jack didn't doubt that. Rio had long ago learned to detangle the mess in Jack's head, whether or not Jack admitted what bothered him. He'd given good advice, too, and Jack stood in need of that. "I don't want to ruin—" He waved a hand, the motion encompassing the house and the people in it. "Everything."

"You won'. Trust me, Jack. You won' ruin anythin'. Your family is strong. An' has it never occurred to you tha' they want to protect an' comfort you as much as you want to protect an' comfort them? Why don' you give them tha' chance?"

It was a good question.

Attempts to answer it occupied Jack's mind while he helped lay out a buffet on the dining table, poured drinks, fed treats to Bagpuss, and ran his fingers along Gareth's back every time the man swung past him.

"Did you really find a house full of hostages because

someone got a speeding ticket?" Nico asked when Jack came from the kitchen with a tray of glasses.

Jack flipped through his mental catalogue of cases he'd worked. "I think it was a company paying their water bills twice that started me thinking. The speeding ticket came later."

"A bit like Jon in the good ol' days." Rio waved the bottle of rum, and Jack nodded. "He caught a spy once because the man went to the post office too many times. Couldn' happen now, of course."

"Yeah, what's a post office?" Jack fell onto the sofa and listened to Rio and Gareth argue spycraft in an age of mobile phones and surveillance drones. He didn't speak of his misgivings. He didn't mention his anger or his grief. Instead, he raised his first glass of rum to Jon's memory and saw the others follow suit.

Their Christmas Eve party became a cheerful affair after that. They ate their way from one end of the table to the other while Bagpuss hopped from Rio's lap to Jack's and back again.

"Middle of a gang fight was when Ah met Jon," Rio said, answering Daniel's question. "He wanted to talk to me, so he walked righ' in the middle of it as if he had no care in the world. Half an hour later, there Ah was, sittin' opposite him eatin' curry goat. Insane he was when he got goin'."

"Remember the night we spent shooting pool?"

"An' drinkin' that expensive Italian wine. Barolo or somethin'."

Jack smiled, having found a memory that wasn't tinged with pain. "Seriously good stuff, that. Thank God I never saw the bill. Jon kept saying he needed the wine to keep his brain warm."

"Yah, tha' was it. He was bald as a cue ball tha' night. He'd shaved his head, so he'd be convincin' wearin' a wig."

"And he needed to wear a wig because?"

"That's where he'd hidden the data he carried."

Nico had coaxed Bagpuss onto his lap by then, but the boys' laughter sent him looking for a quieter place. He found it on Gareth's lap, and Jack approved his choice. He'd been leaning against Gareth all evening, letting his warmth ground him, and accepting the support he offered. Jack still couldn't think with equanimity of Jon being gone, but Rio's presence filled a hole in their family he'd not been aware of and watching Bagpuss make himself at home in their midst no longer hurt.

FOUR

C hurch bells clamoured in the distance as Jack woke. He stretched out a hand, unsurprised to find Gareth's side of the bed empty and the sheets cold.

He'd crashed after their Christmas Eve wake, sleeping through Gareth getting up to start preparations in the kitchen, and Bagpuss draping himself over him for a nap.

The cat was a warm weight on Jack's chest, his breaths huffing against Jack's neck. But he wasn't as deeply asleep as Jack had been because the moment Jack opened his eyes, Bagpuss followed suit. He lifted his head and bared his throat, and Jack obeyed the silent command, scratching around the cat's ears and under his chin.

When the purr started, Jack chuckled. "Why are you up here? Why aren't you downstairs in the kitchen where Gareth is making delicious breakfast?"

"Because he knows that a delicious breakfast is about to arrive right here." Gareth carried a tray and had a huge grin on his face.

Jack grabbed Bagpuss and squirmed until he sat with his back against the headboard. "Why didn't you wake me? I was supposed to be downstairs, helping."

"Save it. You needed sleep, and we had Nico to fetch and carry, until Daniel complained he kept getting underfoot."

"I doubt that."

"So do I, but Daniel is having fun, and he's looking forward to hosting the Open House, so let's not interfere."

"Definitely not." Jack took a sip of coffee and stared at his plate, which held muffins, scrambled eggs, smoked salmon, and crispy bacon. "Wow. That's a spread."

"It's Christmas." Gareth handed him a fork and settled on the bed beside him. "There's more coffee in the pot, too. And Rio said he's gonna be back later with a bunch of people. And more Jamaican food. That fish paste you like?"

"Solomon Gundy."

"That. He promised to bring more of it. He said you eat that with a spoon and a box of crackers. Why didn't you ever say so? I'm sure we could have found a recipe."

"You're..." Jack breathed out, suddenly unsure what to say. "Thank you. For breakfast. And inviting Rio. For—Everything."

"Having the wake was the boys' idea."

"Really?" Jack thought about that while he crunched bacon. "Remember how scared the two were that first year?"

"Yeah. They didn't talk. Wouldn't look at anyone. Didn't let go of you. And they ate for four."

"It's nice to see them have fun. Even with the crap last year, they've come a long way."

"We all have," Gareth said, sipping his tea. "We're slowly finding our way together as a family. I never thought I'd have a family, you know?"

"Don't look at me. I'm the poster child for that sentiment."

"And here you are. House. Children. Cat."

"And a surprise trip to Japan that didn't happen."

He stroked Bagpuss as he spoke, wanting to convey that he didn't blame the cat for the failure of his plans. And that was silly, in the same way that worrying about Jon and Rio was silly when one of them was dead and the other a fully functional, capable adult.

"Don't think so hard. And don't feel guilty for what we've built here. It doesn't take away from what you had with Rio, or with Jon Briggs. Your family is just getting bigger."

"Rio told me that last night."

"If Jon had been there, he'd have told you the same."

"Trust you to make sense of the mess in my head." Jack let himself lean. He soaked up Gareth's warmth while his other hand played with Bagpuss's silky ears. And there they sat, two men who were making the best of their second chance and worked through the horrors in their past one step at the time.

"There has to be something I can do to help," Jack said a long while later, when his breakfast was eaten and his coffee drunk.

Gareth was right there with an answer. "Take Nico out for a run? It's still early enough and it will do you both good, give you some peace before everybody else arrives."

"You've got it." Jack lifted the tray off his lap while Gareth slid out of bed.

Gareth was his rock, the man to whom Jack gave anything he asked for, and going running with Nico was a kindness and not a hardship. He leaned over the tray and dropped a kiss on Gareth's lips. "Happy Christmas, Gareth."

Gareth returned it with interest. "Happy Christmas, Jack. Now get out of bed and get your skates on."

Their guests started arriving just after eleven—work colleagues, friends from their service days, people Gareth had met while working Aidan's jobs. Gareth's mum and sister stepped through the door, and then Aidan and Alex. Rio brought half a dozen Jamaicans and soon they had music, with Frazer joining in enthusiastically.

Jack greeted each one, mellow from his run, a hot shower, and a large mug of Irish Coffee. The house smelled heavenly of fir and spices, and conversations washed around and over him. It wasn't Tokyo, but to his surprise, the feeling of contentment and peace that came to him was similar.

Gareth's Open House was about food and drink, and time spent with friends, but this year, every guest arrived with a memory and a treat for Bagpuss.

The Christmas tree in the corner of their living room gained tiny photos and hand-painted baubles. Nico draped a small locket of his parents over one of the higher branches. Gareth's mum added a photo of the Flynn family when there had been four of them and Gareth's hair had been dark. Rio's memory showed four young men, none of whom Jack had met. And Aidan added a photo of a young blond woman holding a baby.

The tree became a space where people spent quiet time. The fireside, where plush mice, feathery toys, jingly balls, and things to scratch and chew piled up, was anything but quiet.

Bagpuss took it in stride. He slept on Jack's lap, then on Nico's, and eventually even condescended to investigate the pile of new toys.

"It's a Bagpuss Christmas," Nico whispered, when the cat jumped onto the sofa, a catnip mouse clamped between his jaws. "Everyone loves him, and he loves the company. We only warned people that we'd adopted a cat and look what's happened."

"I'm sure you've said more than that."

Nico shook his head. "I put on the card that Christmas

was a time to remember. You don't mind, do you?"

"Of course not." Jack took a sip of his wine and slung his arm over Nico's shoulder. "Between last night's party and today's, it's been a fabulous Christmas."

"Even though we didn't go to Tokyo?"

Jack shrugged. "Tokyo won't disappear. While you and Bagpuss have helped me realise something important."

"Which is?"

"That I'll never be comfortable about bringing my troubles home, but that it won't hurt our family if I do." He picked up Bagpuss and buried his face in the shadowy fur. "We're here for you, fur ball, just as Jon was," he breathed, not really minding whether or not Nico heard him. "You're part of our family now, and we look after our own."

Grand Union Hunt

COMPROMISES

G areth lifted the casserole dish off the stove and set it to cool on the rack. Gusts of wind drove raindrops against the kitchen window, the uncoordinated splatter masking the soft taps coming from the monitor on the sideboard. Jack had installed the feeds months ago to alert them when Nico or Daniel had nightmares, but the fancy tech suite served more than one purpose.

Gareth used it to keep an ear on the activity in Jack's den.

Talking to Jack when he was in the middle of a search was pointless. He was more receptive in the quiet phases in between. Gareth waited until the rattle of fingers on keyboard stilled before he poured a large mug of coffee and piled a plate with lemon and cinnamon shortbread.

Jack wasn't alone in his den. Bagpuss snuggled into one corner of the sofa, a shadowy curl of fur in the dim light. Blackout shades covered the windows, keeping reflections from the seven screens Jack had arranged in three tiers. The desk light illuminated the notepad in Jack's lap, while Jack yawned and stretched in his fancy chair, his neck cracking when he turned his head from side to side.

"Sounds like you're ready for a break." Gareth set the

mug and the shortbread on the corner of Jack's desk, not surprised when Jack blinked up at him a little owlishly. The glow from the screens ghosted over Jack's face, highlighting dark eyes, darker brows, and a layer of scruff—and Gareth's mind took him back to the desert and their shared deployment.

The memory came in a jumble of fragments: Fierce cold. A lack of water. Jack cross-legged on the ground with his head over a keyboard, squinting to make out the data on the screen. And all of them unshaven, dusty, and ragged like a bunch of bandits.

He shook his head to dislodge the images and focussed on the man in front of him. "You realise you've been stuck up here since yesterday morning, yes?"

Jack blinked. "I hadn't, no. What is it now?"

"Wednesday. Just after one."

"Right." Jack sipped the coffee, his attention still on the four active screens. "Baxter asked me for help. We're tracking this gang, and it's trickier than we expected." He snagged a finger of cinnamon shortbread and took a bite. "Their offline security was so sloppy, we thought it'd be a quick job. But they've taken far more care to protect their online assets."

"So online is where you'll find the gold dust."

"That's what I'm thinking."

Gareth wanted to offer dinner and suggest a few hours or a night's worth of sleep, but Jack wouldn't appreciate it. When he hunted, he stuck to his screens until he'd snagged his target or—at the very least—found a substantial lead. Gareth had learned that the hard way, but in the wake of their first big fight, they'd reached a compromise. "We agreed I'd tell you when I feel you're getting lost in the chase."

Jack reached for Gareth's hand and dragged him close enough to rest his head against Gareth's stomach. "And I promised to listen."

Gareth ran his fingers through dark hair, lank and dishevelled from Jack tugging at it. "You are listening, but you won't stop working just yet, will you?"

"There are children in the mix."

Gareth's heart sank. Trafficking cases involving children were the worst. They challenged Jack on every level, professional and personal. "That sounds bad."

Jack tapped keys until lines of text scrolled across one of his screens. "I've found a thread to pull on. I'll give it a couple more hours. If I get nothing, I'll break for a nap."

"Right. Two hours." Gareth stepped out of Jack's hold, even though it was the last thing he wanted to do. "Don't think I won't check on you."

Jack's smile drooped at the edges, but it was a smile. "I'm banking on that. I could do with a bowl of whatever you're cooking. It smells heavenly."

"Chilli beef stew."

"Definitely." Jack shoved another shortbread finger into his mouth.

The sugar and caffeine did their work, and Jack's fingers resumed their dance on the keyboard. "Two hours," Gareth reminded him, and returned to the kitchen, marvelling at the power of compromises.

With Jack otherwise occupied, the food shopping fell to Gareth. Not that he minded. They ordered their staples online, keeping the weekly shop for fresh food and treats. Gareth had simplified the task further by limiting himself to the greengrocer and Rachel's deli, where both Daniel and Nico worked the late afternoon shift.

He found Nico at the large table in the backroom, preparing the schedule for the next day's deliveries, while Daniel finished ringing up the last customers, and got the cash ready to take to the bank.

"Where's Rachel?"

Nico looked up. "We told her to go home. She couldn't concentrate on anything and was too upset to talk to customers."

Gareth waited, but Nico had nothing to add. "Are you going to tell me why? Or is it a secret?"

"Rachel has a friend who makes cakes," Daniel called from the store. "Mrs Harmon has a stall at the farmers' market and caters parties. Things like that."

"And?"

"The police arrested her, saying she's selling drugs."

Gareth chewed on that while he watched Nico and Daniel close the deli. They'd done it before, with and without Rachel present, and it gave Gareth a thrill that his friend trusted her business to the two boys. Ten minutes later, Daniel crossed the road to deposit the excess cash in the bank's night safe. It was rarely a lot, seeing that most people paid by card or came into the deli to collect the food they'd ordered online. But Rachel had made rules for her business and Daniel followed them.

"Tell me again what Rachel said," Gareth ordered as they battled the afternoon traffic out of Richmond and towards their home in Kingston Hill. "What actually happened?"

"The police arrested Rachel's friend," Nico said. "Which is ludicrous. I mean, she must be sixty and looks like a TV granny. But people got sick after eating the cupcakes she sold at the market. Or hyper."

"And that brings the police rather than food standards? Why?"

"Dunno. Rachel said they took everything from her

friend's kitchen. Even the dishes and spoons."

Gareth wished Jack wasn't asleep or—more likely—back to chasing traffickers. He knew more about street drugs than Gareth ever would and could have made sense of Nico's vague comments. He watched the boys in the rearview mirror, hoping for more information, but the two seemed at a loss.

"It isn't just Rachel who's upset, is it?"

Daniel leaned against Nico, seeking comfort. "Mrs Harmon must be so frightened. Imagine being arrested and put in jail when you've done nothing wrong. How do you even prove that someone isn't a drug dealer? Do you think Jack could—"

"Jack's helping Clive."

"Is that why he's not been sleeping?"

"Yes. We need to leave him alone until he's done."

"But that takes days! Can't we do anything?"

Gareth didn't like the note of panic in Daniel's voice. "Speculating and worrying won't do us any good. Let me talk to Aidan and find out how we can help. We can discuss options over dinner tomorrow night. That okay?"

Being presented with a plan of action eased Nico's and Daniel's anxiety. They didn't share random events of their day as they did on other drives home, but they stopped clinging to each other for comfort. Gareth took that as a win.

HORSE'S MOUTH

T he relentless staccato typing coming from Jack's den told Gareth that Jack had returned to his hunt after little more than a nap, and that he'd found a thread to pull on. Though he wasn't so caught up in his work that he missed Gareth poking his head around the door.

"Coffee?"

"Please." The question was a formality, and they both knew it, but Jack raised his head and sent a smile Gareth's way before he returned his attention to his screens.

"I've started the coffeemaker," Nico said when Gareth stepped into the kitchen.

"Good call." Gareth surveyed their purchases. Feeding Jack while he was hacking required delicate balancing. Coffee and shortbread topped Jack's list of preferred foods, but—in Gareth's considered opinion—Jack needed more than sugar and caffeine.

"How about sausage rolls?" Daniel, now changed into jogging bottoms and fleece top, came to stand beside him. "We have bread dough and chilli relish in the fridge to make the picnic ones. They won't put crumbs all over his chair."

"That's a great idea. Can you get started while I call Rachel?"

"She'll like that. She was so—" Daniel dragged in a

breath. "I've not seen her so upset before."

Gareth wrapped an arm around him, wishing he had a simple solution to the problem. "I'll tell her we want to help. Maybe she'll let me talk to her friend and get the details before I speak to Aidan."

"Yeah. Aidan's big on details." Nico made for the door, brimming coffee cup in hand. "I'll take Jack his coffee."

"Tell him we're making sausage rolls for him," Daniel called after him before turning to Gareth. "I've got this."

"Excellent." Gareth wandered out into the garden, appreciating the fresh, rain-scented air. He'd meant to call Rachel in the morning, but the boys needed reassurance and if Rachel had been upset enough to leave the deli to Nico and Daniel to deal with, she might appreciate the support, too.

She answered on the third ring. "Gareth. I didn't expect to hear from you. Is there a problem?"

"With your store? Not at all. The two closed up like pros. Nico entertained himself by planning tomorrow's deliveries while he waited for Daniel to finish."

"Then why—"

"They told me about your friend. How is she?"

Rachel sighed. "The police released her on bail, and she's staying with us. That's why I couldn't concentrate. I knew Martin was bringing her home and—" Distress pushed up the pitch of her voice.

"About that. I was wondering if we can help straighten it out."

"Bless you. It's hogwash, of course. Lucy hasn't put a foot out of line in her whole life. She's never even had a parking ticket! The police are picking on the wrong person and goodness knows how long it will take to sort it out."

Rachel wasn't just worried. She was angry, too. Angry, and a touch fearful, and Daniel and Nico had picked up on that tone. Gareth had seen it before. Those who knew fear understood more than people who'd never been afraid.

"Do you think your friend would talk to me? Tell me what happened? Hearsay isn't a good starting point."

"I'm sure she will, though not tonight. I've given her something to help her sleep."

"Tomorrow morning, then? After I've done the school run."

"Don't you have to go to work?"

"I'll go in a bit later." He heard her breathing while she thought. Did she hesitate because she didn't want to distress her friend further, or because she didn't believe in her innocence?

"You'd really do this? Help her without even knowing her?"

So it was *his* support she wasn't sure of. Gareth smiled. "Have you ever known me to offer, if I don't mean it? How about nine?"

She exhaled in an audible sigh. "Bless you, Gareth. Yes, please."

"He's older than I am, and I'll be sixty this autumn." Lucy Harmon wrapped her hands around her mug of tea, drawing comfort from its warmth. With her styled white hair and fluffy dark green cardigan, she resembled the TV granny Nico had described.

"Do you remember his name?" They were sharing tea and biscuits in the backroom of Rachel's deli, talking while Gareth took notes.

"Of course, I remember his name! I'm not senile." Her mug clinked as she set it down. "His name is Thomas

Fitzgerald. He's from up north—somewhere in Yorkshire—
and he's been a market trader for at least as long as I have.
We used to have a race to see who set up faster." She shook
her head. "A friendly smile makes a difference when you're
having a tough day, you know? His frosting was to die for.
When he offered me the recipe ... of course, I didn't turn
him down."

Gareth held up a finger. "Can we back up a step? You
met Mr Fitzgerald at the market. What did he sell?"

"Honey. He kept bees and sold the honey. He also
made honey elixir, which he sold to restaurants, and a
honey frosting that was out of this world. Do you bake, Mr
Flynn?"

"More than my waistline appreciates, though I don't
think I've ever tasted honey frosting."

"It's the stuff of dreams, I swear. It's light as air and
tastes like spring. Like sunshine and freshly opened
flowers, only better. That's not the point, is it?"

"It seems to me as if it's very much the point. Why
would he share the recipe with you?"

"He wanted to retire. Running a market stall is tough,
especially in the winter. The damp gets to you after a while.
My bees are sleeping, and I feel I should do the same, he used to
say. Then he asked me if I'd be interested in selling his
honey alongside my jams—wholesale or for a commission—
and he offered the frosting recipe as a thank you."

"And you agreed?"

"Why not? I already sell jams and jellies. Honey fits
right in. Plus, my cupcakes always sell well, and cupcakes
with that honey frosting ... I didn't have a single reason to
turn down his offer. And before you ask, my solicitor drew
up a supply agreement for us. It's all above board."

Gareth approved of the belt and braces approach. He
added the solicitor's name to his notes. "This agreement
has been in place for how long?"

"Just over a year. Thomas quit the market in February last year. The week after Valentine's Day, if that's important. It gets quiet for a bit after Valentine's."

"How does it work? He sends you honey, and you sell it?"

"Pretty much. I started by taking the stock he had with him that last week—honey and elixir—so I had products for the next few markets. When I'm running low, I text him an order and he sends me more. It's not a huge volume business, but it's steady. I do three markets a week and sell between five and ten jars at each one."

"Do you also make honey frosting?"

"Yes. That's what the elixir is for." Her hands worked, clenching and unclenching without her being aware of it. "I decorate my cupcakes with it and sell it in tubs as ready-mixed frosting for home bakers."

"What about the elixir? Do you sell that?"

"No. Thomas makes this especially for professional chefs."

"Any reason? Is it expensive?"

"It's not cheap. A thirty-millilitre bottle sells for sixty pounds. It's highly concentrated, so you only need a drop or two to get the taste. The issue is shelf life."

"It doesn't have one?" Gareth guessed.

"Only about two weeks once it's open. If you're not baking professionally, you'd be wasting most of it."

"Yes, I can see that. Are you sure it was the elixir causing the problem?"

"Must have been," Rachel threw in, passing through the back room. "If customers really blamed the cupcakes for getting sick."

"I just can't see how!" Two spots of red bloomed on Lucy's cheeks. "I've been making this frosting for over a year, and Thomas made it for even longer. He's been supplying restaurants with honey elixir ever since he started

128

his business. If it made customers sick, I'm sure we'd have heard about it before now."

"Could it have been a spoiled batch? Or a contaminated one?"

Lucy shrugged. "I noticed nothing amiss. I didn't get sick, or delusional, or whatever."

"You probably don't taste test much anymore," Gareth said. He was so comfortable making his favourites, he'd long stopped tasting while he cooked.

"I suppose not. But the restaurants haven't complained, either, and they have more customers than I do."

"What's your connection there? With the restaurants, I mean. You said they haven't complained..."

"I didn't say, did I?" She took a sip of tea. "Thomas includes their deliveries with mine. Makes shipping easier and keeps the elixir bottles safer than if he shipped them separately. Couriers can be rambunctious, you know?"

Gareth had little personal experience with courier companies. "You make up the deliveries for the restaurants?"

"Oh, no. The orders for the restaurants arrive wrapped and labelled and with invoices attached. All I do is hand them over when someone from the restaurant comes to my stall to collect them. None of them has come back to complain."

"They could have taken it up directly with Mr Fitzgerald, I suppose." Gareth capped his pen. "Thank you so much. That's enough to get started."

She considered him over the rim of her cup. "Why are you doing this? Rachel said you're the helpful kind, but still..."

"Maybe I was bored?" His flippant answer surprised him more than Lucy Harmon's question. What was it about this case that had rattled his cage? He busied himself with his briefcase until he was ready to face the woman again. "I don't like anyone to suffer for something they didn't do," he said. "And I know a few people who'll listen to me."

A Ray of Pitch Black

"Are you having me on?"

Gareth crossed his legs and matched Aidan's glare. "Why would I do that?" They'd met for lunch at Aidan's club and sat snug in a corner of the library, while a vicious April shower lashed the windows.

"Because this sounds like a fucking sob story."

"Hardly. Rachel's a sensible, down-to-earth woman who doesn't fall for sob stories."

"Hm." Aidan watched Gareth over the rim of the brandy glass, a frown between his brows.

Gareth had suggested they meet, convinced that helping clear Lucy Harmon's name was the kind of job Dwight & Conrad had been founded to tackle. Aidan had listened to the story, but judging by that frown, he had yet to find the sense in it.

"Run that by me again," he said. "This friend of Rachel's has a stall at the local market where she sells honey and cupcakes. She's done so blamelessly for years until, a few days ago, the police suddenly arrested her on suspicion of supplying drugs?"

"Exactly. People ended up intoxicated after eating her cupcakes."

"Last time I checked, alcohol wasn't illegal. The most they could charge her with is selling booze without a license."

"It wasn't booze. People were vomiting and disoriented, or they hallucinated and lost their balance."

"And they're blaming the cupcakes?"

"They're the one thing most people will buy and eat right away. It's not as if you'd buy a jar of jam, come home, and stick a spoon in it."

"You tell me. You're the kitchen wizard."

"We make our own jam and relish. We've not bought any in ages."

"What happened to ... Lucy Harper, was it?"

"Harmon. Out on bail while they're testing everything she had in her kitchen."

"After which, they'll either let her go when they find nothing or charge her with possession if they do. I can't see where you come in."

Gareth remembered the fear in Daniel's face and Rachel's voice, the way Lucy Harmon had clutched at empty air in her distress. People who'd done no harm shouldn't fear the judiciary. If they did, the system was broken.

"Lack of evidence isn't proof of innocence," he said. "Even if the police find nothing, Lucy Harmon will always be under suspicion. Nobody should have to live their life like this. We need to prove she's innocent."

Aidan cradled the brandy snifter in his palm. "You know that's not how Dwight & Conrad operates, right?"

"Isn't it? You and Marcus got together to clear the names of people who'd been unjustly accused. You've done it for years. Just because you're usually the last resort doesn't mean you can't step in earlier."

Aidan picked up Gareth's untouched brandy and held it out. "Flynn, you've worked with me. You know how fine a line we're treading. Breaking the law in pursuit of justice is still breaking the law."

"That's never stopped you. You act every time you feel it's justified."

"Those are the keywords right there!" Aidan stabbed the air with a forefinger. "When *I* feel it's *justified*. I'm the last resort for a reason. I get involved when there's a high probability of a miscarriage of justice. Rachel's friend isn't on that road yet."

"If we sit on our thumbs, she will be. Shouldn't we step in as soon as possible, rather than wait until it's nearly too late? It might stop the eternal rush jobs."

"You're not listening," Aidan said with maddening calm. "Dwight & Conrad has a reputation for defending the falsely accused. I do not want one for defending the indefensible, and that includes drugs."

Gareth set the glass back on the table, contents untouched. "Aren't you a little ray of pitch black? You're going to do nothing to help."

"When her defence counsel asks for my help because they're sure she's not going to get the justice she deserves ... that's when I get involved. I'm not sticking my head in the fire one moment sooner. That's how it works, Flynn."

"Okay then." Gareth swallowed the words crowding his tongue. Aidan wasn't in the mood for a discussion, and he wasn't ready for a fight. He checked his watch and stood. "I'd better get back. Sorry for dragging you out for nothing. And thanks for lunch."

The doormen outside the club sheltered under large black umbrellas.

"Taxi, sir?"

"Yes, please." The gutters ran like rivers and Gareth didn't fancy returning to his desk soaked to the skin. He climbed into the taxi, and as the cab fought its way through the late lunch rush, he wondered what had crawled up Aidan's arse. The barrister had never shut him down in such an abrupt fashion, even when they'd disagreed.

Had the failure been his fault?

Aidan believed in justice and rarely needed more incentive than an unwarranted accusation to get involved. And in over five years, he and Aidan had never disagreed about the merits of a case.

Had that made him complacent?

Should he have prepared better or backed up his conviction with more data?

When the car pulled up outside Nancarrow Mining, Gareth had neither solved the riddle, nor shaken off his disappointment. He only knew he had to make another attempt and do better this time.

NOT YOUR JOB

Back in his office at Nancarrow Mining, Gareth shrugged out of his coat and settled at his desk. During his taxi ride, the resolve to make Aidan reconsider his stance had replaced his irritation.

When Aidan involved himself in a case, he started with the data: every scrap of evidence collected during the police investigation, everything the prosecution thought proved their case, and the information the defence team had amassed in their corner. Aidan made sure he heard every side of the argument.

Gareth had data for only one side of Lucy Harmon's case. He had her story, which Aidan considered insufficient.

Fine.

He dialled Lisa's number.

She answered on the second ring. "Gareth. Are you going to read me the riot act?"

"Do I have a reason?"

"I heard Baxter called Jack for help."

"He did, yes."

"And that's not an issue?"

"It isn't. Jack's careful. Sensible. We both are." The silence dragged while Lisa digested that. Gareth didn't explain the compromise he and Jack had reached, or how it was working out for them.

"If this isn't about Jack, then to what do I owe the pleasure?"

"I was wondering if you'd let me pick your brain."

"Pick away."

"I'm looking for information on an ongoing investigation," Gareth cautioned.

"Oh?"

"Do you remember Rachel Whitestone? She runs the deli in Richmond High Street."

"I remember."

"The police arrested a friend of hers on a drugs charge. The woman, Lucy Harmon, sells jams and cupcakes at the local farmers' market."

"And drugs on the side?"

Gareth snorted. "Never in a month of Sundays. She's sixty, Lisa!"

"That's no deterrent. And no, I'm not mocking you."

"I know. I was just—"

"Wondering how to help, no doubt."

"Is that irony I'm hearing?"

"No. It's cute that you still have that mindset after a couple of years of living with Jack."

"I think I'll not ask you to explain that one." Gareth mashed his lips together before his irritation spilled over. "Do you know what's going on?"

"Let me see what I can find out. But Gareth ... I understand that she's the friend of a friend and you want to help. Just remember that this isn't your job."

Gareth's jaw dropped. For a few heartbeats, he stared at the handset as if he'd never seen one before. "How many times have you told Jack that it wasn't his job to help you?"

He sensed, more than heard, Lisa's amusement.

"Touché."

"Hey."

Gareth set his shoes on the rack and turned. Jack stood at the far end of the hallway, coffee mug in hand. He'd scraped the scruff from his cheeks and jaw and, judging by his wet hair, he was fresh from the shower. When he saw Gareth, he smiled.

"You're home early."

"Nothing happening at work." Gareth had cut himself an early afternoon, hoping to sort out the chaos in his head in the peace of his kitchen. Knowing that Nico and Daniel were staying with his mother after spending the day at a food and science exhibition, brought on the sudden urge to tell Jack about Lucy Harmon and how Lisa's words— coming right after Aidan's refusal to help—had raised a wash of doubts. The shadows under Jack's eyes and the slight tremor in his hands held him back. Jack was running on cussedness and caffeine. He needed to be taken care of, not solve Gareth's problems while still dealing with his own.

"Are you done?" he asked as he reached for his briefcase to take it upstairs.

"Not to say done. We're getting there, but it's hurry up and wait right now, so I grabbed a shower and came down for more coffee."

"Do you have time for dinner?"

Jack leaned against the kitchen counter and looked Gareth up and down. Not with the banked heat that led to upstairs fun and games, but with a tiny, puzzled frown. So much for wishing that Jack hadn't heard the trace of hope in his voice.

"I could eat."

"Yeah? How about steak and salad? Feed that brain of yours some protein and not weigh you down with too many carbs."

"Sounds fantastic. Want me to do anything while you change?"

"Your job is babysitting itself?"

"I can take an hour."

"Then get the grill pan hot and decide what kind of salad you want."

"Making me do all the work, I see." Jack stretched and the ratty green T-shirt pulled tight across his chest. "It's actually nice to move after sitting for so long. Go. Off with you. I've got this."

The prospect of dinner with Jack pulled Gareth from his foul mood. Bagpuss, sitting upright on his pillow waiting for him, cheered him a bit more. He cradled the cat and crossed to the window, scrutinising the sodden garden.

"You're a sensible puss, staying indoors," he cooed, grinning when Bagpuss tilted his head, demanding to be scratched under his chin. He hadn't known that having a cat about the place could be so soothing. "If you go down to the kitchen, Jack will feed you," he promised as he set the cat on his feet.

Bagpuss yawned and, as if to prove that he'd only come down to greet Gareth, he took the stairs up to Jack's den and his favourite corner on Jack's sofa. Gareth shed the corporate attire and returned to the kitchen in jeans, a T-shirt and—knowing it would make Jack smile—a bright blue cardigan.

They got the steaks going and when Jack held out a beer, Gareth took it with a genuine sense of pleasure. He loved to be surrounded by people, but being alone with Jack was a treat. In his current state of mind, it was exactly what he needed.

"Wish we'd gone to this food history thing, too, to be prepared," Jack said, when Gareth showed him a photo of Daniel turning a stone quern. "Heaven knows what we'll be eating for the rest of the month."

"I'm sure Daniel won't poison us."

"Maybe Nico will want to help, seeing there's science involved."

"Now you're pushing it." Nico's help in the kitchen extended to shopping, washing up, and cleaning. "Though I noticed that he's been making salad dressings."

"Chemistry. I told you. And he doesn't have to touch any raw ingredients."

Jack's mind was too full of his job to allow for much conversation, but the silences soothed Gareth as much as Jack's company. Sharing dinner fed Gareth's need to look after Jack, and Jack had stepped away from this work for long enough to let him do it. It showed their compromise in action, especially when Gareth fixed a plate of shortbread and a mug of coffee for Jack and sent him back to his den to continue his hunt.

He washed the dishes and cleaned the kitchen, not surprised when his mind returned to the thoughts that had bugged him all afternoon: Lucy Harmon, Aidan's refusal to help, and Lisa's opinion that it wasn't his job to right this wrong.

It was too early to turn in, and with his mind gnawing on the problem, he didn't have the peace to read or even watch TV. Instead, he settled on the couch and called his mother.

"They're perfectly fine," she answered without bothering with a greeting.

"Did they enjoy themselves?"

"I think so. Daniel loved the food, of course. Nico couldn't get enough of the science behind it, so prepare to answer the weirdest of questions."

"You mean it's a day ending in y? We have no issue with questions. Never have."

"You want to talk to them?"

"No, leave them to their fun. I just wanted to check in."

"Right. Tell me what's bugging you."

Gareth didn't even attempt to deny it. He'd known as he'd dialled his mother's number that she'd catch on to his discontent with whatever extra sense mothers possessed. "Rachel asked me to help a friend of hers. Aidan is dead against it, and then Lisa told me it wasn't my job," he summarised. "It left me ... a bit out of sorts, I suppose."

"Did you talk to Jack about it?"

"He has enough on his plate."

"While you're attempting to fix everybody's problems single-handed?"

"What? That's—"

"Sorry if I got the wrong end there. That's what it sounded like."

Gareth didn't believe that for a moment. His mother wasn't shy about getting her points across. "I need to think about that," he said.

She didn't push. They chatted about nothing important for a few minutes, and then Gareth was once more alone with his thoughts.

IRONY

His mother's words hadn't settled Gareth's unease. If anything, they'd left him even less able to relax.

Tackling every problem in his vicinity heart-first was Jack's MO. Gareth approached challenges with logic and logistics, and Aidan sent him to negotiate precisely *because* he focussed on outcomes instead of egos.

The decision to help Lucy Harmon hadn't been a logical choice. He'd decided with his gut, spurred by the fear he'd sensed from Daniel, Rachel, and Mrs Harmon herself. He felt invested in Lucy Harmon's problem now. So much so that Aidan's refusal to help had left him feeling let down. Not by their difference of opinion, but by Aidan. And why had he been so tempted to rip into Lisa for what had been well-meaning advice, but had sounded like hypocrisy to him?

The empty living room offered no answers. Neither was he in the mood for TV, music, or the history of London's Underground he was reading. A strange restlessness kept him buzzing and—short of other distractions—Gareth returned to the kitchen, poured himself two fingers of single malt, and went hunting for flour, sugar, eggs, and spices.

Jack had to be sick of cinnamon shortbread. The boys would be back home the following day. And everyone in the family loved apple cake.

The mixing and stirring soothed him, but by the time he had a loaf of lemon drizzle cake and a tray of apple and cinnamon cake cooling on their racks, the unquiet thoughts and restless feeling were back.

"Oh, for fuck's sake!"

The last time Gareth had felt so unmoored, Jack had been undercover, Lisa hadn't called with an update on Jack's status when he'd expected it, and Gareth had spent a sleepless night half-angry and half-worried, as he often did when events were outside his control.

Was this what bothered him now?

Gareth grabbed a notepad and pen and went to bed.

Propped against the cushions, he took a deep breath and pushed his emotions aside. Then he did what he did best: outline problems and brainstorm solutions.

When they'd first started living together, Jack had offered to sleep on the sofa when his hacking stints stretched into the early hours.

Gareth had nixed that idea the very first morning. He'd insisted that Jack come to bed whatever the clock said, and he'd grown used to the mattress dipping in the middle of the night and icy feet sliding against his shins. The knowledge that Jack was safe beside him made up for being woken.

The previous night, Gareth had barely set his notebook down and turned out the light when he'd heard Jack's zombie shuffle on the landing. Pulling Jack under the quilt and wrapping his arms around him had been the work of moments, and they'd both been asleep before they knew it.

Jack's sleep hadn't been restful. He'd tossed and turned and jerked awake in some half-formed terror more than once. Gareth had soothed him back to sleep each time, but it needed his alarm clock to scare them awake in the morning, and he promptly joined Jack in his hunt for coffee to kick-start their tired minds.

"You can go back to bed, you know?"

Jack wasn't fully awake even after two mugs of liquid caffeine, but he shook his head at Gareth's offer. "I'm okay. I only stopped because I started making mistakes. Now that I've had a few hours of shuteye, I'm good for another session."

"How's it going?"

Jack shrugged. "Slowly. I'm sending stuff to Clive as I find it. With a bit of luck, he'll get to them before I do. It's taking so much longer because I'm documenting as I go."

Jack didn't like to work this way, Gareth knew. Having to record each keystroke slowed him down and made him second-guess himself. Worse, it interrupted his flow when he didn't need the interruption. But since clear, consistent documentation meant the police could use his data as evidence in court, Jack accepted the limitations.

"I'm going to stash sandwiches in the fridge for you. There's also cake, apple, and lemon drizzle," Gareth said as he took the empty breakfast dishes to the sink to rinse them.

"Thank you. I know there was a reason you didn't want me to set up a coffeemaker in my den," Jack said as he wrapped his arms around Gareth's waist and rested his cheek between his shoulder blades. "Don't think I haven't noticed that something's bugging you. Can discussing it wait until I'm done with Clive's stuff?"

Gareth turned and returned the hug. A little, because he wanted to hug Jack just then, and also because Jack had surprised him, and he didn't know how to answer. "If I haven't worked it out by the time you've fixed Clive's problem, I'm happy to discuss it."

Jack relaxed and gave him more of his weight. The kitchen was silent and warm and filled with the comforting scents of coffee and bacon. Between familiar surroundings and familiar touch, Gareth's unease dissolved just as it had the previous evening, while he'd attempted to work out how this problem differed from all the others he'd faced in the last years. As he had last night, he wondered whether to tackle Aidan with the data he had or wait for Lisa to call him back.

Jack felt it when he reached a conclusion because he squeezed his arms around Gareth's waist one more time and then stepped back. "Tell me later," he said. Then he refilled his mug of coffee and left the kitchen with less of a droop to his shoulders than they'd had when he'd entered it.

ANOTHER GOOD REASON

A t Nancarrow Mining, the stack of issues needing his attention had grown taller overnight. Not surprising, given his unplanned, premature departure the previous day. Gareth ignored them in favour of watering his lemon trees and the pots of herbs along his windowsill. He started fresh ones as soon as he had cropped the existing ones into oblivion, and despite the gloomy April weather, the new pots of mint were doing well. He picked a sprig to chew on and settled to clearing the most urgent items off his to-do stack—signing requisitions, approving payments, and authorising the latest surveillance job.

He slogged through the work, his powers of concentration like a sprite on crack while his mind chewed on the problem of how to help Lucy Harmon.

"Arrange tasks in logical order. Brew a fresh pot of tea. Get stuck in." He repeated it twice, then fished the notepad from his briefcase and studied the previous night's scribbles.

Right at the bottom of the sheet he'd written in big, blocky letters: *Aidan is the roadblock* and *what would you do if Aidan wasn't in the picture?*

The untidy scrawl proved Gareth had struggled to keep his eyes open at that point, but as always, when exhaustion bypassed the filters in his mind, what came spewing out was the actual issue.

Which appeared to be Aidan Conrad, and Gareth's work for his unconventional law firm.

Gareth knew he was a caretaker. When he'd been looking for his second career, Aidan had offered him the chance to do what he loved, and he'd followed Aidan's lead as he'd once followed the orders of his command.

If Aidan hadn't sought him out, would he have built himself a life without extracurricular activities or gone looking for people who needed his help?

And if he'd found those people, what would he have done then?

He stared past his miniature herb garden at the cloudy April sky, waiting for his mind to produce a solution. Nothing occurred to him, and after a while he returned the notepad to his briefcase. He was familiar with this state, when the problem was plain, but the solution eluded him. It usually meant that he lacked data, and he decided that he'd think more about that on the way home.

The phone on his desk interrupted him in the middle of a first-pass supplier assessment. "Flynn speaking. How can I help?" he answered, grateful for the chance to leave his chair and stretch.

"You weren't wrong."

Loudspeaker announcements and the hum of a busy crowd almost drowned out the voice at the other end of the line. "Lisa?"

"You weren't wrong," she repeated with more volume.

"Lucy Harmon's in the clear?"

"I don't know about that. Not yet. It appears—"

An almighty crash from the main office made Gareth spin to face the door. Cheers, shouts, and the quick back and forth of snarky banter dialled down the spike of alarm. The new kit had arrived, and the last thing he wanted was to be treated to a fashion show. He wasn't in the mood for it. "Is there a chance to meet for coffee?" he asked.

"Funny you should say that. I'm at Charing Cross."

"Want to come here? I'm sure I can find us pastries to go with the caffeine."

"Yes, please." As expected, she jumped at his offer. "Give me a few minutes."

Gareth called the cafeteria before he took the stairs down to the lobby, arriving just in time to greet Lisa as she came through the door.

"You must have read my mind," she said. "I've been on the go non-stop and a civilised meeting over a cup of decent coffee is what I need."

"That works out nicely, then." He led her to the small meeting room beside the cafeteria, finding that Sara had set out a full afternoon tea: sandwich bites, pastries, and petits fours. He raised an eyebrow in question.

"You skipped lunch, Mr Flynn. I thought you needed a bit more than a pastry with your tea," she said as she poured coffee for Lisa and tea for Gareth. "Call me if you need anything else." She disappeared in that silent way she had, fluid and graceful despite her towering heels.

"It must be nice to be known like that." Lisa fell into her chair.

"Sometimes."

They looked at each other over the rims of their cups before they both broke into smiles.

"We've not done this in a while," Gareth said, while Lisa snagged a sandwich and stuffed the bite into her mouth. Meeting for coffee and a snack had been the norm when they'd first met, a way to fit private time into two busy schedules. They'd kept in contact after they'd ended their relationship, but the coffee meetings had stopped.

"The first time I came here, I was meeting Jack," Lisa said. "He explained why he'd agreed to work for Nancarrow."

"Let me guess: real coffee a few steps from his desk?"

"That got a mention."

"I'll never understand how he doesn't bounce off the walls." The moment he said it, Gareth realised his error. As he'd promised, Jack prioritised his family over his crusade. Clive's most recent job had pushed Jack's buttons, but he hadn't buried himself in his den with coffee, energy drinks, and chocolate bars, and hadn't worked until he fell asleep where he sat.

Instead, Jack had taken the time to share dinner with Gareth, and he'd come to bed, even though dreams and old memories had marred his few hours of rest. "He told me this morning that they're getting closer to the end on Clive's job."

Lisa's smile was a beautiful thing. "I haven't had time to catch up with Clive yet, but this sounds like the news we need. My overtime budget is going through the roof."

Gareth didn't ask questions, but it occurred to him he and Lisa were in the same boat. Clive worked as hard as Jack and was as ready to step up when someone asked for his help.

"Let's talk about my mess," Gareth said when they'd finished the sandwiches and started on the pastries. "You said I wasn't wrong."

"You certainly weren't. Your Mrs Harmon isn't the only cake-selling market trader who had something unusual happen to them."

Gareth reached for his pen, then stopped. "Can I take notes?"

"Scribble away. I'm also happy to send you what I have."

"You're saying it's serious?"

"I don't know yet. Reading the details made my nose itch, and when I searched with the parameters from the casefile, I found more. I've been up north," she said. "Birmingham, to be exact. Talking to a ... suspect, witness, victim. Not sure what he'll turn out to be. It's a young man who loves to bake and who sells cakes at the local market. He met an older gentleman—also a trader—who sold honey and wished to retire and just keep bees. Signed a supply agreement with the man to let him do that. Got a recipe for honey frosting made with a funky elixir that comes in a small bottle. Passes on packets of these small bottles to a local chef, who's been the old man's customer for years."

Gareth nodded. "That sounds about right."

"Yes. Until, one day, the delivery failed to turn up. Not sent or lost in the mail maybe, but when the guy from the restaurant came by our man's stall, there was no package to pick up. Two nights later, someone ambushed the cake seller, beat him up, and threatened him with worse."

"Over the elixir?"

Lisa shrugged. "The attackers accused him of stealing."

Gareth didn't have Jack's suspicious mind, but he connected the dots just fine. "The packages he passed to the restaurants didn't contain honey elixir."

"My thoughts exactly. The local force is treating it as a case of mistaken identity, because the young man leads an entirely blameless life. But two bee-keeping gentlemen wanting to retire from market trading..."

"... and offering honey frosting recipes..."

"Quite. Too much of a coincidence for me. Plus, my search turned up two other cases that I haven't checked out yet."

"Definitely not a coincidence."

Lisa set her empty cup down and stretched. "I'd still like to point out that clearing Mrs Harmon's name isn't your job—but your instincts may have linked four cases in different parts of the country and, well, I know you. I'll mail you what I have, but I'd appreciate it if you kept the whole thing quiet and me in the loop."

The thought of Jack and his pattern tracing skills ensured Lisa's cooperation, Gareth knew, but he didn't argue. Because, for this one case at least, his needs, and Lisa's were perfectly in sync.

ON THE SPOT

I t was nearing seven when Gareth made it home, to-do list vanquished, but still without an idea of how best to help Lucy Harmon. The lights were on; the house was warm, and Jack sat on the kitchen bench, with a beer and pretzels on the table in front of him.

"Is Aidan going to take the case?" Daniel called as Gareth trooped in. He'd texted earlier about making sausages for dinner and was up to his elbows in minced pork and spices. Which explained why Nico kept as far away as possible from the counter where Daniel worked. Or maybe he'd heard the car pull up, because he was raiding the fridge for a cold beer to set beside Gareth's plate.

"Good thinking, Batman." Jack clapped a hand on Nico's shoulder before turning his head Gareth's way. "You look like a man who's earned his beer."

"I have." Gareth snagged the bottle. He took a deep draught and dropped into his seat with a sigh. "Supplier evals," he groaned. "My brain hurts, I swear."

"You do those a lot," Nico said. "Why do you need so many new suppliers? Can't you make a list of companies you like and use them over and over?"

"We do." Gareth wasn't in the mood to discuss the economics of mining operations, but ignoring Nico wasn't fair. "Mining needs a lot of supplies, and keep in mind that we work in different countries. Julian prefers to use local suppliers, but they need vetting. Can we trust them with our money and confidential information? Are they punctual? Will they compromise our operations if we let them on site? Mining can be a profitable business, but only if you keep a close eye on the moving parts."

"And don't let the competition steal a march on you," Jack added.

"Do they try?"

"Gods, yes. Do they ever." Across the kitchen, Daniel reached for a frying pan. Gareth took it as his cue to push to his feet. "Do I have time to shower?"

"Sure. I'm just going to start the sausages."

"Mash is ready?"

"Three flavours." Daniel waved at the row of pots on the stove. "Garlic and cheese, creamed horseradish, and Colcannon. Gravy's done, too, and I'll put the peas on when we're almost ready to eat."

"I see you have it under control." Given the excess of mash, there'd be fishcakes in their future, or a Shepherd's Pie. Gareth didn't mind. He took another pull from his beer, then set the bottle down. "Right. I'll be back."

Jack watched Gareth as he left the kitchen, briefcase in hand and charcoal pinstripes hugging broad shoulders. A moment later, his tread sounded on the stairs.

Nico settled on the bench beside Jack. "Is he mad?"

"Nah. Frustrated."

"Why?"

"I haven't asked him yet, but something's been bugging him. What happened while I was hunting perps?"

152

Nico thought. "Nothing much. We went to the food and science exhibition and stayed with Gareth's mum overnight. Oh, and Gareth phoned her yesterday evening."

"Checking how you were doing?"

"He didn't talk to us."

That wasn't Gareth's standard MO. Jack chewed on a pretzel. "What kind of case was Aidan supposed to take?"

Daniel paused a moment in his effort to fit sausage skins to piping nozzle. "It's this friend of Rachel's," he said. "The police arrested her for drug dealing. It's ludicrous, because she sells jam and cakes at the farmers' market and she's about a hundred. Can you imagine your grandmother selling drugs?"

Jack had never known either of his grandmothers, but his mother hadn't batted an eyelash at supplying. "Rachel believes she's innocent," he said instead.

"Of course, Mrs Harmon's innocent, so Rachel asked Gareth to ask Aidan..."

"That sounds like Chinese whispers."

Nico giggled. "I think that's why Gareth went to talk to Rachel and her friend before work yesterday morning."

To be ready for his conversation with Aidan, Jack was sure. Only, he'd come home distracted, hadn't mentioned Aidan when he'd shared dinner with Jack, and had called his mum without speaking to Nico or Daniel, even though they were spending the night away from home.

Jack slid off the bench. "Let me see what I can find out." He took a detour to the centre island, where Daniel's sausages awaited the frying pan. "Twenty minutes?"

Daniel shot him a look. "Max."

"Got it."

Jack smelled Gareth's cedar and leather shower gel as he came up the stairs, but his hope of glimpsing water-dewed skin died a quick death when he spied Gareth staring out the window.

His hair was damp, and he was barefoot, but he'd found tracksuit bottoms and a T-shirt before his thoughts had derailed his activities. He didn't turn, though Jack hadn't been quiet on the stairs, and the tension in his shoulders stretched the T-shirt's soft, faded fabric.

"What did Aidan say?" Jack got right to the point. "I assume it's his response that's been bugging you?"

"Look at you, all scary cat ears." The affection in Gareth's tone failed to hide his frustration.

Jack hated it. He wanted to pull Gareth into his arms and tell him that Aidan's opinion didn't matter. He knew better. Gareth radiated *don't touch me*, and if the situation were reversed, Jack wouldn't appreciate being caged and held either. He flopped backwards onto the bed. "I know you respect Conrad. Disagreeing with him must be difficult."

"Do I ever?"

"In operational matters, yes. Though I'm guessing that what's bugging you right now isn't operational."

Gareth turned. He braced his hands on his hips and looked down at Jack. "Daniel asked for my help, and I don't know what to tell him."

Jack patted the bed. "Tell me. Then we'll sort it out."

"You have enough on your plate—"

"Flynn." Jack growled the word. "You said you'd share if you hadn't sorted this shit out by the time I finished Baxter's stuff."

"I said that, yes. You're done?"

"I've cleared my plate. And now you," Jack pointed, "owe me an explanation."

Gareth dropped onto the bed beside him. "Daniel will

kill us if we let dinner go to ruin. How about I give you the short version and we discuss the whole thing later?"

"Works for me."

"How much have they told you?"

"Only that the police have accused a friend of Rachel's of peddling drugs, that Rachel asked you to help clear her name, and that you spoke to Rachel's friend before talking to Aidan."

"That's about it. Though I called Rachel because Daniel asked me to do something."

"I wonder why he didn't say so?" Jack contemplated that for a second, then shook his head. "Never mind me. Carry on. You went to see Rachel."

"Yes. Her friend struck me as somebody who's been taken advantage of very cleverly, and I thought it'd be a case Aidan would relish." He ran a finger down Jack's bare forearm and traced idle circles on the back of his hand.

"And Aidan said?"

"That it wasn't his problem."

"In those words?"

"He said he's the last resort for a reason."

Jack narrowed his eyes at him. "What else?"

"Can't get anything past you, can I?" Gareth sighed. "He said he didn't want a reputation for defending the indefensible, which includes drugs."

"Bullshit. We've worked plenty of drugs cases." He turned his palm up and laced their fingers together. "You have every right to be mad."

"I'm not mad. Not really. What sticks in my craw is that he wasn't listening to me. I should have been better prepared."

"You. Unprepared. Not in a month of Sundays. Tell me the rest?"

Gareth shrugged. "I called Lisa, who told me it wasn't my job to fix this. And then…"

The smile on his face was so sheepish that Jack made an *out with it* gesture with his fingers.

"When I called my mum, she reminded me I shouldn't solve all the world's problems by myself."

"Hah!" Jack burst out laughing, and a moment later, Gareth joined in.

"Dinner is ready!" came a shout from downstairs.

Jack stood and pulled Gareth up after him. "They piled it on, didn't they?"

"Maybe I had it coming. I'd not mind so much if I saw my way through. As it is…"

"You realise this isn't the army, right?" Jack offered cautiously. "Aidan is not your chain of command. You don't have to abide by his decisions. Especially not if your heart tells you different."

Gareth ran a hand over his hair, making sure he was presentable. "Part of me knows what you say is right. Another part of me feels…"

"Disloyal?" Jack suggested. "Let down? Betrayed?"

"Yeah. All of that."

Another shout came from downstairs, and Jack started for the door. "Let's have dinner. Unwind a little. We'll think better once we've been fed."

SAUSAGES AND SPECULATIONS

D aniel had added paprika and dried herbs to his sausages to enhance the flavour of the pork, and black pepper and chilli flakes to add a kick. They spent the first quarter hour digging into their dinners, comparing flavours and giving Daniel the praise his creations deserved.

When they'd all had seconds, and Nico and Jack were working on thirds, Gareth zeroed in on the thread of agitation Daniel was attempting to hide.

"You weren't worried about making sausages, were you?"

"Why would I worry about that?" Daniel frowned. "You showed me how to do it."

"Okay, then. What is it?"

"What's what?"

"Whatever is upsetting you. Share it."

Daniel didn't. He took their plates to the sink and grabbed a baked cheesecake and the dish of strawberries. Setting them on the table, he then returned to the centre island for plates, forks, and a cake slice.

Gareth waited him out, watching Jack and Nico share the last three sausages.

"You know we went to the food and science exhibition," Daniel said when he'd arranged the dessert ingredients to his satisfaction. "It was in a massive hall with cookery demos on every corner and it was heaving. I..." He wrapped his arms around himself, uncomfortable with the memories. "All these people. Bumping into me. Touching me..." He swallowed.

"What did you do?" Jack asked before Gareth got there.

"I went upstairs. The rooms there were smaller and not so packed." Animation returned to Daniel's tone, masking the remembered discomfort.

"Removing yourself from a situation is a valid choice." Gareth said. "Did you find anything interesting up there?"

"An exhibition about unusual foods and ingredients."

"Yeah," Nico chimed in. "Like that fruit you're not allowed to take on a plane because it stinks."

"Durian."

"That's it, but they didn't have one. Do you think it smells too bad to have in an exhibition?"

"I don't know. I've only read about them, same as you." He lifted a slice of cheesecake onto his plate. "So, no stinking fruit. What did you find that got you excited?"

"Psychedelic honey."

"I beg your pardon?"

"That's what it said. You know how honey tastes different depending on where the bees get nectar? Rachel sells lavender honey, and thyme honey, right?"

"Right." He met Jack's eyes across the table. Saw the wheels turn and felt an answering curl of interest. "And psychedelic honey comes from?"

"Rhododendrons," Daniel said. "It must be a special type of rhododendron, right? Or psychedelic honey wouldn't be so rare."

Daniel's unease was making a comeback. Jack's knee bumped his under the table and Gareth felt lighter. Here was a problem he could help with, and Jack was letting him do it. "Go on, put your theory together," he requested, and held up a hand when he saw Nico was ready to jump in.

"I don't like..." Daniel trailed off. "I'm happy to cook, but constructing arguments makes me uncomfortable."

"You were uncomfortable in the exhibition and worked out how to handle it. You'll deal with this, too." Gareth stuck a fork into his cheesecake. "It's only us here and we're happy to wait."

"And eat cheesecake."

Daniel rolled his eyes, but the hint of panic faded from his gaze. "It's not a theory," he said at last. "It's ... speculation, because we only have a story and not much data." He looked to Gareth for confirmation.

"That's right," Gareth said promptly. "Start there. With the data you have."

"We know Mrs Harmon bakes cupcakes and makes frosting with honey."

"Right. What else do you know for sure?"

Daniel thought. "Bees can make psychedelic honey from rhododendrons and eating it makes people feel loopy. But I only know that because the panel in the exhibition said so. I've not seen the honey or tasted it."

"Let's assume that the people who put the exhibition together did their research. Now what?"

"If Mrs Harmon used psychedelic honey in the frosting, the cupcakes might have made people feel strange."

"That's reasonable. The police took Mrs Harmon's ingredients for testing," Gareth said. "If the honey has psychedelic properties, they'll find out."

"And since she bought the ingredients, she can't be in trouble, right?" Once more, his gaze moved between them, and Gareth suddenly understood why Daniel was so keen to clear Mrs Harmon's name. Here was a cook in trouble for the food they'd made. No wonder Daniel felt sympathetic to her plight.

Jack got it, too. "I'm no lawyer," he said. "But unless she doctored the cake to poison people, I can't see how she's at fault. Especially as she buys honey from the same supplier and has done so for what? A year?"

Gareth nodded. "Just over. The beekeeping gentleman retired in February last year."

"We have to wait for the police to finish their tests?" Nico made a face. "That's kinda ... lame."

"You can keep speculating to pass the time," Gareth said. "See if something else occurs to you that fits the facts we have and explains what happened."

"Or find out more about that psychedelic honey," Jack said.

"If I found some, you wouldn't eat it, would you?"

Jack shook his head. "I'll stick to booze or exercise if I want out of my head. But it would prove that it's possible to get it here in England without having to jump through hoops."

"And that it might contaminate real honey?"

"That, too."

Daniel looked a bit brighter.

FACE IN THE MIRROR

"Feeling a touch better about yourself now?" Jack crossed the room and wrapped his arms around Gareth's waist. They'd spent the rest of the evening thinking up scenarios where psychedelic honey ended up in regular products and landed regular people in trouble until even Daniel had joined in.

"I love how you know me so well."

"Do you really? Then what am I going to do next?"

"You'll let me take care of you?"

Jack's hands crept from Gareth's waist up his chest to his shoulders and from there into the silver hair. "Nope. I had something else in mind." He rubbed circles over Gareth's scalp, loving it when Gareth tipped his head back like Bagpuss wanting scritches. "You rarely need an appointment with a bottle of massage oil, but right now you're wound so tight ... and I'm in the mood to unwind you. Get you all slippery and loose."

Gareth's breath hitched, and Jack gave him no time to think. He fetched a bath sheet and the oil—frankincense and arnica to soothe and relax—and returned to the bedroom already stripping.

"What brought this on?" Gareth shed his own clothes. "After the last so many days, you should be the one in need of sleep."

"Don't you worry, I'll sleep. I'm also not as spun out as

you think. Breaks were a thing, you know?"

"I know. Really, Jack, I know."

"So let me take care of you. You did it for me after the club when my mind was such a din, I couldn't hear myself think. You'll need a quiet mind if you want to reach a sensible decision."

"I've never needed that before."

"Don't kid yourself. When you're out in the field, making split-second decisions, you're focused on the outcome, on your goal. There is no room for self-doubt, second-guesses, or failure. Right now, you want to beat a heavy bag into submission. Or Conrad's face. Right?"

"Perhaps."

"Either way, not the sign of a peaceful mind."

"How did you become so wise?"

Jack didn't even have to think about that one. "I watched you, and then I spent seven years *not* watching you. Hones the mind wonderfully."

"Even if it's rather lonely?"

"That's not the issue." He gave Gareth a little push, and Gareth went with the programme, stretching out on the bath sheet and presenting his bare back to Jack's gaze. The sight of that beautiful vee turned Jack's crank every single time, but he ignored his simmering arousal. They could have sex later. Or the next day. This was about Gareth allowing Jack to tend to him and giving himself permission to be vulnerable.

He straddled Gareth's hips and poured oil into his hands, rubbing lightly to warm it.

"This case is scaring Daniel, and I don't like it." He set his palms on Gareth's back and spread the oil in long strokes.

"I'm more annoyed that I didn't catch on right away. Before we brought the problem home, I mean."

"You? I thought Daniel and Nico suggested we help?"

"I could have nipped it in the bud and told them to let the police take care of it." Gareth tucked his hands under his chin and spoke into the pillow. "Daniel's response makes sense, you know? He cooks, and it hasn't occurred to him he can hurt as well as feed people."

"Or land in trouble with the law and have it all taken away from him."

"That, too." Jack's fingers dug into a knot at the juncture of neck and shoulder, and Gareth groaned when something cracked and gave. "Damn, that's good! Talking of trouble with the law ... are you really done with Clive's stuff?"

"In this round of whack-a-mole. It's not as if the trafficking ever stops."

"Sometimes, I wonder how you keep going."

"Same." Jack rested his hands on the small of Gareth's back, sharing warmth while drawing strength and comfort for himself. "And then I look at you."

Gareth's breath hitched and evened out. He didn't push for more than the quiet admission, and silence settled over their bedroom.

Jack worked his way from Gareth's neck across his upper back, down to his waist, over his arse and along his legs. He took his time, alternated digging into Gareth's muscles with long, soothing sweeps of his palms until Gareth melted into the sheets and groaned his appreciation.

"I didn't mean to treat you to my Victor Meldrew impression," Gareth said when they curled up under the quilt afterwards, limbs tangled together.

"Grumpy cat, maybe. You weren't that bad. Besides, I meant it when I said that you have every right to be mad at Aidan."

"It's never been an issue before."

"Doesn't matter. Whatever Aidan's reason for turning

down this case, his choice doesn't sit well with you. So make a different choice."

"You make it sound so easy. Choosing differently might mean stepping outside the law."

"And I thought I was the sleep deprived one. We've done plenty of work for Aidan that's been skirting the law and jobs that have outright broken it. That's the whole point of his outfit."

"Yes, but..."

Jack yawned. He was losing the fight to keep his eyes open, but he wanted to make sure Gareth heard him. "You want to help, right? Then let's help. Talking to people isn't illegal. We can nose around and send anything we find to Lisa. This isn't a job you have to do alone. I'll back you to the hilt."

Now and then, Gareth understood Jack's need to go running at 03:00 a.m. His body was loose and heavy after Jack had worked the knots from his muscles, but his mind didn't let him rest. Jack's words ran on a loop, and he considered them from every angle.

Taking orders from Aidan shouldn't force him to ignore his own instincts—that much he agreed with—and his instincts told him to step up when someone needed help.

Did that make him a crusader like Jack?

Jack's moral code was simple. He protected himself and those who needed protection using every tool at his disposal and accepted that his actions had consequences. Neither the letter of the law nor people's expectations had a place in his decisions.

Gareth had never seen himself that way. He was a protector, but he believed in law and order.

Or did he?

He'd accepted Aidan's job offer and continued to help others using skills he'd learned and honed over many years, but he'd made no rules for himself. He'd skirted, bent, and broken the law while working Aidan's jobs, but he hadn't done it honestly, for want of a better term, hadn't decided what he could accept and what he wouldn't tolerate, hiding behind Aidan's authority, Aidan's choices.

Gareth shifted, the soft bed linen like sandpaper against his skin.

Was this the reason for Aidan's refusal? Had Aidan told him he couldn't help whomever he wanted while he expected Aidan to take responsibility for his actions? Had Aidan Conrad ... called him a coward?

Shame heated Gareth's face and neck, and he was grateful for the darkness. Cowardice was unacceptable, especially when the choices open to him were straightforward ones. Follow the law, let the system do its work and accept the occasional imperfect result, or stand beside Jack and Aidan and help in any way he was able.

Grey light crept into the room as Gareth rolled out of bed.

Jack stirred. "You okay?"

"Fine." Gareth dropped a quick kiss into Jack's hair. "Sleep. It's early. I'm going for a run."

Jack snuggled back under the quilt. His lashes drifted down, even as the corners of his mouth turned up. "I knew you'd work it out," he muttered. "You're clever that way."

FAMILY AFFAIRS

Gareth dished bacon strips onto four plates and handed them to Nico to take to the table, before he cut up the last strip and placed the pieces into Bagpuss' dish. "We're going to help Rachel's friend, with or without Aidan's blessing," he said. "It'd be wrong not to."

Jack rested his cheek on his hand and watched Gareth flip pancakes and fry eggs, dressed in jeans and a T-shirt and with his hair standing in damp spikes. Despite the sleepless night—and yes, Jack knew Gareth hadn't slept—he was a thing of beauty: competent, focussed, and free of doubts. Nico and Daniel looked like lost puppies by comparison, while Jack went along for the ride, mellow and content after Gareth had ambushed him in the shower.

A mountain of work waited for him after his days away helping Clive, plus he had unfinished business with Aidan Conrad—but both could wait while he basked in the glow of Gareth's returned confidence.

"Do we have a plan of attack?" he asked.

"Find out who grassed up Mrs Harmon." Nico was quite serious.

"Why do you think that'd be helpful?"

Nico shuffled the bacon strips to the side of his plate to make room for a heap of scrambled eggs. "In books, they suspect family, friends, and neighbours first, right? Aidan said that's true in real life, too. If someone had it in for Mrs Harmon, it proves that it's not her fault." He swallowed a forkful of eggs. Then his eyes went wide. "Oooh! Maybe someone poisoned the honey frosting to get her in trouble!"

"Who poisoned the frosting?" Daniel blinked, still half asleep.

"Whoever wanted to hurt Mrs Harmon—keep up!"

"I'm not sure the police will share their information source, even if we ask." Gareth stopped the brewing exchange. "Besides, Mrs Harmon isn't the only market trader who met a beekeeper wanting to retire."

"What?" Jack felt the hair on his neck stand straight up. "Lisa said that?"

Gareth nodded, too classy to speak while chewing. Daniel wasn't so restrained. "There are more people in the same situation as Mrs Harmon? Accused of dealing drugs when they didn't?"

"That's what Lisa told me, and that's why stepping in to help is our best course. If you have time after school, write me a summary about this psychedelic honey. What it is, where it comes from, how you make it ... everything you can find out. Lisa's people may not think of food when they're looking at drugs. She also promised me notes about the other cases. I'll chase that up."

Jack crunched the last of his bacon. "What do you want me to do?"

Gareth shot him a look. "Rescue Janet and Frazer from overwork."

"Fair enough." Knowing the two, they'd piled work on his desk until it appeared—to Gareth, Julian, and especially the guys from exploration—that it'd be weeks before he had time to even return an email. "You know there won't be much for me to do beyond making sure I know what went down, right?" Jack had no doubts, because Donald Frazer was just that good, and Janet was getting there. All the two lacked was confidence.

"I know. Though the state of your desk suggests otherwise."

"Excellent." Jack wasn't sure how he'd got so lucky, but he wouldn't jeopardise what he had. "I'll take them to Simpson's for lunch." And then, rather than wait for Lisa to share her data with Gareth, he'd find his own.

Aidan wasn't at Nancarrow Mining that morning. Jack could have taken the short walk from the Strand to Aidan's chambers in the Inns of Court, but he focused on Janet and Frazer and the work on his desk instead. Aidan had issues, but had they been serious, Jack would already know.

He resumed his 'at work' persona—aloof, industrious, watchful—and kept an eye on Gareth even as he caught up with projects and reviewed task logs. Just before lunch, the system alerted him to Aidan's arrival. Jack needed to talk to the man—for his own peace of mind if nothing else—but he stuck to his plan and dragged Janet and Frazer across the road for a slap-up thank you lunch.

Tackling Aidan could wait.

It was nearing three when Jack finally breezed into Aidan's office and threw himself into the visitor's chair. "When did you turn into such an insufferable arse?" Aidan raised his head from the stack of papers in front of him and when Jack saw the dark smudges under his eyes, he knew that he'd been right. "Emily okay?"

"Emily's fine. And you're fucking scary."

"Fucking pissed is what I am. Gareth didn't deserve

that."

"Wrong," Aidan fired back. "I hadn't planned to tell him quite this way, but he needed to hear it sometime."

Jack mulled that over, not surprised when Julian's secretary arrived with a pot of tea and a cafetiere of freshly brewed coffee on a tray. Arranging china and pouring drinks bled some of the tension from the room. "You're the king of ambiguous statements, but you're not entirely wrong," Jack said at last. "Now tell me what's bugging you that isn't Gareth being a boy scout. With details."

"Nothing you need to worry about."

"I beg to differ. You're off your game. You made Flynn doubt himself."

Aidan swallowed. "I hadn't meant to do that."

"I sure hope not." Jack sipped his coffee and watched Aidan fiddle with his pen, his teaspoon, his ... anything within reach. The very picture of a man who had something on his mind.

"Has it never bothered you that Flynn was coasting?" Aidan asked when the silence was growing a touch too heavy for the topic under discussion.

"Get a grip, Conrad." Jack set his cup down. "He wasn't coasting. He wouldn't have lasted a week with your outfit and you know it."

"Then what is his issue?"

"Chain of command," Jack said. "He's Mr Law-and-Order. When we served, he didn't like me hacking, but he'd order me to do it if we needed the intel."

"You'd have done it anyway."

"Not the point."

"Which is?"

"That, as my team leader, he didn't let me make the choice. If I broke the law, it was on his orders, and he was ready to carry the can for that decision. But–" An image of a worried Daniel pulled at his attention.

"But what?"

"Gareth was career army. That's different from you or me serving, getting out, and starting over. It didn't occur to him that outside of the—what's that phrase?—the institutional envelope, there is no chain of command. Not like he was used to. And he started collaborating with you while he served, right? I think he simply replaced the brass with you and called it good. It's not uncommon."

"Isn't it?"

"No. You see it a lot with former soldiers joining my old crowd. They do what they're told, no questions asked. It rarely ends well." Aidan was listening, and Jack chose to deliver a few truths of his own. "Daniel asked Gareth to help Rachel's friend. He thought it beyond unfair that a lady who made cakes was treated like a criminal. It only occurred to him last night that this could have been him, accused of hurting people when he'd meant to feed them. It scared the socks off him!"

"I'm sorry to hear that."

"You should be. You had to rock the boat, didn't you? And before you say anything, remember that I don't coddle Nico and Daniel nearly as much as they deserve. I lay plenty of hard stuff on them, but they're still kids and don't have to know about all our crap. Especially not if it scares them." Jack drained his cup and set it back onto the saucer. "Now tell me what brought this on, so I can fix it."

Aidan sighed. "Horwood, I'm not ready to tell you. That enough to stop you digging?"

"Fine. Be that way." Jack stood and turned towards the door. "It's not like I can't find out for myself, right?" He threw the challenge over his shoulder as he left.

"I talked to Aidan," Jack said when they followed the long line of traffic from the Strand to Kingston Hill.

"I'd have told you not to, but I didn't think you'd hear me. Anything enlightening?"

"Something bothers him. Other than that, he was an arse because he wanted to be."

"He thought I needed a wakeup call."

"Something like that."

"Why didn't you kick me into line when you saw I let Aidan make my choices? Didn't it ever bother you?"

The question was eerily like the one Aidan had asked him earlier. "No, it never bothered me. I have my reasons for taking the risks I take. In the beginning, I assumed you had yours. Then I realised that you'd replaced one chain of command with two new ones. Aidan hadn't called you on it, and our work relationship is not unlike the one we had while we served, so I fell into the same river."

"Denial?"

"No. Complacency."

"Is that even a river?"

"You know what I meant." Jack shifted in his seat, grateful for their ability to have deep, life-changing conversations on their drive home. As if being cocooned in a car, with half their focus on traffic and weather, created an environment that encouraged admissions and confidences.

"Yes, I know. But chains of command aside, there's a difference. You've always known that you—"

"Break the law? Hell, Gareth, the law, and common decency should have stopped my mother from selling me, but did they? Did they heck! I was fourteen the first time I helped the police. And I offered myself as bait to help them arrest Jericho."

"They let you do that?"

Jack was amazed Gareth didn't slam on the brakes in

his surprise. "Now you're getting it! Rio was the one who tried to protect me. Nobody else considered how wrong it was to send me into that club to help them catch the bigger fish. You grow up like I did, and there are only two rules that matter: stay alive and don't get caught. Which, of course, is exactly the attitude the service was looking for." He brushed his fingertips over Gareth's cheek, enjoying the rasp of late-afternoon stubble. "You have my back and I know it. Everything else is semantics."

"Still." Gareth slowed to a stop at a traffic light. "I should have realised sooner that I was hiding behind Aidan. Acknowledged it sooner."

"You worked it out. That's what matters."

"Is it? I want to help, but I also want to keep the law-bending to a minimum."

"Fair enough. Any reasons beyond your law-abiding tendencies?"

"A few." Gareth found half a smile, though the uncertainty still lurked in his eyes. "I mean, waiting for justice must be stressful and distressing. Shouldn't we work to keep that time as short as possible?"

"Of course. But that's rarely how it goes."

"That's why Aidan offers his help as a last resort, right? He steps in when it's clear that the system has failed."

Jack settled deeper into his seat. "As far as I know, that's exactly why he does it."

Gareth nodded, as if confirming his decision to himself. "I'm not that patient. Nor do I want to see people worry themselves to shreds while they wait for justice. Let's find out what really made those people sick. Clear Mrs Harmon's name. And do it within the rules."

All around them, people headed home from work, minds on dinner and the evening's entertainment. Jack's mind went there, too. To Daniel, who'd settle his misgivings by cooking dinner. To Nico, who'd be eager to investigate the mystery. And to the man beside him who finally had found ground again. He kept his eyes on the traffic and smiled. "I'll have your back, you know that."

POKING AROUND

"Rhododendrons are invasive. Their leaves are toxic to grazing animals, and they poison the soil to stop competing plants." Gareth's eyebrows climbed higher and higher the longer he read through Daniel and Nico's report on psychedelic honey. "I always found flowering rhododendrons cheering. I was even thinking of planting some out front."

"Stick 'em in containers." Jack bent his head over a stack of printouts and muttered around a pen clamped between his teeth.

They'd finished dinner, and while Nico and Daniel cleaned the kitchen, Jack and Gareth had brought Lisa's data and the boys' honey report with them into the living room to read. Gareth now knew more than he'd ever wanted to about the toxins in rhododendrons and the history and symptoms of honey intoxication.

"That honey is potentially nasty stuff, you know? People could have died. Why didn't they?"

Jack spat out the pen and looked up. "It was just contaminated or spoiled honey that had nothing to do with rhododendrons." He ticked options off on his fingers. "It was 'mad honey', but the concentration of toxin is low enough to cause only minor symptoms. Or—and this one bothers me—someone's diluting it."

"Why would that— Oh! Now you're thinking drugs, too."

Nico joined them in the living room, with Bagpuss trailing after him. The cat jumped into his lap as soon as Nico sat down, and Nico stroked the dusky fur without Bagpuss having to prompt him. "I'm sorry I neglected you, big boy," he cooed. "I had a lot of reading to do."

Their research into the history and origin of the honey had kept the two boys busy all afternoon and the data they'd found had surprised them. "Don't you need a lot of rhododendrons to make enough drugs to sell?"

"Not if the toxin concentration is high enough to begin with. Besides, there *are* lots of rhododendrons," Jack said. "Whole hillsides of big, wet leaves."

"And stunning flower displays to go with." Gareth knew Jack remembered the same exercise. They'd spent a week in Wales, and for six days out of the seven it had been grey and raining, but on the last day, the sun had produced an unbelievable display. "Though I can't imagine that many beekeepers want to risk their hives by sending the bees to feed on rhododendrons."

"We need to track the beekeepers the way the police track cannabis farmers." Nico hadn't lost track of the conversation despite the cat in his lap.

"They track cannabis farms by electricity use. Beehives don't use electricity."

"I know. Livestock, then. They can tell where meat comes from. Why not honey?"

"Why not, indeed?" Gareth, ready for their evening ritual, filled two glasses with wine and held one out to Jack.

He took it with a smile. "Because a hive has thousands of bees, and you can't track each one?"

"We'll come up with something," Gareth soothed, before the discussion spiralled out of control.

"I'm sure we will." Jack skimmed Lisa's data for

connections. "He's consistent, our Mr Fitzgerald. He used the same name in every case Lisa sent you details for. Three of the victims reported him as Thomas Fitzgerald. To the fourth one, he was Geoffrey."

"Shouldn't that make him easier to find?"

"He's good at keeping out of sight."

"We have his name," Nico said. "Mrs Harmon placed orders, so she must have an address for him."

Daniel settled on the sofa and leaned against Jack. "She paid him, too, so she had bank details."

"Right. And he has a van, which means he's in the DVLA database," Nico said eagerly.

"You'd think." Jack pulled his slate close and started tapping. Then he stopped.

"Jack?"

"You're right. Mrs Harmon had both an address and bank details for Mr Fitzgerald. And yes, he's in the DVLA database."

"And?" Gareth set his wineglass down, surprised by the odd note in Jack's voice. "What's the punchline? Have Lisa's guys already interviewed him?"

Jack stacked Lisa's papers and neatened the edges, brows drawn tightly together. "The police haven't found him yet."

"But—"

"According to the Royal Mail, the address he's given doesn't exist," he said.

"Google maps?"

Jack smiled and Gareth couldn't decide whether the sentiment behind that smile was approval or irony. "On Google Maps, the closest corresponding location is a derelict farm building on the border between Warwickshire and Northamptonshire."

"He can't just disappear. Not in this day and age." Gareth thought of the hoops he had to jump through every time he placed an online order. "As soon as you enter your post code anywhere—"

"There are ways to disappear," Jack disagreed. "Stay with the same bank and don't update your details. Collect cheque books and debit cards from a branch rather than have them sent to your home. People used to do that even when they had nothing to hide. Besides, Fitzgerald hasn't disappeared. He's just not where his data says he is."

"That sounds like 'disappeared' to me," Nico grumbled.

"Not at all, trust me on that."

The spark of interest in Jack's eyes was a joy to behold. He relished the puzzle that had come their way, and at least this case wouldn't trigger sleepless nights and old, painful memories. Not so with Daniel and Nico. Daniel was seeking comfort from Jack, and Nico had Bagpuss draped like a blanket over his chest.

"Cheer up, you two," Gareth said. "You know these things take time."

"I know. It's just ... Mrs Harmon must be so worried."

Gareth heard the next thought, as if Nico had spoken it aloud. *Daniel is worried, too.* He met Jack's gaze, saw his own feelings reflected there. None of them liked to see Daniel scared.

"He has a phone, right?" Nico tried again. "If the police haven't done it already, can't we ring him and track the number?"

"Maybe." Jack made notes in the weird shorthand he used, and Gareth knew that he'd be heading up to his turret in a short while to verify the data Lisa had sent and stretch out feelers for more.

"Thoughts?" he asked before Jack disappeared.

"The phone numbers the market traders use to place orders are prepaid SIM cards. That's a hint if I've ever seen one. Problem is, since none of the police forces linked their cases together until Lisa went looking, none thought too much of it."

"I thought the police used a centralised database."

"They do. But you can't connect cases from all over the country without the right tags and keywords. Lisa has a knack for that. She takes a scenario and knows how someone writing the report described or classified it. That's how she connected these. But..." He flicked the edges of the stack of notes. "I don't believe that these four cases are the only ones. I think they're the ones where something went wrong."

Nico's eyes went wide. "You think there are more? That he does this all the time?"

"Think about it: four times that we know of he's worked a local market, befriended another stallholder, and got them to sell his honey for him. It's almost a production line. If he was really a beekeeper who wanted to retire, why does he need such a sleek setup?"

Gareth had thought about that. "Honey isn't like butter or milk. It's used more slowly. What if he produced far more honey than one market can take?"

"Then he'd work several markets to make sure he had enough customers, I get that. But I can't see the numbers adding up." Jack woke his slate and scrolled to a page of notes. "One beehive produces ten to fifteen kilos of surplus honey a year. That's fifty or sixty jars. To make a living, he'd need five hundred to eight hundred hives or more and I'm not sure he'd have the time to manage them, not while hanging out at several farmers' markets each week."

Jack was holding forth on beekeeping as if it was a long-practised hobby. Gareth saw the method in the way he gathered and assessed data, and a direction to the conclusions they could draw. "Let's verify the scope of the operation," Gareth said. "We need a list of farmers' markets in England. And a list of their stallholders."

"There have to be hundreds!"

"That'd be the whole point. The surest place to hide a needle isn't a haystack. It's a needle factory."

"Can I do anything?" Daniel asked. "I'm not good at this stuff, but I want to help."

"There's enough work to go around. Jack has Lisa's data. The three of us tackle the markets. If we split the counties three ways—"

"Start in the Midlands, around the area where his supposed address is," Jack suggested. "Warwickshire, Northants, maybe Oxfordshire and Leicestershire. And Surrey, of course. That covers the cases Lisa has found so far. And Daniel?"

"Yes?"

"Could you talk to Mrs Harmon? Ask her how often she passes boxes of elixir to someone from a restaurant."

"Get the names of the restaurants, too," Gareth added. "I didn't think to ask about that."

Daniel smiled. "I'm on it."

COUNCIL OF WAR

"You know what's weird?" Nico sprawled on the sofa in Jack's den, Bagpuss on his lap. "I've been watching you so many times, but I never realised how much patience your work takes."

"That's the way. You won't know how something plays until you have a go yourself."

"Does it get easier?"

"Do you mean less boring?" Jack abandoned his screens and spun his chair around to face Nico.

"Not ... precisely. We made all these calls for a reason. That helped." Nico's voice had a raspy edge, betraying the hours spent on the phone. "And we have a list of markets."

"Which I'm sure Gareth is itching to explore." Over the previous five days, the two boys had compiled a list of farmers' markets across the Midlands before calling organisers to find out about stalls selling honey. "As for your question ... unless you're pulling threads for fun, this kind of work comes in lumps. It's often urgent, and then you pile in until it's done. You've seen me."

Nico's fingers moved around the cat's ears, down his cheeks, and along his chin, over and over in a rhythm that calmed him as much as it pleased Bagpuss. "I know you don't sleep when you hunt. But how do you know when to stop? Or when to keep going?"

"Because you define parameters for the work before you start," Gareth said from the doorway.

He'd traded his workday elegance for threadbare weekend clothes that gave Jack ideas. He sent a smile Gareth's way. "Did we miss the dinner gong?"

"Nope. Daniel is happy as a clam in the kitchen and told me to leave him be."

"Yeah. He's been looking forward to some cooking."

"I know how that feels." Gareth joined Nico on the sofa, pulling boy and cat against his side. "You look peaky."

"Sore throat. I now feel sorry for customer service people."

"Teaches you all kinds of things, Jack's work."

"No sore throats in my line of work, thank you very much. I never ask for information I can dig up in other ways. People lie too often and too easily." The moment the words left his mouth, Jack wished to take them back. Gareth wanted to help while sticking to the rules. Jack had to respect that or tell Gareth he was going his own way.

Gareth smiled the crinkly-eyed smile that gave Jack butterflies. "You're a cynic."

"The market organisers won't lie about their stallholders," Nico argued. "If customers came from a long way away to buy honey and there wasn't anyone selling it, they'd leave negative reviews."

"You're right. What you've been doing is standard investigative work. Jack just likes to snoop. He's nosy that way."

"Right." Jack wasn't touching that with a ten-foot pole. At least Gareth wasn't mad at him. "Wanna share what you found out?"

"Wait." Gareth waved at Jack's screens. "Are you babysitting anything?"

"Not really."

"Then why not have that discussion downstairs? That

181

way Daniel can hear, and it saves us going over everything twice."

"Or have Daniel interrupt us when dinner is ready." Nico hopped up, the cat cradled in his arms. "It's time for Bagpuss to have a treat, anyway."

Gareth waited on the landing when Jack emerged from his den after shutting down his screens.

"Hey."

"Hey yourself." He took a step closer, caught a hint of leather and spice, and went pliant when Gareth reeled him in by his belt loops to kiss him. Gareth tasted of basil and mint as if he'd been picking at the herb pots on his office windowsill, but Jack soon forgot about that and focussed on what mattered. The stubble under his fingertips as he traced Gareth's jaw. Gareth's grip tightening over the waistband of his jeans. Their tongues touching and twining.

Kissing Gareth never got old.

"I appreciate you following my lead," Gareth said, drawing back to let Jack catch his breath. "I won't get mad if you question it now and then."

"You'd get mad if I went off and did things my way."

Gareth shrugged. "Rules of engagement. For now, at least. Without Aidan standing behind me, I'm making this up as I go, you know that. I might learn that the straight and narrow isn't a suitable road."

"Then you'll find another one, and I'll walk it with you."

"I know you will." Gareth let him go. "Come on. There's a beer that's calling my name. Let's see what Daniel has to go with."

What Daniel had for them that night was ... street food. Kim bap and pho, bao buns, and short ribs, gyoza dumplings, fried shrimp, and chicken skewers. An enormous plate of shredded vegetables took up the centre of the table and everyone helped themselves, mixing and matching to their hearts' content.

The explosion of dishes represented the level of Daniel's anxiety. Gareth knew that, but he also thought it the perfect Friday night dinner. A chance to disconnect from the week, discuss food and cooking, and plan holidays. He waited until after he'd opened a bottle of wine and Daniel had set a box of chocolates on the table to serve as dessert to turn their evening into a council of war.

"Lisa called. They found no drugs in the items taken from Mrs Harmon's kitchen. The honey was honey, and the elixir was exactly that."

"So Mrs Harmon's in the clear?"

"Not yet. The working theory is a spoiled or contaminated bottle of elixir. Of course, she could have disposed of the incriminating evidence before the police got to her. I know it's not likely she'd do that." He stopped Nico before he started a tirade. "They're the police. They're paid to think that way."

"And they've been in a gazillion situations where that's exactly what happened, right?"

Daniel, still flushed from his dinner success, bit into a chocolate shaped like a seahorse. Gareth had caught him watching YouTube videos of a French chef who made chocolate sculptures and wondered if he needed to invest in slabs of marble and other chocolate-making equipment. "Did you finish with the market list?"

"We did. But we had little luck."

Gareth reached for his notepad. "Tell it in order."

"There are a shocking number of farmers' markets across the middle of England. And farm shops."

"That's not a bad thing."

"Unless you have to phone them." Daniel made a face. "Only fourteen had honey on their product list."

"Fifteen." Nico picked a chocolate for himself. "I got through to the Kettering one just before they closed."

"Fifteen, then. But all the farm shops and most of the markets buy their honey from a franchise or a cooperative or something like that. They say on their website the honey is local, but how do you know?"

"How indeed." Gareth made notes. "No Mr Fitzgerald?"

"Only one," Daniel said. "Hazelworth lists a Mr T.G. Fitzgerald. But that's a pop-up market, and they didn't have a date yet for the next one. Or know if he'd be there."

"Maybe Jack can check if—"

"No. We're doing this the legal way. There's no need for Jack to get himself in trouble." Gareth kept his voice calm and low, the way he did at work when an argument erupted during the team meeting.

"Wait." Nico sat up straighter. "Knowing where he's selling honey right now doesn't really help us, does it? Shouldn't we phone the markets where there isn't an exclusive honey stall and see if they had someone in the past? Someone who retired?"

"That's an idea." Jack took a sip of wine and snagged a chocolate from the box. "It's more difficult to do, though. If you phone the organiser of a market and ask if they have someone selling honey, they have no reason not to answer and little reason to lie. If you ask if they used to have someone and where they went ... that sounds like snooping and potential trouble. They may even refuse to tell us. If, on the other hand, we know where he's selling now, we can check him out. Or point Lisa his way."

"Pop-up market, remember? Last year, they only had five of them and they only announce dates a fortnight in advance. I'm sure Mrs Harmon doesn't want to be called a drug dealer for three months." Daniel reached for another chocolate, the line between his brows making a comeback. "Did you know she's not allowed to sell at our market while the police are investigating her? They made a mistake, and she can't earn any money. That's so unfair! Imagine if she had no savings, or can't pay her mortgage, or—"

"Daniel, breathe. We're right here, helping to get this resolved." Gareth wrapped an arm around his shoulder and hugged him. "I've not been sitting on my backside while you've been wearing out your vocal cords. There are legal ways to find out what we want to know."

"Are there now?"

Jack's suddenly heavy-lidded gaze heated the tips of Gareth's ears. "Just because I don't enjoy working with computers doesn't mean I don't know how." Gareth riffled through his notes. "Most of the markets have websites listing the products they offer. And their stallholders."

"But that's for current markets," Nico complained.

Jack started laughing, and Gareth enjoyed the sight. "There's an archive," he explained. "Goes all the way back to the beginning of the internet."

"Really? It shows you what the BBC looked like when they started?"

"Yep. Works even for websites that aren't around anymore."

"It must take ages to find anything."

"Probably. But the list of markets and farm shops you compiled told me where to look."

"Did you find anything useful?" Jack woke up his slate, ready to take notes.

"I'll mail it to you," Gareth said. "So far, I've found four markets where he used to have a stall. They also had a stall selling cakes and such."

"Nice."

"Daniel, did you remember to ask Mrs Harmon about the restaurants?"

Daniel relaxed a tiny fraction. "Yes. She said there are three. Carmelo in the High Street, The Golden Ball in Sutton, and the Striped Cat in Cheam." Daniel's voice was still thin with fear, but a touch of interest crept in.

"Excellent." Gareth's mind was off and strategising. "You're not working tomorrow, are you? How about we check out these restaurants? Nico can stay home and rest his voice."

Daniel and Nico looked at each other, and Gareth let them have their silent conversation. He understood their need to help, but the two had worked hard all week and deserved a break, especially since they had a history exam coming up. He'd take Daniel to explore food, while Nico got more enjoyment out of a morning spent with Jack.

"Can we have lunch at Carmelo?" Daniel asked finally, falling neatly in line with Gareth's plans.

"We can indeed."

SURPRISES

Gareth followed Jack into their bedroom, not surprised to see him switch on the monitor on his bedside table. The discussion had shifted to food for the rest of the night, and Bagpuss had joined them and demanded cuddles, but Daniel hadn't relaxed much. They saw nightmares in their future, and Jack took the boys' needs seriously, whatever else they had going on.

"You're going to do something illegal, aren't you? You have that gleam in your eye."

Jack rolled across the bed, reached for Gareth's hand and pulled him down to the quilt. "I promised I'll walk this road with you, and I'm going to do just that," he said, voice serious. "I'm not sure Lisa has enough for a warrant, but I'm prepared to wait and see."

"A warrant?"

"For T.G. Fitzgerald's phone and banking records. We need to know how many market traders he's working with."

"What if he uses a different pre-paid SIM for each trader?"

"I doubt he has a different bank account for each one."

"Fair enough." Gareth's expertise lay in logistics and leadership rather than data mining, but he saw the usefulness of phone and bank records. "I thought you wanted to gauge his level of sales."

"While getting a peek at his customer list, yes. Lisa has four victims with similar stories. I have the feeling they're not the only ones. Especially with you finding markets he used to work but doesn't anymore."

"Do you really think we've stumbled onto a drugs ring, or was that something to keep the boys interested?"

Jack rolled onto his back and lay staring at the ceiling. "It's a clever setup, even the little we've glimpsed so far," he said, and Gareth imagined the cogs whirring in Jack's mind as he wove patterns from the facts they had. "All in plain sight and seemingly legitimate. And God only knows what they're brewing."

"I can't see what you see."

"You're not supposed to. Besides, Conrad usually sends us to find evidence to clear suspects of charges. You've never gone up against traffickers," Jack soothed. "I used to unravel traffic systems for a living, and I imagine this one grew out of the honey frosting. You cooks can't ever resist a good recipe."

"You mean there was a man selling honey frosting and one day he got the idea to sell drugs alongside it?"

"Nothing so crude." Jack warmed to his topic. "The best traffic system is one where the distributors aren't aware that they're doing anything illegal. The frosting is the bait to recruit innocent, oblivious distributors. People who believe they got a bargain on top of an excellent business opportunity and wish to be helpful in return. Don't look at me like that. It happens!"

"I take your word for it. I just never considered it this way."

"Imagine you're dealing with camouflage, deception, and misdirection. Same difference. It's even possible that the whole honey operation is completely legitimate, and that someone's piggybacking onto it."

"How?" Gareth got a kick out of seeing Jack's mind at work.

"Consider the setup. Mrs Harmon places an order for honey and elixir. Her delivery holds her order, plus a few wrapped and labelled parcels. She passes those to representatives from local restaurants when they call for them."

"And instead of elixir, they hold drugs?"

"Maybe. It's possible that our Mr Fitzgerald is an oblivious innocent himself."

"How?"

"Imagine you're a dealer with a product to distribute. You monitor Fitzgerald's phone or email, so you know when Mrs Harmon has placed an order. You intercept Fitzgerald's parcel—by pretending to be from the courier company, for instance—open the thing up and add your product to the honey and elixir already in the delivery. Then you'll send it on its way as planned, and Mrs Harmon takes care of the rest."

"Doesn't work." Gareth saw the snarl in the logic the moment Jack finished speaking. "According to Mrs Harmon, it was Fitzgerald who asked her to pass on parcels to restaurants. Which means he must know about that bit, at least."

"He may not know that there's an extra parcel in the delivery. One that doesn't go to a restaurant."

"Are they really so bloody devious?"

"This isn't devious," Jack said. "Just a bit clever. And speculation. First, we need to get a handle on Fitzgerald. Let's email Lisa in the morning, and then you have restaurants to check out."

Gareth pulled his T-shirt over his head. "What's on your to-do list tomorrow?"

"Besides teaching Nico about the Way Back Machine?" He stripped his own clothes and slid under the quilt. "I had no idea you even knew about that."

Jack's skin was soft under Gareth's palms. "Impressed you, did I?"

"You know it. But then, you're always good for a surprise or two."

"Yeah? Let's see..."

Kissing Jack never got old. Gareth loved the hint of hesitation before their first touch of lips that charged the air with heat and static. The taste of cinnamon and wine, laced with the sugar-burn of hunger. The tiny sounds of want he coaxed from Jack's throat when he cradled Jack's jaw as they kissed.

So many things about Jack turned him on, but none more than Jack letting him take charge in bed. With all he knew about Jack, that level of trust was breathtaking. It caught him in the feels every single time, ramped his determination to see to Jack's pleasure.

He drew Jack closer, loving the way skin slid against skin while they devoured each other's mouths. Jack gripped Gareth's shoulders, held on while he rocked against Gareth's thigh.

"Impatient?" Gareth breathed the question against Jack's lips.

Jack chuckled, voice rough with desire. "Ravenous."

And not in the mood for games, if the way he wrapped himself around Gareth was any indication.

Well, they could play later.

Gareth slid a hand between them and grasped both their lengths together. Jack's groan was a thing of beauty and heartfelt relief, and Gareth's toes curled in answer. He started a slow, long rhythm while they kissed and Jack's hands roamed his back, the touch like fire on his skin.

Cocooned in warmth and wanting, they rocked against each other, drawing out every sensation. They tried to make it last, but they knew each other too well. Far too soon, Jack's movements grew jerky, and then he slid his fingers up to the gold ring in Gareth's nipple, and Gareth's world caught fire.

Daniel and Gareth returned from their lunchtime sortie laden with shopping bags, and Jack breathed a sigh of relief. Caught between work and snooping, he hadn't placed their usual order for groceries.

There was something else beyond ideas for dinner, though. Gareth's expression made him think of canary feathers, and Daniel's grin was so wide it threatened his ears. Before Jack got around to asking, Gareth crossed the room, took Jack by the neck, and kissed him as if he meant it, not stopping until Jack's vision blurred at the edges from lack of oxygen.

"You. Are. A genius!" Gareth took a step back, still grinning.

Jack blinked. Stared at Gareth. Turned his head to check on Nico and Daniel. They made no secret of their relationship, but they rarely mauled each other in the middle of the kitchen. Or in front of an audience. "What brought that on?"

"You. Being right. So damn right!"

"How nice for me. What am I right about?"

"It's a drugs ring!" Gareth's piecemeal delivery was too slow for Daniel and didn't explain the matter any better.

"Explain while using actual sentences?"

Daniel rolled his eyes. "Mrs Harmon hands parcels to three restaurants. But there are only two."

"After what you said last night..."

"Gareth called Lisa and told her. She's going to apply

for a warrant."

Excitement painted a flush into Daniel's cheeks. It looked good on him, but it was Gareth who held Jack's attention. They'd found another piece of the puzzle and Gareth's elation was a damned fine sight. Much better than the tense figure who'd doubted himself just because Conrad had had to be an arse.

Daniel sidled up to him, and they watched Gareth unpack the food they'd bought while fending off Bagpuss, who was determined to investigate each bag and parcel. "We had lunch at Carmelo, and I swear they'd put honey elixir on their roast beef, and into the spun sugar basket they put over the baked plums."

Jack bit back a sigh. Stopping Daniel when he was gushing about food was as impossible as stopping Nico from sharing his latest science discovery.

"Worth having dinner there one night," Gareth said. "Food's good. Besides that, the Golden Ball is where it says it is, and has a website. We couldn't find hide nor hair of The Striped Cat. Not in Cheam."

"Did you find it anywhere else?"

"We drove Google Maps insane, but no. No Striped Cat."

"Now, isn't that interesting?" Jack straightened. "Well done, you."

Daniel wasn't as lost in food as Jack had thought. "You know it could be nothing, right?"

"Nothing? Why buy boxes of honey elixir—which isn't cheap—if you have no kitchen to use it in?"

"They have no *restaurant* to use it in. What if The Striped Cat is a catering service? For dinner parties and birthdays and such."

"Good thinking." Jack was glad Daniel was managing his expectations rather than let himself get carried away. He had a hunch, though. That weird tug in his gut that warned him he was onto something. "Let's see what we can find."

PATTERNS

J ack breathed a sigh of relief when Lisa emailed him Fitzgerald's banking records. He hated unsolved problems, and after days of doing little more than watching Nico and Daniel grow anxious and distracted, he'd come close to stepping outside the lane Gareth had him running in. Now he didn't have to.

Fitzgerald's account showed plenty of activity and a healthy balance. Mrs Harmon was far from the only person placing orders for honey and elixir, and most of the outgoing payments were cash withdrawals. Whether Fitzgerald was part of the distribution network, or an oblivious innocent was still open for debate.

They agreed to split the work with Lisa chasing down the deposits—the people buying honey—while Jack tackled the withdrawals.

Plotting the markets and the locations of the cash withdrawals didn't take long, and Jack scrutinised his map from this angle and that, seeking to spot a pattern in the accumulation of coloured dots. He ran progressions by time and market. Nothing jumped out at him, nor did the added tangle of lines suggest any new avenues of attack. In the end, he went running, stretching his muscles while letting his mind work in peace.

The kitchen and living room were empty when he

returned, but the music was a dead giveaway, leading the way up the stairs to his den. Nico lay flat on his back on the sofa, holding his tablet above his face to read, while a cable trailed from the sofa to the nearest socket.

"That doesn't look comfortable. And why the heating pad? What did you do?"

Nico dropped the tablet to his chest. "Everything hurts," he admitted. "Sorry, I snuck up here. Your sofa is comfier than ours. Or the floor."

"Don't be silly. I know you won't compromise anything I have running." Jack dropped to his knees beside the couch. "Define everything."

"Shoulders to knees. Not sure what I did. I stuck to my exercise plan, I swear."

"I believe you. Do you think you're coming down with a cold? You had a sore throat yesterday."

"That was from the phone calls."

"Maybe." He touched Nico's forehead, relieved to find it cool and dry. Nico and Daniel were prone to episodic muscle and nerve pain, and both ran hot when that happened. "Well, you don't have a fever. Can you move? Bend? Twist?"

"Yes."

"What's the pain like?"

"It hurts?" Nico managed a small grin. "It woke me up early this morning, but it doesn't feel as if I've pulled a muscle or need physio. It's sort of ... diffuse. Like there's a storm coming?"

Jack's gaze went to the window. They'd been having a typical April, and it had been raining on and off for the last couple of weeks, but his phone alert for major air pressure changes hadn't pinged. "I don't think we're expecting weather. Let me check."

He crossed the room to his workspace and—one by one—the seven screens came to life. Finding the weather channel took only a moment. "No storms."

"Then why am I so sore?"

"Not sure." Both boys carried scars from the abuse they'd suffered. They had regular physiotherapy appointments and exercise schedules to help them deal with the damage as they grew, and Jack and Gareth had learned massage techniques and stretching exercises to loosen tight muscles. They were never without ice packs and heating pads and kept painkillers for the worst days. "How about a massage?"

"I don't think that will help. It's all over. Even my skin hurts."

Jack stilled, the memory coming unbidden. His younger self huddled on Rio's living room sofa, hurting as if he'd taken a major beating. And Rio saying—

"It might be a growth spurt. Unfortunately, the only thing for it is heat and painkillers, and gentle stretches when you don't feel so sore."

"Growing ... hurts?"

"It was more of an all-over ache for me," Jack said. "Came and went a few times. The worst was losing my balance, so take care with that skipping rope once you feel better. Painkiller?"

Nico pushed himself to sitting, moving as if he was decades older. "Yeah. Maybe." He stared into the middle distance, eyes blank, and Jack wanted to hit something.

Someone.

But that ship had sailed.

Jack held out a hand, waiting until Nico took it and hauled. "Up you come." He wrapped an arm around Nico's waist and Nico leaned, revealing just how miserable he was. It shoved a giant lump into Jack's throat, and more helpless rage into his heart.

"How about ice cream to wash down the pills? Assassin's Creed?"

"Can we watch something distracting? Daniel's revising and I don't want to bother him."

"That's fine. Want me to carry you down?"

"Don't be silly."

They turned towards the door, but before they reached it, Nico's head snapped back around. "Jack!"

"Hm?"

Nico's gaze stayed glued to Jack's work-in-progress, aches and pains momentarily forgotten. "On your second screen ... what are those markers?"

"Green for markets, red for the cashpoint withdrawals? Why?"

"Because I've been staring at them while I lay here. The pattern reminded me of something, only I didn't know what it was."

Two long strides returned Jack to his console. He magnified the screen and scrutinised the array of coloured dots. "And now you have an idea?"

"It sounds stupid."

"There are no stupid ideas, only premature ones. You know that."

"Right. Do you remember that project on transport routes I did last year? For the history class. I've been revising it and these...." He waved at the markers on Jack's screen. "... remind me of the canal network."

Canals? How the fuck did canals fit into this? Jack wanted to sit down and explore the new angle, but he was too aware of the heating pad on his sofa and Nico standing beside him. Excitement tempered the pain for only a little while. "Let me print this and get some pills into you. Then we sit down with a map and see if we can work it out."

"You don't think it's daft?"

"Why? Just because I know nothing about canals doesn't mean you're wrong."

The tiny smile on Nico's face was hard won. To Jack, it was a thing of beauty.

"They built the canals by subscription," Nico explained, fingers busy stroking the cat in his lap. Jack wasn't sure if all cats sensed when their humans needed comfort, but the moment Jack had dropped two pain pills into Nico's palm, Bagpuss had arrived and draped himself across Nico's lap. Now the laptop on the coffee table showed the network of canals crisscrossing the Midlands, while Nico told Jack everything he remembered about this period in history. Jack listened and made notes, glad it both distracted Nico from his pains and helped with his revision. "Factory owners and landowners banded together because taking goods by water was faster and the roads were awful."

"That hasn't changed," Jack muttered.

"Building the canals employed lots of people," Nico continued. "The workers needed looking after, so pubs, and workshops, and restaurants started up along the canals. Where possible, the canals ran alongside existing roads to make transferring goods easy. Here. See?" He pointed at the map where the canal and the road ran side by side.

"The trains follow that route, too."

"Trains came later."

"True."

Nico deflated at the monosyllabic answer. "Oh, you mean the train lines or the roads cause your pattern, rather than the canals? I suppose so." He scrutinised their map again, and Jack let him work it out for himself. "It's not a complete overlap. See here? These three cash withdrawals are at marinas. If he was travelling by train, it'd make more sense to take cash out at the station."

"True. What else do you see?"

Nico's gaze flitted back and forth between the map and the list of transactions Jack had printed. Then he saw it. "That lonely black dot is his address, right? The one the post office says doesn't exist. It's right beside the Grand Union Canal!"

Jack hugged him. Carefully. "Well done. I'd never have considered canals. Not in a month of Sundays."

"I can be useful." Nico shifted in Jack's hold, loosening and stretching aching muscles, while taking care to keep hold of Bagpuss. "I feel better, too. Not so achy. Will you explore the canal? See if you find him?"

"Let's see what Gareth thinks. Besides, it was your idea. You should come."

Nico shook his head. "We have to revise."

Everything in Jack revolted at the idea of leaving the two alone at home. "Is revising easier when we're not here?"

"No. Or maybe?" Nico didn't look up from the cat in his lap. "I don't know about the revision, but you and Gareth have so little time for yourselves. This is ideal. And productive."

"Productive?"

"An efficient use of all our time." Daniel stood in the doorway. "You don't have to go for weeks, just a couple of nights to find where he stays."

On Nico's lap, Bagpuss purred like an engine. "We look after Bagpuss."

"Heaven forbid that he fends for himself for a night," Jack muttered under his breath. "And how do you propose we find the man?"

"Rent a narrowboat and cruise the canal! Then you can tell us about it. Just in case it turns out to be an exam question."

Jack didn't roll his eyes at the obvious scheme, but it took effort. "Right."

WORRIES

Nico looked peaky. The colour in his cheeks wasn't the glowing pink of a recent workout. Neither were the small dots of perspiration along his hairline.

"I was in Jack's den, reading. He had a map on his screen showing the markets and the places where T.G. Fitzgerald has withdrawn cash. I stared at it so long that suddenly the dots made a pattern," Nico said. "I wish that worked for other subjects, too."

Gareth could spot a distraction from a mile away. Nico was … prickly. Daniel wasn't any better. Even Jack wasn't completely himself.

Did it have anything to do with Nico's discovery?

"Why don't you tell me, too? Since I assume everyone else already knows." His tone must have been sharper than he'd realised because Daniel jumped in to make peace.

"Nico and Jack worked it out. I only know because I walked in on them when I came down for a drink."

"And I only saw it because I've been revising for the history exam," Nico continued. "The pattern was like the network of canals built in the 1800s. I did that project last year and–"

"He lives on a canal boat?" Gareth turned to Jack for corroboration.

"We don't know that. He uses cash machines near a

canal or directly in a marina, and he attends markets in locations close to a canal."

"Except for our local one," Gareth argued. "Richmond's nowhere near a canal."

"True enough. Maybe proximity to a canal isn't the only criterium he uses."

"But they're the distinguishing factor?"

"We think so. His address—the one that doesn't exist— is right beside the Grand Union Canal, too." Nico looked like an eager chipmunk.

"You and Jack should rent a boat, cruise the canal, and see if you find him," Daniel suggested.

"That is ludicrous." The words spilled from Gareth in a rush. Spending time with Jack wasn't a hardship, but leaving Nico and Daniel?

"Breathe." Jack sounded amused. "Their suggestion took me the same way."

Though perhaps not for the same reason. Gareth had promised himself that he'd help without breaking the law. Hiring a boat to spend a few days on the Grand Union Canal wasn't in any way illegal, but it felt way more involved than he was comfortable with.

Jack knew without having to ask. "We don't have to hunt Fitzgerald ourselves," he said. "We can bundle what I've found and send it to Lisa. Leave it to her to despatch officers to check on the boaters and the marinas."

"Or?" As if he didn't know.

"Or we sit on our data for a little while longer, treat ourselves to a weekend away, and attempt to narrow down the most likely part of the canal. Active resource management, right?"

The grin curving his lips held understanding, acceptance, and a tiny hint of challenge. Gareth wasn't sure how to respond to it.

"Can I bother you?"

Jack turned his head. Daniel's pout was cute enough for an audition with a boy band, and Jack had a decent idea what had prompted the puppy dog eyes. He waved Daniel into his den and held up two fingers, finishing the line of code he was writing before he spun his chair around.

"What's he doing now?" he asked, not minding—or hiding—the indulgence lacing his tone. Gareth hadn't reacted well to the idea of leaving the boys at home while going out hunting for T.G. Fitzgerald, and for the last couple of days, he'd been working out his frustration in the kitchen.

"He's cooking as if you'll be gone for months and I've never picked up a wooden spoon in my life," Daniel complained, just as Jack had predicted.

"He's worried."

"There's no reason. We're not planning a rave or a bank heist, or whatever it is he imagines. We're going to be here, revising." He pulled his knees to his chest and rested his chin on them. "We won't do anything risky, Jack. We want you to find out who's taking advantage of Mrs Harmon!"

Jack had a thousand things to say in response, but he kept silent until Daniel relaxed his tight control.

"We're worried, too," he admitted in a whisper. "Nico and I, we talked about it, and we agreed we can't keep hiding behind you and Gareth."

"That's really not what you're doing. You've not missed a day of school, or one of work. Doesn't look like hiding to me."

"Maybe not. But Jack, listen! You can't always stand

guard over us. We agreed that if we no longer feel safe here, we ask you about moving and you'll listen to us. Do you think Gareth has forgotten our discussion?"

The plea was an unexpectedly eloquent one for Daniel, showing just how much Gareth's worries affected him.

"That's not it. Gareth doesn't think you're helpless, reckless, or lazy. He's worried about you revising without him here to feed you."

"What? Why?"

"He went to the parents' evening, remember? Revision time means teenagers who throw tantrums, don't sleep, and live on junk food and bottles of coke."

"What?"

"Don't blame me. I didn't come up with it. But parents talk, you know?"

"He doesn't have to listen."

Jack shrugged. "He always listens unless he's been there, done that, and came away with the T-shirt. Now he's making sure that you have peace to revise and healthy food to eat when you stagger downstairs like zombies."

"Don't you find it weird?"

"Gareth cooking his heart out?"

"Not that. Us taking exams when you never did."

"I took exams. The army tests you all the time. They're hot on everyone improving their skills. I had to defend my thesis, which is like an exam." Jack had never worked out why Daniel liked to hear of him growing up. He never refused to answer, though he focussed on the positive parts and censored the rest.

"Nico is going to do so much better in history than I," Daniel sighed.

"Wouldn't surprise me in the least. He loves history." He shot Daniel an encouraging grin. "You love other things. Not even identical twins have the same likes and dislikes."

"There are twins in the year below us," Daniel said, momentarily diverted. "Maybe I should ask them."

"And remember that you're not competing with Nico, only with yourself."

"I'll remember."

"Right. Then cut Gareth some slack. He's stressed, and he's working it out. Besides, I don't think he's taking all the fun of cooking away from you. He's more likely to stuff the fridge with ready-prepped ingredients for you to rustle up your favourites at the drop of a hat."

"That's something he'd do, yes." Daniel looked brighter, as if voicing his concerns had eased his mind.

Jack added another dollop of emotional balm. "Why not cook for us when we come back on Sunday? That way, we sit down and tell you what we've discovered without you having to wait."

"I've caused a bit of a stir, haven't I?" Gareth surveyed the kitchen and larder. He didn't appear pleased with his efforts. More ... resigned, and Jack hated hearing that tone in his voice.

"You've gone a touch overboard." Jack went hunting for a bag of soy-flavoured rice crackers, his current snack of choice to go with an ice-cold beer. "We're going for three nights, not three weeks."

"I know."

Gareth opened a beer for himself, and Jack slid over to make room on the bench. To discuss work or the logistics of their lives, they invariably sat facing each other. For heart-to-heart conversations, they often ended up sitting side by side.

"I didn't realise that leaving them alone bothers me so much."

"I'd offer to check out the canal lead by myself, but that won't fix the problem in the long term. You can't keep them caged."

"Yes, I know." Gareth took a swig from his beer. "I'm making a mountain out of a molehill."

"There's no shame in being concerned for Daniel and Nico," Jack said. "They're ours. We protect them."

"You don't want us to be afraid."

Jack twisted around, not surprised to see Nico and Daniel standing in the doorway. The two had radar for discussions with topics that concerned them—and rightly so.

"It's more than that." Gareth waved them to the table. "We protect each other, yes, but what we're about to do now isn't the same thing. Actively pursuing a suspected drug dealer isn't safe. I'm concerned that we'll make ourselves visible to people who could harm us."

Dead silence.

"I never thought of that," Nico admitted.

"You shouldn't have to," Jack said. "Unfortunately, we're not a normal family. Even with Gareth working his socks off to make us feel and behave like one."

"Don't make it sound as if I'm the only one."

"I wasn't. But taking this beyond collecting data affects all of us, so it needs to be a family decision."

"You've already booked the boat," Daniel reminded him.

"We can cancel the booking," Gareth said. "Jack is right. We should have made it a family decision from the start."

Daniel assembled a large plate of snacks, placed the plate in the centre of the table, and returned for bread and olive oil. When he resumed his seat, he finally said what was on his mind.

"I think it's been a family decision from the start. Nico and I asked you to help Mrs Harmon. You listened and made it happen."

"Are you still in favour of us helping, knowing it could get dangerous? Or shall we hand over everything we've found to Lisa?" Gareth popped an olive into his mouth and kept his eyes on the toothpick in his hand. Jack picked at the pickled chillies, staying equally silent.

"The police are so busy, they may not get this sorted for weeks," Nico said after a while. "And all this time, Mrs Harmon can't work because people think she sells drugs. We should help."

"Agreed," Daniel said. "Besides, we're already careful."

Jack slapped his palm on the table. Nico, who got it first, added his own on top. Daniel followed suit, and then Gareth settled his hand on top of the stack, sealing the deal.

A RAFT OF FRUSTRATIONS

"T here she is, gents. Your home from home for the weekend." The man from the boat hire company, who'd introduced himself as Roger, stopped beside a deep blue narrowboat with gilt-painted decorations and brass trim. It was one of the smaller boats moored in this part of the marina, not that this was saying much. As far as Gareth was concerned, the boats were rather too long, and from where he stood on the jetty, he was taller than every single one. Maybe he should have brought a hard hat.

"She's six feet and ten inches wide and forty-seven feet long. An ideal weekend boat for two. I'm not joking!" Roger had caught Gareth's incredulous look and waved a hand at the boats moored two spaces over. "These are seventy-two feet long and sleep eight to ten people. Largest size possible on this part of the canal."

Only his experience of barracks and long-distance army transport let Gareth imagine ten grown men fitting onto such a boat without bloodshed or a crowbar. "They're all the same width?"

"Narrowboats are, yes. You might see the odd widebeam or barge, but they designed these canals for narrowboats, so that's what most people are familiar with and what we hire out. Let me show you around and give you some pointers before you set off."

Jack followed right along, curious and eager to learn something new. Gareth needed a moment to take it all in. Almost fifty boats moored in this section alone, with further rows of jetties on the other side of the marina building. Boating appeared to be a popular pastime.

Gareth had never imagined himself on a narrowboat. Truth be told, he'd never given the canal network a second, or even a first thought.

The jobs he did for Aidan had been more or less predictable. His first solo foray was not.

How had his decision to help a fellow food enthusiast led to spending a weekend on a narrowboat trawling the canal for a drug dealer? He could neither plan nor prepare adequately for something like this. Was this what bothered him? Or was he losing his sense of adventure?

"Gareth, did you get lost?"

Jack's voice startled him from his musings. At least he had Jack, who stopped him from feeling maudlin without breaking a sweat.

"On my way," he called back, and prepared himself for claustrophobia.

He needn't have worried. From the platform at the stern, where the pilot manned the tiller, steps led into the interior of the boat. Which was roomier than he'd thought. He had to duck under the lintel going in, but the inside space was high enough to let him straighten without fear, and from his place at the foot of the ladder, he had a clear view to the front of the boat.

Instead of the cramped confines he'd expected, the interior was a light, neat space that calmed his nerves. He and Jack had space to spread out, and the boat had room for Nico and Daniel, too.

"Right, gents," Roger reminded them of their reason for being inside. "First, the kitchen. You have an electric hob and oven, microwave, kettle, and toaster, and a fridge with built-in freezer. Cutlery and dishware are in the cupboards along the wall, pots and pans are underneath. Some boats have a dishwasher, but most of our customers moor up for lunch and dinner at a pub along the canal," Roger said. "It's for the same reason we didn't put in a bigger freezer."

"Do you live on a boat?" Jack asked before Gareth had the chance to do so.

"For over thirty years. We're on our second boat. Our first one was like this one, and we outgrew it. Children, you know, they need more stuff than two practical adults and a dog. By the time they left for uni, we'd got used to the bigger one and kept it." He moved into the centre of the boat and waved at a sofa and armchair with a coffee table between them. "This is your living area. The log burner works if you want to take the chill off in the evening. Logs and kindling are in the bow. And the sofa folds out into an extra bed. I'm guessing you won't need that?"

"Not if there's a bedroom."

There was. Separated from the main part of the boat by a partition, the bedroom had an airy feel with built-in furniture painted a pale grey. The bed—definitely spacious enough for the two of them—ran along one side of the boat and cast-iron drawer handles along the edge suggested it doubled as storage.

"The design is ingenious," Gareth admitted. "I didn't think there'd be so much room." He pointed to the small round windows. "Or so much light."

"Dark and claustrophobic, eh? We get that a lot." They

watched Jack open a door. "That's your bathroom and shower."

"And again, roomier than expected." Jack's grin revealed his fascination with the boat, and Gareth's disquiet took another step back.

"Now we know where we'll sleep," he said. "How do we move this thing?"

Roger shooed them back to the ladder. "There's not much to it, you'll see."

He took them through starting the engine, steering the boat, and using the mooring lines. "We usually recommend that you go up this part of the canal for a bit to get the hang of piloting a narrowboat. You get a few miles of clear water, then a lock. Above the lock is a mooring if you want to stay overnight, or there's a marina a little farther if you'd rather have people around you and pub food to go with. In the morning, you can either come back here and go up the Oxford arm of the canal or carry on from where you are until it's time to turn around and head back. This will help." He handed Jack a folder. "Distances, travel times, locks, and moorings. Plus some general FAQs and contact numbers if you need a hand."

"We're longer than the canal is wide, right? How do you turn around without getting stuck?" Gareth had visions of holding up a stream of boats while he attempted a fifteen-point-turn.

"Junctions. Winding holes." Roger grinned as if he'd guessed Gareth's thoughts. "The canal's a touch over twenty-six feet wide. That—as you've already realised—isn't enough to let you turn the boat. Canal junctions have room to turn. So do most marinas. For the rest of the time, we have winding holes. There's one just by the next marina, so you can turn there." He watched them start the boat's engine, then waved for Gareth to take the tiller. "Let's get this show on the road. I'll guide you out of the marina."

Gareth caught Jack's eye, saw the amusement there. No pressure.

"Oh, for fuck's sake!" Gareth barked his shin on the stepover, hopped on one foot, and then promptly banged his head on the lintel. "I hate narrowboats!"

"So you keep telling me." Jack accepted the dewy bottle Gareth held out. He took a sip, then set it on the roof beside him and returned his attention to his laptop. As far as he was concerned, working from the roof of a narrowboat outstripped working from an office. He had fresh air, moving scenery, and regular beer deliveries. "You were the one who agreed to the trip."

"I've been regretting it ever since I've seen this crate."

"Really?" Jack smirked and didn't mind that Gareth saw it. "I'm letting you drive."

"Drive." Gareth scoffed. "Two miles an hour? Three? I fucking walk faster."

"That's the idea, I think."

"Huh?"

"Keep up, Flynn." Jack took another sip of his beer. "Narrowboat holidays are supposed to be a way to unwind. Slow down. Relax."

"We're not on holiday. We're working. And if your next smart-arse comment mentions age, you're going in the water."

"Is that supposed to be a threat? It's a canal, Gareth. It's barely four feet deep."

"I'm sure it's deep enough to drown your laptop."

"In which case, there'll be war. You may want to rethink

that approach."

Gareth huffed and stomped back to the tiller. Jack watched him. He knew what this was about. However much Gareth ragged him for feeling responsible for everything in his vicinity, he was no better.

Not that he'd see it this way, but Jack would deal with that one later. For the moment, it was easier to stay out of Gareth's way and give him a chance to find ground again. He was busy making sure Nico and Daniel took breaks in their revision by sending them photos of the canal, the clouds, and a scowling Gareth at the tiller.

MAKING IT WORK

"Jack!"

"Hm?"

"That contraption ahead looks like a lock to me. You're up."

Jack considered the obstacle in their path. The huge wooden gates were closed, which he interpreted—after his crash course in canal boating—as the lock being full. It meant that first he'd have to empty the lock, lowering the water table inside to their level. Then he'd have to open the lock gates and guide Gareth and the boat inside, before closing the gates behind them. Only then could he let the lock fill up and open the upper gates.

Since the logic of the operation appealed to him, Jack abandoned his roof and jogged on ahead.

Gareth's grumpy mood evaporated now that he had something more to do than guide the boat along a straight stretch of canal. He paid close attention as Jack opened a gap between the massive lock gates, shifting their boat out of the way of the wash of rushing water. And he had a grin on his face when Jack put his back to the boom, pushing wood against water to open the gates wide enough for their boat.

Gareth's problem, Jack realised as he worked, was control. He'd been off-kilter from the moment he'd clashed with Aidan and stepping out of the man's shadow had helped only a little. Gareth had decided on a goal, had made choices and decisions designed to reach it, but for most of the time, he reacted to the data they turned up. As time passed and their investigation expanded, Gareth had grown frustrated by his own lack of leadership.

Jack could relate. He remembered the untethered feeling from his time just after leaving the army when he'd taken his own missteps while searching for a meaningful second career. Only to find the place where he belonged exactly where he'd left it, both in his professional and his private life.

Gareth wasn't a follower. He was a leader, a strategic thinker. If he needed help to realise that he hadn't left those skills behind when he left the army, then Jack would relish the job.

The thought of Gareth in charge sent a delicious shiver down his back. Time to do something about it.

He jogged back to the boat and hopped aboard.

"There's a mooring half a mile up the road." He paused as the phrase struck him as wrong. "Up the canal? Whatever. The mooring Roger mentioned is half a mile away. Let's stop there."

"Did you find something? Fitzgerald?"

"What? No. Wrong part of the canal for that."

"Then why the fuck did we come this way? Do you enjoy wasting my time?" It was an impressive amount of steam for such an innocent question. Proof, if Jack had needed it, that Gareth was indeed struggling.

"Get off your high horse. You haven't earned that ride." Jack wasn't above a little needling to move matters along. Especially if it resulted in Gareth scowling as he did right then. "Roger sent us this way to let us get comfortable with the boat. You know that as well as I do. We can continue to the marina, or we stop at the mooring he suggested and have a little privacy. Your call." He slid down the short ladder into the interior of the boat, leaving Gareth to stew up top. Fighting with Gareth was so much more enjoyable when he wasn't mad and had a game plan.

Forty-seven feet by seven made for a surprising amount of room. Jack, with his renovating hat firmly in place, inspected their floating palace more closely than he had during the earlier whirlwind tour and wondered why the double bed hadn't been built into the front of the boat where they'd have had an extra six inches of usable space. Did nobody make a mattress that size?

Curious, he pulled out his phone. A quick check revealed a choice of suppliers of oddly shaped beds and mattresses. Jack dismissed his curiosity as unimportant. The bed on offer was roomy enough for them.

The shower, on the other hand, was a squeeze for one. If they tried to share, they'd end up with bruises. Or stuck like a cork in a bottle and unable to shift. The image made him smile and move from the bathroom towards the living quarters before the mischievous part of his mind took over.

The centre section of the boat was cosy and inviting with a woodburner, comfortable seating, and even a TV. Roger had pointed out kindling and logs, and Jack wanted the experience of sitting by a fire while on a boat. He'd see to that when they moored up.

For the moment, he settled on a detailed inspection of the kitchen, and was stashing beer bottles in the fridge when he heard the engine sound change. Gareth's shout rang through the open hatch a heartbeat later.

"Jack! Give me a hand tying up this boat."

Roger had given instructions on this, too. Jack joined Gareth by the tiller, smiling when he saw the boat glide towards a mooring on the canal bank.

"This private enough for you?" The bank offered two mooring spaces, and neither held a boat.

"Unless the local wildlife is planning a rave..." Jack

balanced the length of the boat and picked up the mooring rope while Gareth brought the craft close to the bank. Then he hopped onto the towpath and pulled until the boat rode snug in its mooring space. "And ... we've arrived."

The sound of the engine died away and, in the sudden silence, Jack felt Gareth's eyes on him and returned the scrutiny.

Gareth let go of the tiller. His chest expanded as he filled his lungs to capacity and breathed out. Tension bled from his shoulders, only for a different tension to take its place. Desire warmed the air, and they were both aware of it, despite the forty-seven feet of boat between them.

For the longest time, neither of them moved.

The prickle of awareness wasn't new, nor was the sense of anticipation. Yet something held them motionless, expectant. Jack's mind quested outwards, catalogued the greenery edging the towpath. Hazel catkins, ragged now at the end of their life, and pale green leaves just past unfurling. Drifts of tiny white flowers covering the blackthorns, and the swelling buds on the prickly sloes. He listened to birdsong and breathed air that still held a hint of diesel fumes. And he never took his eyes off Gareth.

Gareth broke the spell, turning towards the hatch that led into the boat. "Dinner in or dinner out?" he rumbled a question.

"In." Jack said immediately. "I know you've packed food, and I want to get that woodburner going."

"Good call."

Gareth's grip on the door frame relaxed, and Jack hid a grin. A fireside dinner wasn't the sum of his plans for the evening, but it got them started. The contents of Gareth's food cooler were a mystery to him, but he had no doubts that the resulting dinner would be to his liking. Besides, he knew what he'd buried at the bottom of his own overnight bag, and between food and Japanese whisky, he was sure he could help Gareth unwind.

The absence of engine noise was blissful. Gareth stood in the centre of the boat, engaged in nothing more strenuous than breathing. His frustration was counterproductive when he and Jack had a night and a boat to themselves. They didn't have so much alone time that he wanted to ruin a night with a fit of temper.

Jack didn't deserve that.

He'd waited without complaint while Gareth sorted out the mess in his head, but even Jack's patience wasn't endless. He'd expect Gareth to deal with his midlife crisis or career crisis, or whatever he wanted to call it, like a sensible, responsible adult.

And Gareth would, now that—

"Don't drown in that river again," Jack admonished as he squeezed past, carrying a bag of kindling. "You've brought food, but it won't cook itself."

Startled out of his thoughts, Gareth floundered. "River? What river?"

"Complacency. Keep up, Flynn. We had that discussion."

"We did, yes." Only he hadn't immediately grasped all the implications. Hadn't understood that changing his goals and the way he approached problems wasn't enough. It had taken his family and a crazy-arse case that scared Daniel to make him realise he needed to change himself, too. "And I'm still a way away from shore."

Jack knelt in front of the open doors of the woodburner, intent on stacking kindling into a neat pile.

At Gareth's words, he turned his head. "You know where you are and you know where you want to be," he pointed out. "That's the hardest part done."

"You think so?"

"I do, yeah. It's all risk assessments now, and ethics, and logistics. Right?"

If he took a step back and considered the issue with no heartburning, he saw Jack was right. "How many times have you been around that mulberry bush?" he asked, suddenly curious.

Jack held up a hand, fingers spread. "When I escaped from Jericho, when Rio found me stealing booze, when I agreed to help the police take down Jericho, after I left the army, and just before we met again," he listed. "Not my idea of a fun time, but you come out stronger at the end."

And that, Gareth thought, was the whole point of bothering to change.

He found a smile for Jack, who deserved a treat for his display of patience, and turned to face the kitchen. It had a hob and an oven, and he'd stashed chilli beef casserole and mashed potatoes in his cooler. Time to get dinner started.

The woodburner produced enough heat to combat the evening chill. Unlike an open fire, though, it didn't give enough light to see by. They augmented the subdued red glow with candles and listened to soft jazz while the night grew darker. They'd enjoyed their dinner, had shared a fine Burgundy, and had discussed nothing more complicated than replacing Gareth's ageing Range Rover with a new set of wheels. Gareth's blood hummed with contentment and then Jack reached for the bottle on the low table and charged their glasses with another shot of whisky.

"You're getting a taste for the good stuff, aren't you?"

"I love how it tastes on you," Jack said, not embarrassed admitting as much, and a flash of heat zinged down Gareth's spine.

He hauled Jack across the sofa and almost into his lap. Close enough, at any rate, to kiss the blue bejeezus out of him.

Jack didn't object. He kissed with the same focus he brought to his hunts, all tight clutches and hot mouth, and Gareth felt his body harden with so much need he almost lost it.

"Damn, brat! That's—" He gasped the words against Jack's lips, images of everything he wanted to do to Jack flipping through his mind like options on a menu of pleasure. "Will you let me play?" he asked when he could form actual words.

Jack shivered. Clung for a heartbeat longer, and then pushed himself out of Gareth's hold. "I'm game. Though I'd better check the pillows are in decent condition. Wouldn't want to startle the wildlife if you make me scream."

"How do you know that's just what I want to do?"

"You have that look." To Gareth's delight, Jack started stripping. Revealing skin slowly and with intent to rile, the newly poured whisky forgotten.

Jack rating him higher than premium-quality malt heated Gareth's blood better than any alcohol. Jack giving him a show fanned the flames. "We'll need the bed for what I have in mind," he said, voice husky.

"Yeah? Then what are you still doing, sitting there and gawping? Get the boat locked up, and the candles dealt with."

They'd always been swift with the chores when the

mood took them. Tonight was no exception, and securing the boat didn't need much work.

Jack stood beside the bed when Gareth joined him, contemplating the wide mattress. Gareth pulled him close, slid one hand into Jack's hair, twining his fingers into the soft strands, and let the other hand rest on Jack's flat stomach. "With you here, I can take on the world," he said.

"Didn't see that on the schedule for tonight." Jack grabbed the hem of Gareth's T-shirt. "Get out of these togs, will you? Or I might think you're all bait and no tackle."

"I'll show you tackle." Gareth hooked a foot behind Jack's knees, tipped him over on the mattress, and manhandled him into the centre. "On your side," he ordered.

Jack rolled obediently, then turned his head to smile over his shoulder. His eyes were wide and dark, and Gareth shucked his clothes, desperate to join him.

"Provisions," Jack reminded as he set a knee onto the mattress and Gareth growled and went to grab lube from his wash bag. Shiver after shiver rippled through him when he slid onto the bed, want like a rope around his chest. And then Jack was right there.

They fitted together, warm skin against warm skin, Jack's delectable arse against his groin. Jack twisted to let them kiss, and it was almost too much skin, too much heat, too much … of everything. Gareth held Jack tight and buried his nose in Jack's hair, trying—one deep breath after another—to come back from the brink.

Jack didn't help. He rocked in Gareth's hold, pushing his arse into Gareth's aching cock in an imitation of what he wanted Gareth to be doing. And the tiny, hungry noises coming from his throat drove Gareth insane.

Gareth groaned, gripped Jack's hip tight enough to bruise, and held him still.

"That bad already?" Jack chuckled, but he sounded as if

he had as little breath to spare as Gareth.

"You turn me on like … nothing … else," Gareth gasped, and smashed their mouths together. Jack's mouth tasted of whisky and heat. Gareth stroked his tongue along Jack's, got another moan for his efforts, and decided that teasing was a road too far that night.

He needed to get off now, not in a couple of hours.

The thought sent more heat into his blood until he felt the flush rising from his neck to his hairline. His cock fit snugly into the crease of Jack's arse, and he ground himself against the tense globes over and over while he bit and sucked on Jack's lips.

"Lube. Get the damned lube," Jack panted.

"Got so fucking lost in you." Gareth groped for the lube, his fingers clumsy. "I need—"

"Gareth…" The growl was sexy as hell, but Gareth heard the warning, too. If he didn't get to fucking soon, Jack would take over. And while that was just as exciting, it wasn't what he wanted right then.

He coated his fingers with the slippery stuff and set to work while Jack writhed and twisted. In no time at all, Jack was swearing. Gareth pulled him closer and took his mouth in a bruising kiss while he worked himself inside Jack's body.

They both stilled when Gareth bottomed out, panting against each other's lips.

"Love this. With you," Jack gasped and clenched every muscle until Gareth saw stars. "Now move."

Gareth didn't need telling twice. Holding Jack wrapped in his arms, he snapped his hips over and over until their disjointed groans became a symphony and bliss exploded through their bodies, shutting out the world.

Breakfast Conversations

"Don't you dare apologise." Jack accepted the mug of coffee Gareth had ready for him when he stepped out of the shower. They'd both slept well, but Gareth now seemed pensive. "I'm the last person to call you out for changing tack. You realise that, yes?"

"You could have called me out for not getting my head out of my arse."

"Bollocks. Change depends on the right time and right attitude. It also needs a trigger. Practice what you preach, will you?" Jack pulled a T-shirt over his head. "You were comfortable where you were. There's nothing wrong with that. I was comfortable when I first joined the service, and even when that changed, I didn't leave immediately. That's not how it works, and you know it."

Gareth finally smiled. "I know it. And while we're at it ... how about we head to the marina for breakfast and do a bit of snooping?"

"As long as they have coffee. What kind of snooping?"

"I know nothing about people who live on boats. What's it like? Does boating attract a crowd of solitary wanderers, or is there a community? What if they all know each other and can point us right to Fitzgerald's boat?"

"If he has a boat. What if he's marina staff or maintenance or a boat builder?"

"Exactly. So ... breakfast?"

Jack didn't let his man get away so easily. Catching up with Gareth took only two steps and kissing him felt right. "You're going to charm intel out of people," he said when they drew apart. "What am I going to do?"

Gareth laced their fingers and tugged Jack to the short ladder. "Eat breakfast and snoop, of course. Your kind of snooping. If my charm draws a blank, you may get lucky and pick up Fitzgerald's phone."

Gareth didn't mind that breakfast was a quiet affair. They'd aired a lot of issues over the last few days, and while he was still busy processing, he also felt clearer about his own wants. Jack had been right. He mentored others on personal change, but hadn't considered his own state of mind for far too long. He had—as Jack had pointed out—been stewing in his own complacency.

He was done with that.

For now, he topped up Jack's coffee and then pushed away from their table, leaving Jack hunched over his phone.

The marina was a bustle of unfamiliar sights and sounds. Gareth strolled between moorings, careful where he put his feet. He marvelled at the variety of colours and designs in use on narrowboats, stopped to watch a crane lift a long-arsed boat out of the water and into a dry dock, and stuck his head into a chandler's workshop. It was, he concluded at the end of half an hour, not unlike walking across an army base.

"Are you thinking of buying a boat?" An older man stood beside him. He had bushy eyebrows and a weathered face, and his clothes were sturdy rather than stylish.

"Still a wide-eyed innocent, I'm afraid," Gareth admitted. "It's our first morning waking on one."

"You've come up from Braunston, then."

"We have, yes. This morning, I'm supposed to turn the boat around and head back down."

"Ah. Have you seen the winding hole?" He walked off without further ado, expecting Gareth to follow.

The winding hole wasn't so much a hole as a deep, narrow notch in the canal's side.

"Point the front into the hole and swing the stern around. How long's your boat?"

"Forty-seven feet."

"That'd be easy, then."

Gareth pictured the manoeuvre and nodded. Yes, he could do that. "Do you live on your boat?"

"Yep. I've got a residential mooring in the marina, but we cruise half the summer." He shot Gareth a glance from under bushy brows. "Ask questions if you'd like."

"Are you sure? I have quite a few. Mostly about the logistics of living on a boat. What do you do for an address, for example? What about post? Deliveries?"

"Ah. Can of worms, that. You bring time to listen?"

"Of course." He checked his watch. "It's a bit early for beer, but how about a cup of tea?"

They returned to the cafe in the marina and settled by one of the large windows with tea and a plate of pastries. Jack was nowhere to be seen.

"Now," the man said. "The first thing to understand about boating is that there are two types of people. Relentless cruisers and boaters who hold a permanent mooring."

Gareth returned to their boat at lunchtime, head bursting with information. He'd thought he understood the principles of an itinerant lifestyle, but being moved from post to post and heading off on deployment wasn't in any way comparable to the life he'd had just described to him. The army had plans, processes, and procedures for postings and deployments. Not once had he had to worry about his mail, council tax, bank statements, or the delivery of things he'd bought online. Living on England's waterways was a whole other ballgame.

Jack sat on the roof of their boat with a laptop across his knees and a large mug of coffee beside him. He also had a silly grin on his face. As Gareth came closer, he realised Jack was talking to Bagpuss, telling him to make sure Nico and Daniel took regular breaks. It was adorable on so many levels that Gareth stepped across the narrow gap between the towpath and the boat, swung himself onto the roof, and settled beside Jack.

"I see you're having fun." He waved at the screen where—on hearing his voice—Nico and Daniel's faces appeared with flattering rapidity. Before he'd opened his mouth for a question, Daniel held up a plate containing the remains of their breakfast.

"We're fine," Daniel said. "Jack's been reminding us every two hours to take breaks and eat. He's even roped Bagpuss in to help."

"I've also given them a video tour of the boat and caught them up on the best practices for navigating a lock and turning a narrowboat in an even narrower canal."

"You're going to do that next, aren't you?" Nico said.

Gareth wanted to hide his face in his hands. "I've had

a chat with a delightful man who showed me the winding hole and explained to the nth degree how to use it."

"So that's what you were doing," Jack said. "I thought you'd needed a second breakfast."

"It was bribery. Or a thank you for telling me about living on a boat. We'd better get going, or we won't make it to Braunston at a reasonable time to do more investigating. Fridays seem far busier than Thursdays."

"I can't imagine a canal ever getting busy," Nico said, but he and Daniel didn't linger. They waved goodbye, and Jack closed the laptop and stretched.

"Thank you for doing that," Gareth said. "For their peace of mind, and mine."

Jack narrowed his eyes at him. "You hadn't expected me to leave them unsupervised, had you?"

"I was wondering if you thought you should."

"Too soon for me," Jack admitted. "I didn't tell them, of course, but I don't want them out of my sight while I can keep eyes on them. Did you learn anything useful?"

"Oodles. The man I talked to? He's been living on a boat for thirty years. You buy and sell them like you do houses when you outgrow them. They had one like ours when they started, and now they have one of those long-arsed affairs—much like the guy who rented us this boat. I'll tell you about that over a beer tonight because I wasn't kidding. It's going to be much busier today."

Jack chuckled. "If four boats an hour constitutes traffic, then yes, there's more than there was yesterday."

"How many boats were there yesterday?" Gareth asked idly as they made their way aft to stow Jack's laptop.

"Just the one." Jack disappeared down the ladder and reappeared a moment later, shrugging into a deep green fleece jacket. He hopped onto the towpath and untied the mooring lines, while Gareth started the engine. "Let's get this show on the road," he said, and then stopped. "Canal, at any rate. I wonder what they'd have said back in the 1800s?"

Gareth didn't know. He smiled at the magpie tendencies of Jack's mind and got their boat moving.

LUCKY BREAK

The canal *was* busier than it had been the day before. They met other boats, first at the winding hole, and then on their journey, and Gareth curbed his impatience. The boat cruised at walking speed. They waited their turn at the lock, and by the time they'd covered the distance back to Braunston Junction, it was late afternoon.

"Early dinner, early start?" Jack asked, taking in the bustling marina and the groups of people walking the towpaths.

Gareth consulted their notes. "There's a pub a little way up that arm."

"You want to stay at the marina?"

"That wasn't in my plans. There are moorings on the northbound Oxford Canal. That'd be quieter. Park the boat, hike back down here, cross the bridge, and wander down the other towpath to the pub?"

"Sounds good to me." Jack brushed fingertips along Gareth's nape in passing. "Carry on, captain. I'll watch out for parking spaces."

A breeze stirred the trees and creased the surface of the water until a passing barge trailed larger ripples and gently rocked the boats moored along the canal. The temperature dropped as the sun dipped behind the trees, and Gareth was glad for the warmth enveloping them when they finally stepped into the pub.

They'd arrived early enough for the lounge bar to have a few empty tables, and the dining room at the back of the pub was less than a quarter full. Gareth nodded to a couple of barstools in a corner, and Jack shrugged out of his jacket and handed it over.

"This will do," he said. "I'll hunt up beers and a menu."

Gareth had heard the abstracted note in Jack's voice. "That's not what you meant to say."

Jack grinned. "You're good. I was wondering if you can get seasick on a canal boat." He headed for the far side of the bar to book a table for dinner and order beers without waiting for a reply.

"It's been known." The reply came from a woman occupying a barstool in the same corner. "Some poor sods get seasick in a bathtub."

Gareth turned his head. The woman was lithe and petite with short auburn hair in a pixie cut—very much his type.

"I'm Pam," she introduced herself, scrutinising Gareth's fleece top and trainers before sparing a glance for her own sturdy work clothes. "I drive the coal boat."

"Gareth," he replied and pointed at Jack, who approached with a beer in either hand. "That's Jack. The coal boat?"

"I thought I hadn't seen you two here before. Boating virgins?"

Jack grinned at her. "You know it. What have I missed?"

"Nothing yet. Pam's about to explain what a coal boat is. Or does."

The woman cackled. She was on shots, and Gareth waved to the bartender.

"Thank you," she said. "I appreciate it. Been up since four this morning. Have you been out on the canal yet?"

"Yes, we rented the boat yesterday and went up the canal for a bit and back down."

"Then you've seen all the boats moored along the bank, yes?"

"We did."

"The one issue cruisers have on the canals is supplies. In the old days, workshops, pubs, and stores lined the canal. Now you're lucky if you find a pub in between the marinas. Makes for a quieter environment, but it's crap for shopping. That's where the coal boat comes in. I travel up and down the canal with provisions: coal, logs, matches, tea bags, milk, cat food. You name it, I probably have it. I take orders, too."

"Like a mobile corner store." Jack sounded impressed. "How long have you been doing this?"

"Technically, since before I was born. Third generation family business, you know? My granddad was a chandler, here in the marina. My grandma used to run the coal boat, then my dad. I took over when he retired."

"You're based at the marina?"

"Yes. The junction is one of the busiest spots on the entire network. There's enough business here to make a living."

"Has it changed much?"

"You bet. Not all for the better, either. But I get by and I'm not complaining." She knocked back another shot, and Gareth ordered another refill.

"What brought you to the canal if you've got no roots here?" She asked after a pause.

"An unusual weekend break," Jack said.

"And honey," Gareth added, when it occurred to him

that—given Pam's business—she must know each man and his dog along the canals.

"Honey?"

"Allergies. I'm told that consuming honey in the winter helps with hay fever symptoms come spring."

"I wouldn't know about that, but if you want honey, you need to go up the Oxford for a stretch and find Tommy Fitzgerald. He keeps bees at what used to be Honey Vale Paddock."

"He has a mooring there?"

"That he has. Not sure if you'll catch him at home, though. He cruises. Hi, there!" She waved to a party entering the pub. "That's my crowd. Thanks for the drink. Say hi to Tommy for me." She hopped off the bar stool and disappeared into the depths of the pub with another wave.

"Do you think the beekeeping Tommy Fitzgerald is the man we're after?" Gareth asked over dinner. The group seated closest to them had left, and he was no longer worried about being overheard.

"I've no more information about that than you do." Jack set down his cutlery. "But it's one more coincidence in a line of coincidences. Two more, actually."

"Two?"

"A beekeeper named Tommy Fitzgerald," Jack said. "And the no-longer-existing address."

"I'm not sure you've ever said what his address actually was."

"Honey Vale Lodge."

Gareth took a breath. "I see."

"I'm sure you do. Coincidence after coincidence."

"You don't believe in those."

"Exactly my point. Besides, we'd already planned to go up the Oxford Canal. It'd be criminal not to check it out."

Gareth leaned back in his chair to let the server remove his empty plate. "True. Question is, how far up the canal are we talking?"

Jack squinted at his phone. "Best guess? Twenty miles, maybe? Twenty-five?"

"Do we have enough time to make it there and back? No driving at night, remember? And I can't put my foot down and make that crate go any faster."

"Occupational hazard. Let's see how far we get in the time we have," Jack said. "I know you want results, but time limits opportunities. Especially in freelance jobs. We have new intel. We're a small step further forward. Take that as a win for now."

Jack was right. But Gareth didn't want a small win. While puttering around the canal at walking pace, talking to people he'd never otherwise have talked to, and watching the scenery drift by, he'd become caught up in the hunt for T.G. Fitzgerald. Not as an intellectual exercise, to differentiate himself from Aidan, or even to ensure Daniel's peace of mind, but because he wanted to know. He'd finally sunk his teeth into this problem, this injustice that needed fixing, and he didn't want to let go until he'd done so. Family and day jobs be damned.

It felt exhilarating, but also scary as hell.

Gareth saw Jack watching him and breathed out. "I need a drink."

And Jack, grey-green eyes alight and amused, understood perfectly.

A HILLSIDE FULL OF
BIG WET LEAVES

T oo antsy to sleep in, Gareth was out of bed as
soon as the dawn chorus started. The chill air
raised goosebumps on his flesh as he dressed,
and he grabbed an extra fleece top from his bag. Jack, still
buried in the pillows, would wake at the first waft of coffee.
One reason Gareth had primed the coffeemaker the night
before. He flipped the switch on his way past and let the
machine do its thing while he went topside.

It was beautiful.

The deep sense of peace along the canal reminded him
of frost-rimed mornings enjoying the hot tub in his garden.
Sunrise was a hint of lighter grey behind the trees and thin
ribbons of mist drifted over the water in a breeze too gentle
for Gareth to feel. Soon, he'd see birds hunting for
breakfast, the local rabbit population laying claim to fresh
greens, and the first joggers appearing on the towpath.

For now, though, his world was silent.

It felt like sacrilege to tear the serenity with engine
sounds.

Gareth did it anyway. They had thirty-six hours before
they had to return their boat to the holiday company.
Nowhere near enough time to explore the entire length of
the Oxford Canal. Pam had been vague about the exact

location of Tommy Fitzgerald's mooring, and Google Maps showed far too much land along the canal as belonging to Honey Vale Farm. But Gareth thought that with a business based at Braunston Junction, Pam was unlikely to travel the canal further than halfway.

They'd go up the canal and see what they found.

Gareth untied the mooring ropes, then shoved the boat clear of the bank and jumped aboard. The engine grew louder as the propeller whipped the water into eddies, and the narrowboat moved out into the canal.

Jack stuck his head out of the hatch fifteen minutes later. "You got the coffee going, but you haven't even made tea," he admonished and held out a mug. "Bacon sarnies okay?"

Gareth took the mug. "More than." His stomach grumbled. He imagined the mouthwatering aromas of toasting bread and frying bacon, pictured Jack in the tiny galley kitchen, and—despite the greyness of the morning—the canal took on a brighter hue.

Common sense had taken the wheel and Gareth had accepted that their weekend was as much about spending time with Jack as about their investigation. Nico and Daniel, while expecting them to help clear Mrs Harmon's name, had also offered them a gift he was determined not to waste. Whether the man selling honey to Mrs Harmon was the same Tommy Fitzgerald keeping bees beside the Oxford Canal was open to debate, but puttering up and down the Grand Union, hoping to spot his mooring, wasn't their only option.

And while twenty-five miles were a distance in a narrowboat, a car would make quick work of it. If they had to turn around before they found Honey Vale Paddock, they'd drop off the boat and return by car to locate the place.

"It's easier to sneak up on him from the canal side," he

said when Jack brought him a plate of bread and bacon, before going back for his own plus the obligatory mug of black gold.

"What makes you say that?"

"I was working out what to do if he's further up the canal than we have time to travel. Driving up is an option, but if he lives on a boat, he's used to boats passing. More so than to cars pulling up. The residential moorings are all on this side of the canal, away from the towpath and the road."

Jack set his coffee on the roof and shifted to face Gareth. "We haven't discussed how we want to manage this. Do you want to talk to him? Buy honey? Cruise past, and see?"

"Did you really expect to find him? I didn't."

"Neither did I. Still ... the coincidences keep piling up."

"Yeah. If he is a drug dealer, alerting him won't be helpful. Unless he has a sign by the mooring offering honey for sale, I suggest we cruise past. Note the location and get Lisa to check it out."

The decision didn't satisfy him, but until he had more intel, it would have to do.

For the next two hours, they saw nothing more exciting than wildlife, heard nothing but the tut-tut-tut of their boat's engine. They talked little, and the silence between them was easy, companionable. Jack drank coffee, watched the scenery, and let his mind do its thing.

Gareth loved watching him work, sure his guesses about what occupied Jack's thoughts were far off the mark.

"Penny for them?" he asked at one point.

Jack turned his head. "Just wondering whether we'll ever get to see Bagpuss carrying a rabbit. He brought me one—or at least I assume it was Bagpuss who left the rabbit on Jon's doorstep—but seeing the size of those things," he pointed at the towpath, "I'd love to see it. Do you think he can catch a squirrel? Or a duck?"

Speechless didn't quite cover it. Their boat drifted a little towards the middle of the canal as Gareth hung over the tiller, laughing.

"And here I was," he finally gasped, wiping tears from the corners of his eyes, "imagining you dissecting our perp's lifestyle, or planning routes to distribute drugs, or … something. Not Bagpuss, for sure."

Jack didn't take it amiss. "I think about those things. But not consciously. That's not how it works." He patted his pockets, like a smoker looking for a pack of cigarettes, turned his head to contemplate the hatch into the boat. Then he shrugged and stayed put. "Juggling helps if you want connections faster. Or I just sit here and let my mind wander."

"All this time…" Gareth said, amused and humbled. "You're definitely not an open book."

"Neither are you. And flipping ahead to find the good parts doesn't work."

It was an accurate assessment, but it filled Gareth with joy, not frustration. The idea of learning new things about Jack thirty years down the road appealed to him.

Silence returned and lasted while they negotiated a lock and passed under a couple of bridges. Gareth's mind adjusted to the pace, no longer chafing under the need for speed. Part of him saw the appeal of a boating holiday, though Nico would run back and forth on the towpath like a puppy, and demand to be the one to work each lock. Gareth wasn't so sure about the fourth member of their family.

"Do you see Daniel enjoying a narrowboat holiday?" he asked.

And then his jaw dropped.

They'd been rounding a bend in the canal and the view opened before them as the boat straightened. A hillside covered by rhododendrons stretched beside the canal, with drifts of blossom like fluffy clouds cheering the grey day with a kaleidoscope of colour.

"Fuck me," Jack breathed reverently. "That's not a view I expected to see again." He had his phone in his hands, shooting video as they passed. "The flowers are just starting. Imagine how this will look when they're all out. Almost worth coming back for."

"You will be, I'm sure."

Gareth's tone had Jack spinning around, and Gareth knew when he saw it, too.

A narrow wooden jetty stretched at the base of the rhododendron-clad hillside. It had a seating area surrounded by a low fence and manicured flowerbeds and backed onto a meadow dotted with beehives. Off to one side and camouflaged by greenery, Gareth spotted a barn.

They'd found a mooring, but no boat.

GENIUS

"That's the problem with driving a bloody boat. You can't pull up and jump out."

Jack was scrolling on his phone. "There's a pub with visitor mooring a quarter of a mile away. Why don't we stop there and come back for a nose around?"

"Sounds like an idea. I won't even speed."

"Boy scout."

"That's me."

Threads of tension and excitement wove into their relaxed mood, and Gareth blew out a relieved breath when he spotted an empty mooring outside the pub. "I'll book a table for lunch, shall I?"

"Might as well. They won't fuss about us leaving the boat moored while going for a walk if they know we're coming for a meal afterwards."

They locked up the boat and headed down the lane, setting a brisk pace to combat the chill. The weather was typical for April, mixing T-shirt days with chilly afternoons and mornings where gloves came in handy.

The road—narrow and gravelled—led away from the canal, then turned and continued parallel to its path. Now little more than a lane lined by a Saxon hedge on one side and rhododendrons on the other, it must once have been a supply route to bring building materials and provisions to the canal builders.

"I want some of those for our garden." Jack kept snapping photos of the flower-decked rhododendrons.

"They're invasive and poison the soil they grow in."

"I know. They also need acid soil, which we don't have. Is there a reason we can't stick a few in containers? The things are just covered in flowers."

Gareth pictured tubs of flowering bushes in front of their house and found the image inviting. "Go for it if you want them," he said. "You're the garden wizard." Except for barbecue and PE, he was of more use indoors than out. Pots of herbs on a windowsill, a hot tub, and strings of twinkle lights took care of his garden needs. "Go for it," he repeated. "They're a pleasant reminder."

"Of seeing my boots dissolve and coming close to growing webbed feet," Jack scoffed, though mirth creased the skin beside his eyes.

Gareth wouldn't remember the six days of lashing rain when he saw the plants, but Jack's smile on the seventh day, when the sun rose over a flower-covered hillside. He'd learned a little of Jack's history by then, and it had amazed him that Jack had kept the capacity to enjoy simple, innocent things.

On impulse, he slung an arm around Jack's shoulders and pressed a kiss to his temple. "Love you."

Jack leaned for a moment. "What brought that on?"

"You. Flowers. Stupidity."

"Right."

They continued down the lane until a fence and gate barred the road. Jack stopped.

"What?"

"Trespassing?"

Embarrassment sent heat into Gareth's cheeks. "Damn." In the heat of the chase, he'd forgotten his own rules.

"I'll go in by myself," Jack offered.

"No way."

"In that case, let's take the footpath." Jack pointed to a stile and a footpath sign along the fence. His grin was a little evil, and a lot amused.

"Hoist by my own petard?" Gareth queried.

"Just a tad. Though most people wouldn't think twice."

Gareth wasn't going there. He flanked the fence and followed the path as it wound closer to the canal through the meadow dotted with beehives.

"That's the barn down there. The one beside the mooring?"

"I think so, yes."

Jack sounded distracted and Gareth turned to see him heading off across the meadow towards the remains of a farmhouse, footpath, and right of way be damned. The lane they'd come down led right to it.

"The original Honey Vale Paddock, I suppose," Jack said. "Interesting."

"Why?"

"The post office still shows the address, which is why I thought they'd delisted it recently. But this house hasn't been habitable for a long time. Decades rather than years."

Gareth circled the building. The roof had collapsed. The windows were gone, and remnants of the front door hung in a sagging frame. Plaster had come off the walls in chunks, and both carpets and floorboards were rotting away. Here and there, strips of wallpaper had survived, the patterns loud, large, and geometric.

"I wonder why he let it rot," Jack said.

"If he lacked the money to fix the roof..."

"Who'd let a house go to waste?"

"I was being facetious. Though that wallpaper's enough to give anyone a migraine."

"Yes, but ... what about mail? Deliveries?"

241

"He lives on a boat. He doesn't need a physical address."

"You think he forwards his mail to the marina?"

Gareth shook his head. "No. There's a thing called canal post. I haven't told you about that yet, have I? The chap I chatted with yesterday morning explained it to me. It's for hardcore cruisers who don't have a residential mooring."

"How does it work?"

"Well, first you turn your life electronic—do everything online or by email. For the few things you can't do online, you'll use the canal post service. They receive your mail, open it, scan the contents, and email them to you. They also give you a physical address for when you really need it."

"If this service exists, then why do Fitzgerald's bank statements show a non-existent address?"

"Paper trail?" Gareth turned his head from side to side, scanning the meadow. "Or like you suggested, he's keeping below the radar by not updating his address."

"Hm." Jack stared towards the canal, thinking.

Gareth didn't disturb him. He quartered the area and walked back and forth, hunting for whatever had caught his attention. Was the rubble too orderly? Was something out of place? There didn't seem enough beehives to supply half a dozen market traders. "Where do you think he processes his honey? Or makes the elixir?"

"In the shed beside the mooring? Or he rents a space somewhere else, of course."

Gareth opened his mouth to reply when his gaze snagged on a metal hoop sticking out of the grass. He froze, shut his eyes against images of heat and sand, breathed. He was with Jack. Beside the Oxford Canal. Hunting a drug dealer.

He forced his eyes open and took another look. He

hadn't imagined it. The metal hoop was where he'd seen it.

Gareth approached, one careful step at a time.

The hoop was real and ... a handle. Gareth pulled, and a hatch lifted, revealing a set of stairs. The room at their base could have been an ordinary cellar—except for the smell wafting up into Gareth's face. Not stale, damp air nor rotting vegetation, but a mix of metal, acid, and ashes that reminded him of chemistry lessons at school.

Gareth settled on his heels and shone his phone's flashlight into the dark space.

"Jack!"

Jack was beside him in an instant. "What?"

Gareth had the latch in a white-knuckled grip. He pointed at the steps leading downwards and the darkness beyond. "Is that what I think it is?"

Jack knelt and used the beam of his torch as Gareth had done a moment earlier. Once more, the light revealed racks of glass tubes, brown glass bottles of various sizes, marble slabs, and something that looked like an ancient washing machine.

"Fuck, yeah." He played his light back and forth, then grabbed Gareth's hand where it steadied the hatch. "Don't open it wider. But shine your light down here and let me take photos."

Jack stretched out on his stomach, head over the cellar opening. He snapped image after image until Gareth patted his shoulder. "I'm sure you have enough. Let's call the cavalry."

They made sure they'd left no sign of their presence—Jack even wiped the metal latch Gareth had touched—before they walked back to the pub in stunned silence. Despite his mental gymnastics over boundaries, Gareth hadn't expected their outing to yield anything useful. He needed time to wrap his head around that.

"We don't even know what his boat looks like," Gareth said when they'd settled on the pub's terrace with beers, breadsticks, a dish of olives, and the lunchtime menu. "If he passed us right now, we'd be oblivious."

"It's useful, not being able to recognise him," Jack said, fingers busy on his tablet. "The last thing we want is to tip him off."

"True." Gareth smiled as the server came up to them. "A couple more beers, please. And I'll have the pork chops with wild mushroom sauce."

"Coming right up. And for you, sir?"

Jack glanced at the menu. "Duck, cranberry, and port pie with mash and red wine gravy," he read out. "Thanks."

The server disappeared, and Gareth took a sip from his beer. "I'm stumped here. Aidan's jobs have precise parameters. Find this, obtain that, and all past the point where the police get involved. This is—"

"Out of your comfort zone?"

"Yes. But not out of yours, so ... what's the protocol for such a situation?"

"No idea. This one went pear-shaped so fast, my head's still spinning. Lisa needs to get a team in here. I've emailed her the images I took. Fingers crossed it's enough to convince a judge."

"Do they issue warrants on a Saturday?"

"Life doesn't stop at the weekend." Jack kept tapping at his tablet screen, only half his focus on their conversation. "Lisa won't love us, and neither will the judge, but ... whoa!"

Gareth had never seen Jack look as stunned as this—eyes wide, mouth half-open, as if something had jumped out of his screen and yelled at him.

"That is ... not what I'd expected. Fucking genius," he breathed.

"What is?"

"T. G. Fitzgerald."

"What about him?"

"Thomas Geoffrey Fitzgerald, the owner of that mooring, is listed in the land registry as the owner of Honey Vale Paddock. He inherited the place in 1944."

"And never passed it on?"

"Not that I can find."

"If he was eighteen in 1944—which he had to be to buy or inherit property—he must be in his mid-nineties now. No wonder he wants to retire."

"Right."

Their eyes met as they considered this new bit of information, which didn't fit with any of the data they'd gathered so far, nor with Mrs Harmon's description of the man's age. As if by mutual agreement, they stopped talking about the case and, with the skill of men who'd learned to compartmentalise, they enjoyed their lunch and finished their beers, discussing the following week's schedule, and speculating about the questions in Nico and Daniel's upcoming history exam.

They didn't return to the case until they were back on their boat and Gareth had Lisa on speakerphone.

"I truly didn't mean to invade your weekend," he said. "This trip was the boys' idea, and neither Jack nor I believed for a moment that we'd find anything. Certainly not a lab, if that's what it is."

"It looks like one." Lisa sounded distracted. "Tell Jack his photography skills need an upgrade."

"You take decent photos while lying flat on your face

245

and guesstimating where to point your phone. Do we need to go back?"

"No. I was teasing. They're clear enough for what we need. I'll never understand how you went from honey to a drugs lab beside a canal in a couple of weeks."

"Mad ninja skills."

"Right. Well. Go enjoy the rest of your weekend and leave me to—"

"Lisa. Wait."

Jack's voice had gained an urgent edge that made Gareth spin around. "What? What did you find?"

"This keeps getting weirder." Jack held up his tablet, the screen displaying the website of the General Registry Office.

"Weirder than a ninety-year-old who looks thirty years younger cooking drugs beside the Grand Union Canal?"

"I think so. There is no death certificate for T. G. Fitzgerald. Do we think he's immortal?"

COMING TO TERMS

J ack had lit the woodburner again, enjoying its gentle warmth after a day spent outside. They'd settled on the sofa and Gareth held a half-full glass of wine in one hand while the fingers of the other tangled in Jack's hair. Jack loved the rhythmic grip and slide and didn't want to shift from his place. Not even to reach for his own glass of wine.

With the four of them at home, and Jack often pitching in elsewhere, quiet hours were rare. Once, Jack would have made the most of alone time when they had it and not worried himself further. But the last eighteen months had made him realise they both needed time to just be and that sacrificing it brought dangers.

Jack soaked up Gareth's warmth and promised himself to pay more attention.

He didn't plan to discuss his insight with Gareth when the man had finally stopped pacing and settled into something resembling relaxation.

Jack's latest piece of data had rocked the boat, had added the possibilities of identity fraud and even murder to what had been "just" a case of drugs trafficking. Lisa's groan had reached him loud and clear, but convincing Gareth to sit on his hands had been more of a challenge.

Had the towpath not been busy with walkers, he might have dragged Gareth off to bed. But the boat's walls weren't exactly soundproof and putting on a spectacle wasn't on his to-do list. In the end, he'd started a video call with Nico and Daniel and breathed a sigh of relief when Gareth had joined in. Afterwards, they'd headed up the canal to the next winding hole, turned the boat and started the trip towards Braunston.

"This isn't quite what I signed up for." Gareth's sigh interrupted Jack's musings.

"Hm." Jack hid his smirk. Gareth was too law-abiding to be a vigilante, but he'd been itching all weekend to get stuck in and get his hands dirty. It reminded Jack of their army days, of Gareth pushing past collecting intel to sorting out problems.

"We started this to help clear Mrs Harmon's name," Gareth echoed his thoughts. "Not—"

"Unmask identity-stealing drug dealers?" Jack snagged his wineglass and leaned back into Gareth's side. "Do you know, I still haven't met your Mrs Harmon?"

Gareth wasn't up for being distracted. "How do you deal with it?" he demanded. "Finding a lead and then having to wait until the powers that be get their shit together?"

Jack sighed. "Two years ago, I got on with it and ignored the powers that be. Since I've stopped going out to beat the snot out of the predators I find online, I work with Baxter. It works out reasonably well for all of us." It wasn't the entire story, but it was the part Gareth needed to hear.

"It feels damnably flat."

"That's what virtue gets you. A beautiful bunch of hurry up and wait." Gareth's discontented grumble was adorable. "You've had twenty years of service to get used to that," he teased. "Or can't you remember that far back?"

"Oh, shut up." Gareth's fingers slid from Jack's hair and cupped the back of his neck. "Or I'll make myself remember what else you could use that mouth of yours for."

Gareth's grip had no strength, no force directing Jack to move. Gareth's growl alone caused the flash of heat down Jack's spine and the curl of want in his belly. A wide grin followed on their heels. "If you need to *make* yourself remember, then I clearly need practice," he hummed thoughtfully and slid off the sofa and onto his knees.

They returned the boat at lunchtime the next day and hung around the marina for a little while longer, waiting for news which failed to materialise. Then, as if to punish their impatience, the M40 was a snarl of stop and go traffic all the way to London, and Jack—whose efforts the previous evening had only knocked the edge off Gareth's discontent—imagined that Gareth wanted a large drink and a proper rant when he got home.

Not that he'd indulge in either this side of dinner or outside their bedroom.

"Mr Fitzgerald really is a drug dealer?" Daniel queried, pausing while laying the table for dinner.

"Not just a dealer, but also a manufacturer." Gareth dropped into his chair and found a smile when Bagpuss launched himself into his lap and started purring.

"That means Mrs Harmon is in the clear, right?"

"I imagine so. She didn't hide how she met Mr Fitzgerald and how they worked out the business of her selling honey and elixir for him, so I don't think the police will have much more to say to her."

"Why didn't you wait for Mr Fitzgerald to be arrested?"

Jack shot Nico a warning glance. "Because a) that's a matter for the police and b) we'd have been there for a while. He's cruising on his boat. If Gareth hadn't found his lab—"

"And if Jack hadn't worked out that T.G. Fitzgerald is actually dead," Gareth added as a deflection, and Nico and Daniel's enthusiastic questions took over their living room. They didn't stop to hear any answers either, so Jack went and found a beer for Gareth and poured him a decent slug of malt for good measure.

"You've earned that," he said when he set both beside Gareth's plate. He felt more like wine than beer and spirits that evening, so he opened a bottle of red and poured a glass.

Even through the noisy speculations, Daniel heard the oven timer beep. He raced back to the kitchen and presented them a short while later with a dish of crispy, savoury confit of duck, accompanied by an enormous bowl of mashed potatoes.

Gareth's eyebrows shot up to his hairline. "When did you get up to put *that* together?"

Daniel's shrug was a little too casual. "We didn't sleep too well last night, so we came down here to study, and cooking in between the history revision cheered me up."

"The result is cheering me up no end already," Gareth said, inhaling the steam from his plate. Jack saw the moment his gourmet sense kicked into overdrive and gave Daniel an approving nod. "A much better end to the day than I thought we'd have."

"But you are going to tell us about it, right?" Nico took his place beside Jack.

"Every single thing," Jack promised, and held out his plate to Daniel.

Lisa didn't call until Thursday and, by then, Gareth was on tenterhooks.

"I'm sure you'd love to know that you were right," she said, with only a touch of irony in her voice. "We found the lab, ran Jack's data, and then waited for Mr Fitzgerald to return from his cruise along the waterways."

"Did you arrest him?"

"With that lab beside his mooring? You bet. Manufacturing, possession with intent to supply, probably identity theft, too."

"Murder?" Jack had explained his reasoning, and Gareth hadn't liked it one bit.

"Can't say until we find a body. Could be the old man died, and nobody registered the death."

"Can you do that?"

"It suggests intent to commit fraud, but yes, it can be done. Honey Vale Paddock isn't short of land to bury a body. There are no close neighbours, and whoever assumed the old man's identity kept everything else running. Bank accounts, driver's license, even the pension."

"Hard to imagine that nobody noticed."

"It's the age of short attention spans. Besides, quite a few people make the century these days."

Lisa sounded ticked off, but Gareth didn't ask. She'd tell him if he needed to know. He listened to her breathing and wondered what to tell Nico and Daniel.

"What I really want to know," Lisa interrupted his musings. "How did you ever think of a narrowboat?"

"Oh, you need to thank Nico for that one. Jack was plotting the cash machine withdrawals and Nico thought the pattern resembled the canal network."

"And then you went and rented a boat to check it out?"

"When Jack and Nico realised that the address on Fitzgerald's bank statements was next to the canal. We didn't think we'd find anything, but Daniel and Nico needed to revise, and they didn't want me hovering."

"I'm glad you went. Finding the mooring was an excellent piece of work. And that lab was the icing on the cake."

"What were they cooking? MDMA?" Gareth still only had a vague knowledge of street drugs, but he'd been listening to Jack for long enough to know a few things.

"MDMA. Spice. And do you know? There really *is* such a thing as mad honey. He was experimenting with that, too."

"You doubted Nico and Daniel? They spent ages on that honey report."

"And I appreciate it. Honey isn't..."

"What you're usually up against?"

"Hm. That lab was quite something, you know?"

Gareth, with no experience to call on, hadn't known. "I don't understand how Mrs Harmon got mixed up in this. That's what bothering me."

A quick, noisy inhale, and Gareth had an image of Lisa sitting up straight and leaning forward. "How do you mean?"

"The honey elixir isn't suitable for home bakers. It has no shelf life to speak of, and it's so concentrated that a little goes a very long way. Unless you bake at a scale of a restaurant or professional baker, the elixir will spoil before you finish the bottle."

"I've read that, yes."

"Then why don't you have more reports of people feeling sick after eating her cakes? If she used contaminated elixir, shouldn't there have been reports over weeks and weeks?" Gareth had mulled over that while following the canal back to Braunston, and he hadn't found an answer that satisfied him. "Unless you had more reports, of course."

"We didn't. Not over weeks and weeks, at least. The hospital reported several incidents over the course of two days, and the only common factor was Mrs Harmon and her cupcakes. Seeing we found nothing untoward in her home or stock, I doubt we'll ever learn quite what went wrong there."

"You've arrested the fake Fitzgerald."

"And we'll ask him, though I'm not sure how much he'll tell us. We still don't know who he is. He's not in the system and—so far at least—he's exercising his right to remain silent." Lisa's frustration came across loud and clear.

"There has to be something."

"Yes. Because never in a month of Sundays is he ninety-four years old. Sometimes, I really wish they'd microchip every person at birth."

Gareth thought of Jack's way with electronics and chuckled. "Someone would meddle with the chip."

"No doubt. But do you know what confuses me the most? He doesn't act *in character*. He's like a one-man crime wave, but he lives on this tiny boat—"

"Tiny my arse," Gareth scoffed.

"Fine. He lives on a seventy-two-foot boat, but he doesn't live in luxury. Where's the money?"

"You'll find out."

"Of course we will, now that you've done the hard work."

"Right." Gareth smiled, quite aware that Lisa knew how he felt and wanted to cheer him up. "The boys have suggested we get everyone together for a barbecue once they've had their history exam. Want me to send you an invitation?"

"Just text me date and time and we'll be there. Even if I'm drowning in work, I'll make time."

"I'd like that a lot."

STEPPING OUT

Putting on a barbecue without Nico and Daniel seemed wrong. Yet that's what they'd ended up doing when his and Gareth's diaries had finally aligned with the schedules of Lisa, Baxter, Aidan, and Alex. After two weeks of sunshine and showers, they'd been lucky with the weather, and had spent a large part of the day in the garden, sitting around the fire pit. They'd cooked sausages on sticks, steaks on the griddle, and had baked potatoes in the ashes. Between laughter, good-natured ribbing, and plentiful food, they were mellow and relaxed.

All except for Jack.

He checked his phone, relieved when he found both boys where they'd been an hour earlier. Daniel at Mrs Harmon's house, helping her bake, and Nico working the afternoon shift at the deli.

"Stop worrying." Lisa plonked herself down beside him.

"I'm not worried." Jack snagged his beer, careful not to jostle the cat sleeping in his lap. Bagpuss had made the rounds earlier, snaffling bits of sausage, steak, and grilled chicken. Until he'd grown weary of being fussed over and had climbed into Jack's lap, effectively stopping him from moving for the rest of the afternoon.

"Liar. You keep checking your phone. What is it you'll think will go wrong?"

"Nothing," Jack admitted grudgingly. "It's just that Nico and Daniel started this whole thing, and now they're not here to see the end."

"You're not old enough to have memory issues. They got a tour of our forensics lab as a thank you—right after their history exams. Do you know yet how that went?"

Jack shook his head. "Not until August, but they both came out smiling, so we're hoping for decent results."

"Then stop fretting. You're making everyone nervous."

"Right." Jack wasn't buying it. "Finding all the buyers will be a cow. Need a hand?"

"If you're bored and need entertainment. Otherwise, leave it to us. I'm far more interested in understanding how you got from drug-running to identity theft," Lisa admitted.

Jack stroked Bagpuss's shadowy fur while he thought about his answer. "Idle curiosity," he said in the end.

"Bullshit."

"Not. Gareth mentioned residential moorings. That made me think about entries in the land registry. I went to look, but I never expected to find what I did."

"An immortal?"

"A farm that last changed hands in 1944. Then I realised I'd never pulled data on T.G. Fitzgerald beyond his car registration, not even when we found the non-existent address." He shrugged. "And the rest, you know."

"Hm."

She took a sip from her tumbler—whisky, if Jack wasn't mistaken—and stared into the fire. The embers were deep cherry now, ready for another log or two. Jack wanted to relax and enjoy the company, but the itch in his brain didn't give him any peace. He shifted in his chair, and Bagpuss dug in his claws for just an instant. "I'm staying, don't worry," Jack murmured and stroked the cat's ears.

"What is it with you guys? You're sitting on needles, and

Gareth looks like a thundercloud. Can't you be content that you've cleared your friend's name, exposed a drugs ring, and maybe even solved a murder case?"

"We," Jack put emphasis on the pronoun, "didn't do a thing beyond collecting data and sending it to you."

"Ah." Lisa's expression brightened. "Gareth kept you on the straight and narrow."

"He kept all of us there."

"And now he finds it unsatisfactory? Or do you?"

"He does. Can you blame him?"

"Knowing him the way I do, no, I don't blame him. He thrives on results. Getting results by proxy isn't enough. What is he going to do about it?"

This, Jack realised, was the real reason for his unease. Not how Daniel and Nico viewed the case, but what Gareth would decide to do next.

Gareth had managed the whole of the barbecue and enjoyed every minute, just as he'd enjoyed the adult company. He'd fight tooth and nail for his family, but a day without family obligations was an unaccustomed joy, and he was mature enough to own that.

Not that Jack was on the same page. He'd been antsy all day, and even Bagpuss climbing into his lap hadn't made him relax.

Gareth knew the reason, and rather than letting Jack stew, he should have the discussion he needed to have.

He poured himself a shot of Dutch courage when Aidan saved him the trouble of getting out of his seat.

"Proud of yourself?" Aidan took the chair beside him and regarded him over the rim of his beer.

"Not really."

"Why not? You solved the case, saved the lady, and did it without getting your hands dirty."

"Right." Gareth swallowed a mouthful of whisky. He focussed on the smoke and peat dancing on his tongue, on the fire sliding down his throat, and the warmth spreading outward from his stomach. Without that extra bit of help, he'd start an almighty brawl right there in his garden.

"Why did you never tell me that my attitude bothered you?" he asked when he had himself under control.

Aidan blinked. "Because it didn't bother me?"

"Bullshit."

"Not. You do you. I don't have a problem with it."

"Then why did you—"

"Refuse to step in when you asked me to? Because you can't have your cake and eat it, of course."

The words stopped Gareth's tirade before it started. "Having my cake and eating it?"

"Yes. You were content to follow my lead, and I had no problem with that—whatever Horwood tells you. But you changed tack, and you expected me to pivot without warning or a shred of explanation."

"People need help when they need help. It's not something you plan and schedule. Mrs Harmon was in trouble. I didn't want to tell her we wouldn't lift a finger until she was in court. The way the system is creaking, that could be a year or more away, and the whole time she'd be branded a drug dealer, unable to make a living. Does that seem right to you?"

"Of course not. But we can't fix all the world's problems."

"Hah!" Gareth swallowed another mouthful of whisky, convinced he needed it. Either irony was a thing, or this was the strangest case of déjà vu ever. How many times had he said those words to Jack? Then his mother had levelled the same accusation at him, and now Aidan had done it too.

And he was going to use Jack's words to answer them both.

"I can help the people who ask for my help," he said, and faced Aidan squarely. "I *will* help when I'm asked because that's what I've always done. I've just not listened so closely for a while."

Aidan wasn't a heavy drinker, Gareth knew. That he set his half-drunk beer aside and poured a glass of whisky for himself hinted at something important.

"Dwight & Conrad was never designed to be the way it is now," Aidan said softly. "We'd planned for a joint venture, with Marcus running the investigations and me covering the legal side. I didn't wait for Marcus to process out, because I was too keen to get everything set up while he completed his last deployment."

Aidan stared into his glass and Gareth knew he didn't see the amber liquid, but the face of the friend he'd lost.

"With Marcus MIA, I've run both sides of the firm by myself since day one," he said. "I should have a partner, for checks and balances, if nothing else. It's what I thought you could be when we met."

"Good thing you didn't ask me then. I wasn't ready."

"Are you ready now? You said you hadn't been listening for a while, but then neither had I, and it needed Horwood to point that out to me. I'd hate to wake up one morning to find that I'd compromised my principles from short-sightedness."

"From overwork, maybe," Gareth said, buoyed and comforted in equal measure. "You're not the short-sighted type." He clinked his glass to Conrad's. "I'm ready to step up, if that's what you want. No more drowning in that river."

"What river?"

"Complacency."

"Is that even a river?"

"Who cares?" Gareth felt as if he'd had that conversation a lot lately, and he was heartily sick of it. Complacency could go drown in its own river while he and the people he trusted helped those who needed help.

That was how it worked.

"Aidan's asked me to become his partner at Dwight & Conrad," Gareth said later that night, when it was just the four of them—and Bagpuss—in the kitchen. Their guests had left fed, watered, and replete with news, and Gareth had turned the leftover barbecue into a tasty picnic dinner.

"About time," Jack said, filling his plate with sizzling steak strips and dollops of pickles and relish. "What took him so long?"

"He says he was drowning in the same river."

Gareth waited for the questions, but none came.

Jack dug into his food as if he hadn't eaten all day. Daniel arranged small sponge cakes topped with honey frosting on a plate, and Nico fed Bagpuss slivers of grilled chicken when he thought nobody was looking.

It was... disconcerting. "This needs to be a family decision," Gareth started over. "If I accept—"

"Of course, you're going to accept," Daniel said. "You already help everyone. That won't change."

"Nico?"

"Daniel's right. But there's one thing we need a family decision on."

"And that is?"

"When are we going on a narrowboat holiday?"

THANK YOU!

Thank you for reading *When the Law Needs Help*, the first volume of novellas set in the Power of Zero world. I write short stories to help me work out my characters, their motivations and—especially—their backstories. Sometimes these shorts grow into proper stories, and those are the ones you're going to find in the **Dwight & Conrad Casefiles.**

Beyond the ones in this volume, I'm playing with this lot:

Hostile Takeover: Julian Nancarrow, in his early days as CEO of Nancarrow Mining, teams up with Aidan Conrad in a battle against his obnoxious family.

Meet me in the Blue Lagoon: Aidan meets Alex over a dead body and a touch of espionage.

Something Left Undone: Aidan Conrad would do anything for his daughter. When she returns from a backpacking trip with a black eye, refuses to explain what happens, and screams herself awake each night... he has his work cut out to make things right.

Murder in the Middle Lane: A car coasts to a stop in the centre lane of the M1, the driver dead at the wheel. Shortly after, Aidan Conrad's firm receives a request for help. He sends Raf Gallant and Skylar Payne to investigate.

Turn the page to read a sneak peak from Something Left Undone

A Sneak Peek from
Something Left Undone

At 3:00 a.m. on a weekday, Aidan's house should have lain dark and silent. The darkness obligingly stuck to the rules. The silence did not.

Aidan rolled out of bed and left his room on stealthy feet. He knew what had woken him, and the sliver of light outlining the door at the end of the hallway confirmed it.

Emily hadn't slept through a single night in eight months. Not since she'd returned from a solo backpacking trip a day late with haunted eyes, a bruise on her face, and carrying an emergency passport issued by the British Embassy in Colombia.

Seeing it had almost given Aidan a heart attack. He'd fretted through Emily's month-long trip when he hadn't known that she'd travelled to South America.

Now fear shivered through him every time he thought of it.

When he'd asked what had happened, she'd clammed up and Aidan had taken a step back. He'd told her he was glad she was home and that he'd be ready to listen when she was ready to talk.

Waiting had never been so difficult. After three months, she'd begun telling him about the places she had visited and the sights she'd seen. She'd talked about everything except the events that had delayed her return, required a new passport, and landed her with bruises.

It took another two months before he found out that she'd been snatched off the street by a trafficker, and that an undercover DEA agent had saved her life and helped her escape.

Aidan knew his daughter. He also understood nightmares and had long realised that Emily's terrors had nothing to do with her being kidnapped. She sobbed her heart out night after night over the man who'd saved her because she hadn't done the same for him.

Aidan had been a soldier and could have told her that war didn't work that way. But this was knowledge Emily had to learn for herself, just as Aidan had learned to stand back and let her do it.

He took the stairs down to the kitchen and warmed a mug of milk before stirring two large spoonfuls of honey into the liquid and watching them melt. Moments later, he knocked on his daughter's door. "Emily?"

"I'm fine, Dad."

He heard the hitch in her voice and didn't comment on the obvious lie. "I've made you a mug of honey milk," he said instead.

"Come in."

He pushed the door open and squinted into the brightness. Between the ceiling light, the wall sconces, the desk light, and her bedside light, there wasn't a corner that held shadows.

He joined her where she sat on top of the rumpled bedclothes and held out the mug. "Here. This will help you back to sleep."

She shuddered. "I'm not sure I want to."

Her admission surprised him. She normally didn't talk about her dreams.

"I keep seeing his face. He had such an expressive face, and then it just went blank." She clutched at his sleeve as if she was four years old, scared to step out of the car for her first day in school. "I know ... my mind knows... that I had to go through the gate and catch my flight. How long will it take for my heart to believe that?"

Aidan wrapped an arm around her shoulders, careful of the mug she held. He had his own demons, both personal and professional, and Emily's question was one he'd never been able to answer for himself.

He watched over his daughter while she drank her milk, settled back under the covers, and finally drifted off to sleep. She didn't speak, and neither did he.

When her even breathing told him she wouldn't wake again, he slipped out of her room – leaving the lights on – and went downstairs to his gym.

He had to do something about Emily's nightmares.

An hour of pounding out the miles brought the clarity he'd sought. Aidan spent the morning making the phone calls and just before lunch, Raf Gallant walked into his chambers dressed in his customary jeans and a black leather jacket.

"You know, I can't recall if I've ever seen you in a suit."

Raf gave Aidan's charcoal grey Dolce suit a once-over and grinned. "I'm sure I have one somewhere in the back of my wardrobe. Can't remember the last time I wore it, though. It only comes out for court appearances, and these days I mostly sit behind screens."

Aidan knew that. Rafael Gallant was a trained firearms officer, but much of the work he did had little to do with weapons and more with blending into crowds and hiding in plain sight.

"What have you got for me?" Raf asked as he fell into an armchair and snagged a biscuit from the plate in the centre of the table. "I hope it's interesting because I'm dying of boredom."

"It's not a case," Aidan said. "It's more in the way of a personal favour."

"A personal favour? You know what I think about those."

"I know, but … It's Emily."

Raf's face showed his concern. "She's still not sleeping?"

"No. Guilt's keeping her up."

"Guilt?" Raf sounded surprised.

"That she didn't help the agent who blew his cover when he rescued her. She's afraid they killed him."

"Wouldn't surprise me. If she got in the middle of trafficking or drugs and he was undercover DEA ... that fight gets nasty."

"I know. I'm wondering if confirming what happened to the man will help her."

"Closure?"

"Of a sort. I'm not holding out hope that he's alive."

"That'd be optimistic."

"Yeah." Aidan handed three pages of notes across the table. "I don't expect miracles. Any information is better than what we have now."

"And if I learn that he's dead?"

"Then she'll know what happened, and he will be remembered."

For the length of a heartbeat, Raf's expression turned bleak. Then he smoothed it out. "That's the best most of us can hope for. Let me start digging."

MEET JACKIE

Jackie Keswick was born behind the Iron Curtain with itchy feet, a bent for rocks, and a recurring dream of stepping off a bus in the middle of nowhere to go home. She's worked in a hospital and as the only girl with 52 men on an oil rig, spent a winter in Moscow and a summer in Iceland and finally settled in the country of her dreams with her dream team: a husband, a cat, a tandem, and a laptop.

Jackie writes a mix of suspense, action adventure, fantasy, and history, and loves stories with layers, plots with twists and characters with hidden depths. She adores friends to lovers stories, and tales of unexpected reunions, second chances, and men who write their own rules. She blogs about English history and food, has a thing for green eyes, and is a great believer in making up soundtracks for everything, including her characters and the cat.

And she still hasn't found the place where the bus stops.

To chat with Jackie about books, boys and food, join her in her Facebook readers group *Jackie's Kitchen*, or find her in all the usual places.

JACKIE KESWICK

Milton Keynes UK
Ingram Content Group UK Ltd.
UKHW051048021223
433483UK00021B/1166